Waltzing

AT THE

Piggly Wiggly

Waltzing at the Piggly Wiggly

Robert Dalby

G. P. PUTNAM'S SONS
NEW YORK

G. P. PUTNAM'S SONS

Publishers Since 1838

Published by the Penguin Group

Penguin Group (USA) Inc., 375 Hudson Street, New York, New York 10014, USA ·
Penguin Group (Canada), 90 Eglinton Avenue East, Suite 700, Toronto, Ontario M4P 2Y3,
Canada (a division of Pearson Penguin Canada Inc.) · Penguin Books Ltd, 80 Strand,
London WC2R 0RL, England · Penguin Ireland, 25 St Stephen's Green, Dublin 2, Ireland
(a division of Penguin Books Ltd) · Penguin Group (Australia), 250 Camberwell Road,
Camberwell, Victoria 3124, Australia (a division of Pearson Australia Group Pty Ltd) ·
Penguin Books India Pvt Ltd, 11 Community Centre, Panchsheel Park, New Delhi–110 017,
India · Penguin Group (NZ), Cnr Airborne and Rosedale Roads, Albany, Auckland 1310,
New Zealand (a division of Pearson New Zealand Ltd.) · Penguin Books (South Africa)
(Pty) Ltd, 24 Sturdee Avenue, Rosebank, Johannesburg 2196, South Africa

Penguin Books Ltd, Registered Offices:
80 Strand, London WC2R 0RL, England

Library of Congress Cataloging-in-Publication Data

Dalby, Rob.
Waltzing at the Piggly Wiggly / Robert Dalby.
p.   cm.
ISBN 0-399-15367-5
1. Widows—Fiction.   2. Mississippi—Fiction.   I. Title.
PS3554.A4148W35   2006   2006041557
813'.54—dc22

Printed in the United States of America
1   3   5   7   9   10   8   6   4   2

Book design by Stephanie Huntwork

This is a work of fiction. Names, characters, places, and incidents either are the product of the
author's imagination or are used fictitiously, and any resemblance to actual persons, living or dead,
businesses, companies, events, or locales is entirely coincidental.

The recipes contained in this book are to be followed exactly as written. The publisher is not
responsible for your specific health or allergy needs that may require medical supervision. The
publisher is not responsible for any adverse reactions to the recipes contained in this book.

In loving memory of Ellen Sprague Slatter Van Camp

Part One

Chapter One

ONE SUN-KISSED, periwinkle blue, May morning in the first year of the new millennium, Laurie Lepanto, president of the Nitwitts of Second Creek, Mississippi, drove to the local Piggly Wiggly just off the downtown square to purchase a few odds and ends. Nothing she couldn't live without, of course, but one of those trips people frequently make when the pantry needs a bit of tending to.

Beyond that, Laurie knew she might very well run into one or more of her self-absorbed Nitwitts, and they would all catch up on the latest gossip while leisurely pushing around their shopping carts. That kind of lazy morning was typical of the laid-back Mississippi Delta town that was notorious for its quirky citizenry and weather patterns alike. As it happened, the weather was on its very best, late-spring behavior today — nothing out of the ordinary or threatening was going on in the skies above. But that did not mean that something could not materialize at any moment, sending hardy Second Creekers scurrying once again for cover — perhaps even into the well-worn linoleum aisles of the Piggly Wiggly.

The cramped little grocery store smelled of overripe fruit and other pungent produce. As soon as Laurie entered, she was intercepted by Mr. Choppy Dunbar, the longtime owner and manager. "I need to speak with you in my office, Miz Lepanto. Somethin' important I need to tell you today, if you'd be so kind as to give me just a few minutes of your time."

Laurie was caught off-guard but dutifully followed him through the store to his small, cluttered office.

Mr. Choppy looked straight into her puzzled face and said: "I'll get right to the point. After nearly eight decades of the Dunbar family bein' in the hometown grocery business, this store has about three more months to live."

Laurie let his pronouncement sink in. "Are you certain?"

Mr. Choppy impatiently drummed the four remaining fingers of his right hand on his desk. "It's gotten to the critical stage, I'm afraid. I can afford to keep my store open about three months longer — maybe four tops — and then it's gonna die a quiet little death, barrin' some sort of last-minute miracle."

Laurie grimaced but was not totally surprised by the news. "It's that MegaMart out on the Bypass, isn't it?"

He nodded slowly. "Afraid so."

"I knew it. All those bells and whistles and banners and billboards, promising everything to everybody, but, you know, it still feels like an overblown tractor barn."

"To put it kindly."

"All those screaming children and irritated mothers slapping their hands. I can think of at least three businesses that have folded on the town square because of it. They eventually suck the life out of every small business in sight."

"You said a mouthful there, Miz Lepanto. First there was HardWhere to Find, then the Second Creek Newsstand went under, and just last week Dunphy's Dollar Store. That one was really hard on me—I've known ole Clyde Dunphy since grade school." He shook his balding head from side to side and patted the paunch hiding behind his soiled butcher's apron. "It just feels wrong to have your lifelong trade taken away from you like that before you're ready to say when. I mean, whatever happened to customer loyalty?"

"Well, I know I don't have to tell you what the Piggly Wiggly means to me and my generation, and my mother's generation before that. To all of us Nitwitts it's always been something on the order of a social shrine. My mother just adored your father, Mr. Hale, as you well know."

"And he adored her, too," said Mr. Choppy, his smile warm and genuine.

"She always said that if you wanted to know what was going on in Second Creek, all you had to do was go down to the Piggly Wiggly and read all the notes posted on your big cork bulletin boards. There's no better place to gossip while you round up your groceries. I just couldn't stand the thought of this place closing down. It would be like losing an old friend." By now Laurie had worked her fingers into a nervous tangle, and she looked nearly as distressed as Mr. Choppy.

"But it could very well happen, Miz Lepanto."

"Oh, I just can't bear it. As you know, I have the distinction of almost being born in the produce section. That's where my mother's water broke."

Mr. Choppy's pleasant, round face flushed a bright pink. "Yeah, it's not every day a teenage boy nearly witnesses a birth in the middle of the melons like I did."

"Almost born in the produce section," Laurie added, winking at Mr. Choppy. "I must have that inscribed on my tombstone. Centuries from now, historians will wonder what that was all about, I'm quite sure."

"Oh, no—you're still too young to be thinkin' about things like that. Wait until you at least get into your seventies like me," Mr. Choppy replied. He tried to duplicate her lighthearted tone, but his expression drooped noticeably.

Laurie tried to do her best to cheer him up. "There's just so much Second Creek history tied up in your family store, Mr. Choppy. I wonder if there's a way we could get it declared a landmark or something by the state of Mississippi."

"Might could. But then it wouldn't be a store anymore. It'd be some kinda tourist attraction for people to go through and gawk at."

"But maybe you could conduct the tours, Mr. Choppy. People love coming in and talking to you all the time. You see to it that everyone who enters your store leaves the Piggly Wiggly with a smile on their face."

Mr. Choppy looked skeptical, briefly shutting one eye. "Yeah, but there's a reason for that. People come in to ask me if we got any good golden bantam corn right now, or if the catfish fillets we just got in are pond-raised here in the county or caught in the Mississippi River or over on Lake Ferguson or one of the other ox-bow lakes. Our conversation's normally not any deeper than that. I'm no Mark Twain, you know."

"But you have to admit you do know the history of the place. And what an unusual and distinguished history it has."

"Nah, it's just an ordinary, small-town grocery store that's been well-tended over the years, that's all."

Laurie shook her head. "But what about those actors that came through here during World War Two? Wasn't it right in the middle of one of our violent Second Creek thunderstorms that we're so famous for? My mother loved telling me and my sister that particular tale."

"Oh, that was so long ago. Ancient history," he replied, lowering his voice and avoiding her gaze. He held up his right hand and tilted his head in the general direction of his missing index finger. "After all, I have this daily reminder of the whole disaster."

After an awkward silence, Laurie said: "The Piggly Wiggly and the Dunbar family have done far too much for this town for us to give up on this so easily. Lots of people kept their heads above water after the Tornado of 1953 because of all the food your father donated to the community. Then he did the same thing all over again during that terrible thunderstorm ten years later when we had all those strange winds."

"Straight-line winds. Hope we never see the likes a' that again around here. Took that famous finger right off First Presbyterian, as you well know."

Laurie was recalling the traumatic event with her eyes closed. Second Creek's most recognizable landmark—the gold-plated hand with the index finger pointing to heaven atop the Presbyterian Church—had been whisked away over the rainbow early that traumatic evening. It was never spotted again — not so much as a trace — and it had taken more than a year to finance and commission its replacement.

"I remember that evening so vividly," Laurie said with a shudder.

"And I remember tourin' the damage with a buncha' other people after the storm," Mr. Choppy replied. "My daddy had the line of the day when we all came across First Presbyterian and the missin' hand. 'Will ya look at that!' he said. 'God's taken a bite outta that brave little church!'"

Laurie cut her eyes sideways. "Don't believe I've ever heard it put that way before. Why brave?"

He managed a suppressed chuckle and then said: "Well, Second Creek has survived just about every stroke a' bad weather that's been thrown at it over the years. Maybe First Presbyterian's hand had become a symbol of our defiance, I don't know. There are just way too many unusual souls livin' around here to give up so easy."

"Well, you certainly did your part in helping First Presbyterian raise funds for the new hand," Laurie said. Then she drew herself up, looking suddenly inspired. "Maybe the church could help you out now in your time of need. Have you thought of that?"

"The church's money is for the church. No way would I feel right about even askin' 'em. No ma'am, no way."

"Well, what about Jimmy Burke at the bank? Couldn't he float you some money until you work your way outta this jam?"

"Way ahead of you there. I went to him six months ago with that exact pitch," Mr. Choppy replied with an air of defeat. "But things aren't the same anymore in this town. Second Creek

Bank got bought up just recently by one a' those big outta state banks. They don't know Mr. Choppy Dunbar from a can of pinto beans. It's not like the old days when Daddy could ride out the lean times and get credit on his word. Jimmy Burke is a good friend a' mine, but he just don't run things any-more. He takes all his marchin' orders from somebody long-distance now."

"I absolutely hate that this is happening to you."

"Truth is, Miz Lepanto, Second Creek is changin'." Mr. Choppy stood up and offered his hand. "But thank you for lis-tenin'. I didn't mean to burden you too much, but I thought you might want to pass the word along to your gracious Nitwitt ladies about my situation here. You and your friends have always been my most dependable customers down through the years. Seems like not a day goes by when one of you doesn't drop in for somethin' or other. I appreciate that more'n you know."

His affable testimony quickly illumined Laurie's pleasant features and fair coloring—her light blue eyes sparkling, her mouth slowly curving upward into a wide and becoming grin. No wonder the Nitwitts had elected her their leader—not once, not twice, but three times in succession. She had a penchant for peacekeeping and organization, and at fifty-six she was the youngest and sveltest of the assortment of widows whose shift-ing agendas were as eccentric as their thought processes. Nonetheless, their club was always a force to be reckoned with.

Laurie took his strong but calloused hand and shook it enthusiastically. "The Nitwitts will continue to be your best customers. You can count on that." She rose and headed for the door, then turned toward him at the last moment. "Of course,

I'll be making a contribution to your coffers shortly when I pick up the odds and ends I came in for. Try not to worry too much, Mr. Choppy. Maybe we can come up with something to help you. I promise I'll put my thinking cap on and run whatever I come up with past my Nitwitts first chance I get."

AFTER LAURIE had left his office, the delivery bell buzzed rather insistently. Mr. Choppy got up and trudged to the back door to find Billy West Rogers of Memphis Mid-South Foodstuffs hanging his close-cropped head.

"Well, hello there. Is somethin' the matter, son?" he asked when it appeared Billy West was avoiding eye contact.

"I got some bad news for ya, sir," the lanky young route salesman finally answered. He shifted the chaw in his cheek. "We got us a new owner up at Mid-South, and he's been lookin' over all the accounts, includin' yours. He took me aside the other day and got all up in my face. He said I gotta stop deliverin' produce to ya if you cain't catch up on your past-due bills. Frankly, Mr. Choppy, he ain't a very nice feller like Mr. Perry Harvey was, and it's his company now. He says not a speck a' money, not a speck a' produce this trip down. I'm just as sorry as I can be to have to tell ya that."

"But what I've got left has been picked over pretty bad. Bananas goin' black and mushy tomatoes and soggy lettuce —"

"Don't make me feel no worse'n I do, Mr. Choppy. Ain't there some way you could pay on your account this time? I've been carryin' ya for five months now. Cain't ya come up with just a little somethin'?"

But Mr. Choppy knew there was no way. Not without raiding payroll and sending the bag boys and cashiers home with next to nothing to live on for the next two weeks, and that was simply unacceptable. His father would never have done that.

"Just cain't swing it, Billy West. Not right now."

The end result was that no fresh produce was delivered that morning to the Second Creek Piggly Wiggly, and Mr. Choppy had no idea what he was going to do next. Drastic measures were in order.

LAURIE TOOK her Piggly Wiggly purchases out of their paper bags—she detested those clingy white plastic things—and lined them up on her sparkling kitchen counter. She had originally gone in for a quart of skim milk, a box of Cheerios, and a few peaches, but after the disheartening conversation with Mr. Choppy, she had improvised and expanded her order, adding a block of cheddar cheese, a frozen apple pie, some smoked turkey slices, a loaf of sourdough bread, the last firm head of lettuce she could find, one of those little boxes of cherry tomatoes, and a bag of reduced-fat Oreo cookies for dipping in the skim milk. One of her calorie-saving guilty pleasures. She spent the next few minutes absentmindedly moving the various food items around the countertop while trying to sort out the information Mr. Choppy had just laid on her.

Even at that early stage, something he had said was tickling her subconscious, but it just wouldn't come to the surface. She had promised him she would try to come up with an idea to help him out, and she felt instinctively that she was on the verge of a plan of some sort. Five minutes later, she had finally put all the pantry items in the pantry and all the refrigerator items in the refrigerator, but whatever it was that was percolating in her head had still not emerged fully-brewed. Then the phone rang and everything slowly began coming into focus.

"Ah, Laurie, are you having a wonderful day?" asked the basso profundo voice at the other end.

"Powell!" Laurie replied. "How nice to hear from you. But I'm afraid I can't say I'm exactly having a wonderful day." She repeated the gist of her conversation with Mr. Choppy.

"What a shame! I'll bet you any amount of money there are mothers who have lost their children in the deep recesses of the MegaMart and are waiting to see if they're on sale before they claim them. You know, maybe two-for-one before they return them to the fold."

Laurie giggled. "Children on special. I can always count on you to come up with a one-liner, Powell Hampton."

"Ah, that's me. Sometimes I think I majored in cocktail party banter in college."

"Now that's required for a ballroom dancer."

Powell cleared his throat with gusto. "True enough. Ann and I did train quite a few happy couples in the social graces on the dance floor. But by the late sixties, I'm afraid it was all about shaking your booty, as they like to say these days." He sighed plaintively. "I do miss the glamour of the old school. And, of course, I miss my Ann."

"No more than I miss my Roy. But I always get a boost from your unique perspective. We've been around the block a time or two." She paused for a moment and decided to proceed with her just hatched brainstorm. "Powell, I was wondering if you could come over this evening for dinner. I have this brilliant idea I'd like to discuss with you. It just came to me as we speak, and it involves your very special talents as the town's most charming widower. I hope it doesn't embarrass you to hear me say that."

"Ah, the truth never embarrasses me. What time would you like me to put in an appearance?"

"Seven will give me plenty of time to work my magic in the kitchen."

"I'll be there with bells on my toes and the usual silver in my hair."

She laughed out loud. "That's precisely what I had in mind. See you soon."

Laurie hung up and reviewed the brainstorm in her head. Step one was convincing Powell. Step two, Mr. Choppy. Step three, all her yammering, quarreling, self-absorbed Nitwitts. Everything and everyone had to be brought into play.

Then she exhaled. If only it would turn out to be as easy as one, two, three.

BONE-WEARY, MR. CHOPPY shuffled into the fluorescent and neon-bright world of the Second Creek Video Corral later that evening. The video rental store was one of the few businesses near The Square that seemed to be immune to the tentacles of the MegaMart, and if Mr. Choppy was not their best customer, he was surely in the top three. Les, the teenage night-shift clerk who wore his hair in a disconcerting array of moussed spikes, had already spotted him in the parking lot and was prepared to rattle off a long list of the brand-new releases they had just received.

"How's it hangin', Mr. Chop?" he said, shaking hands across

the counter. "Man, have I got some sweet videos with your name on 'em!"

"Nah, son. Not tonight. I already know what I want—*It's a Mad, Mad, Mad, Mad World.* That's four times, you know."

"Four times what?"

"Mad four times."

"Not followin' you."

Mr. Choppy may have been tired, but he found the energy to laugh at the situation anyway. "What I mean is, the word *mad* is repeated four times in the title of the movie. People are always gettin' it wrong. Mostly they think it's in there only two or three times."

Les winked, pointed at him with his index finger for emphasis, and said: "Got it. Cool! You really have the lowdown on all the old movies, Mr. Chop. You could, like, be a critic or somethin'."

Mr. Choppy leaned over the counter. "Tell ya a secret, son. I wouldn't have the smarts to be a critic, but I once wanted to be an actor. Even thought I had a real shot at it for one brief moment in time."

The young man's eyes bulged. "Whoa, that is, like, way cool! What happened?"

"The wrong woman happened, that's what." Mr. Choppy looked at his watch. He wanted to get home by ten and fall asleep watching all those comedians chase each other through the desert. "Well, how 'bout that tape, my boy? Is it in?"

Les gave him a thumbs-up. "We only got one copy, and it should be over there in the comedy aisle on the bottom shelf."

Happily, the video was where it was supposed to be, and Mr. Choppy fell into bed a little after ten, watching as much of the movie as his heavy lids would allow. It was exactly what he needed—something lightweight.

At one point he briefly held up the nub on his right hand in front of his face and sighed wearily. Second Creek and its missing fingers. Frightful storms lifting them off churches and—as it turned out—off of him as well.

Chapter Two

*L*AURIE STOOD over the stove sautéing a couple of plump, skinless chicken breasts with chopped peppers, peach salsa, and onions, thinking perhaps she ought to go easy on the onions. After all, Powell was coming over. Who knew what might happen?

But there would be plenty of breath-freshening parsley in the frenzied inspiration of a salad she was also throwing together from that little box of cherry tomatoes and the lettuce she had just bought, seasoned with fresh-cracked pepper and her special homemade raspberry vinaigrette dressing. In a concession to her spur-of-the-moment invitation, she was baking that store-bought apple pie to take care of Powell's sweet tooth.

Laurie had always loved cooking for people but especially for Powell. The memory of his effusive compliments always brought a smile to her face. "My Ann could waltz until the sun came up, but she could never produce gourmet cooking like this. We mostly ended up eating out," he had told her the last time she had invited him over to sample her shrimp-stuffed bell peppers, sweet potato soufflé, buttermilk biscuits, and freshly made ambrosia for dessert.

"I think one of the worst things about being a widow is not having someone to cook for anymore," she had confessed to him. "I used to whip up all of my best family recipes for Roy and the girls. I always cooked in quantities vast enough to store in my deep-freeze."

"There's something reassuring about that to a man like myself," he had responded.

Then she had really let her hair down. "I don't mind telling you that there are still some frozen packets of vegetable soup, okra gumbo, and Roy's other favorites in the freezer, and it's been nearly seven years since he died. I just can't bring myself to throw them out because that would be admitting that he's really gone." She sighed. "Maybe I shouldn't have told you that. You probably think I'm a little weird now."

But he had laughed brightly and offered the perfect rejoinder. "Everyone in Second Creek is a little weird, myself included. I don't think you can take up residence anywhere within the city limits if you're boring."

Laurie snapped out of her reverie and took a moment to inhale the tantalizing aromas from her stove. She switched the burner to low heat and glanced at the kitchen clock. Fifteen to seven. Now was the perfect time to decant some delicious Delta muscadine wine, light a few scented candles scattered around the house—she was partial to cinnamon and vanilla—spritz a little of her Estée Lauder on her neck, and mentally rehearse parts of her all-important spiel.

Before she knew it, seven o'clock had arrived. As usual Powell was prompt, giving her a peck on the cheek and handing her a bottle of chardonnay. "Ah, I smell heavenly food and fragrant perfume throughout this enchanted little raised cottage of yours!"

Laurie took the wine and indicated the cozy living room with a leftward tilt of her head. "Everything's in a holding pattern with our dinner. Or should I say more accurately—warming pattern? Meanwhile, shall I pour us some of yours or mine?"

He considered briefly. "Muscadine tonight, I think. I haven't had any of the Delta's own in a while."

Soon they had taken their freshly filled glasses and plopped down on her sofa, which was draped with the bright blue afghan she had knitted to ease her grief following Roy's death. Laurie immediately launched into her pitch. "When you walked through the door back there, I got the strangest feeling you might just ask me to dance with you. You give a woman that impression, you know. Fred Astaire and Gene Kelly entered rooms just that way in all those MGM musicals." Those 'sweep 'em off their feet' skills is what I'm referring to."

Powell put his glass down on the coffee table and gave her a curious glance. "My, my. Is this part of that brilliant idea of yours you wanted to discuss with me?"

Laurie swallowed a sip of wine and inched closer to him. "As a matter of fact, it is. I believe in being direct."

Powell faced forward and emphatically put his hands on his big, bony knees. "Then full speed ahead, my good woman."

Laurie set down her wineglass next to his and exhaled. "No one who lives here really cares what the outside world thinks about the way we do things. So what I am about to propose shouldn't seem all that unusual to you."

Powell was squinting, trying to figure out where she was going. "Yes, I have to admit that I am quite happy living out here among the crazies and loons of Second Creek, Mississippi, present company excluded, of course."

"Oh, I've had my moments, I assure you. You just haven't been around to witness them." Laurie paused, gathering up her courage for the final leap. "What I propose is that we help stimulate business for the Piggly Wiggly by using your prowess as a ballroom dancer. We set up special hours each day—two or three should do it, I think—when you offer to dance with the ladies who come in to shop. We could get Mr. Choppy to arrange for some music, and you could waltz them around, or fox-trot them around, or tango them around or whatever they wanted. Meanwhile, the bag boys could round up their groceries from their shopping lists. What do you think?"

There was a long silence. Then Powell picked up his glass and took a big swig. "Waltzing at the Piggly Wiggly?"

"Correct. Now give me your honest reaction. Obviously, this is a no-go if you don't want to do it."

"Give me a minute," Powell said, rising from the sofa. Laurie watched him move deliberately and with grace across the room to the mantel. He leaned his long form against it briefly, then straightened up and caught her gaze. "When you mentioned earlier that you thought I looked like I wanted to ask you to dance, you actually weren't very far wrong. Ann and I used to dance together in the parlor every evening before dinner. Different dances every night. Reminded us of the heyday of our Studio Hampton when everybody was lining up to learn the latest ballroom dance steps. Then, after Ann died so suddenly, I thought I'd never want to dance with anyone again. I thought all the heart had gone out of me—" He broke off suddenly and caught his breath.

"I just can't imagine going through something like that. God bless you."

He soon recovered his poise: "I appreciate that. But all those steps, that posture, that way of moving you just described— everything was just too ingrained in my muscles and tendons and brain cells to fade away quietly. I would find myself holding an invisible partner in front of Ann's full-length mirror, the one she used to primp in front of all the time. All those skills are still here just waiting to be utilized again."

Laurie smiled and patted his spot on the sofa. "Come, sit."

He dutifully obeyed.

"I guess we're both defined by our losses in a way," she began, once he'd settled in again beside her. "Me with all my frozen food and you with all your dancing skills wasting away. So let's cut to the chase. Does this mean you'd be willing to give my idea a try—assuming we can get Mr. Choppy to go along with it?"

"Why the hell not? What else do I have to do with my days?"

"I was hoping that would be your reaction. Now then, do you think this could possibly accomplish what we have in mind?"

Powell screwed up his face for a few seconds while he quickly ran a hand through his thicket of hair. "That's an entirely different question. It seems to me that our first priority must be to get the word out about this."

"That's the other part of my plan. I'm going to put this to my Nitwitts and see if we can't make it an official project of ours. We do have a little money put aside for whatever strikes our fancy. We do more than just play bridge and eat potluck dinners at each others' houses, you know. We have gotten our share of kudos for our civic projects here and there."

Powell reached over and patted her shoulder affectionately. "You haven't forgotten that I attended one of your meetings last year to give a lecture on the subject of Latin dances, have you? Love 'em or hate 'em, the most formidable women in this town belong to your organization."

Laurie gave a deferential little cough. "Thanks for using the word *formidable*. I've heard less charitable descriptions."

"Never you mind. I have an impulsive yet delightful suggestion. To get our project off to a good start, why don't you and I do a little dance or two before our delicious dinner? Do you have any appropriate music around here?"

"We could turn on the radio over there on the little table, I suppose. There's that station up in Memphis that plays the Big Band favorites, swing music, early Frank Sinatra, that kind of thing. Would that do?"

"Perfect. I'll tune it in for us."

"And I'll check on the food while you do that."

A few minutes later they were slow-dancing to "I Can't Get Started" on the radio, and Laurie began to feel certain stirrings again. Here was a man who knew how to lead and how to hold a woman properly while doing so. He made her feel delicate and feminine and as he effortlessly moved her around the living room floor, and she didn't want the song to end. But end it did, replaced by a more up-tempo number—"Saturday Night Is the Loneliest Night of the Week," and Powell quickly segued into a smooth-as-silk fox-trot.

Laurie continued to be putty in his arms and said: "You know, my Roy never liked dancing. I guess it was his one big shortcoming as far as I was concerned. Of course, I never said as much to him—male egos being what they are and all. But the last time I had a partner like you was way back in my days at Ole Miss. It's been that long."

"Well, I'm more than happy to sweep you off your feet, madam."

When the second song was over, the local news came on, and they decided to call it quits. "We should have danced together long before now," Laurie said, while watching him turn down the radio.

"Perhaps we should have. But except for that demonstration I did for your club, the situation just never seemed to present itself."

Laurie had a very self-satisfied expression on her face. "I have a good feeling about this. The dancing at the Piggly Wiggly, I mean. You are going to turn a mundane errand into a lark for a lot of women, trust me, and it's going to give Mr. Choppy a new lease on life. Meanwhile, let me get our dinner on the table. I'm sure you brought that healthy appetite of yours with you."

Powell offered to help her bring things out from the kitchen, and in no time they were dining together with the candles flickering all around and a Tommy Dorsey tune drifting in softly from the other room. As usual the compliments flew Laurie's way: that just couldn't be some form of peaches on top of the chicken—salsa, you say?—what a novel idea!—who would have thought of it?—he had never tasted anything so delicious!—and that salad dressing had to be homemade or his Christian name wasn't Powell Lavelle Dejarnette Hampton Jr. of the Sunflower County Hamptons.

Laurie just lapped it all up, with the combination of Powell and maybe a tad too much wine making her slightly giddy by the end of the main course. She got so caught up in their interaction that she temporarily lost sight of her original objective. There was more work to be done. The nattering Nitwitts and Mr. Choppy had to be convinced that this idea of hers wasn't too off-base even for Second Creek.

Aside from that, however, there was something new to consider. She had come to the realization that she was definitely interested in Powell Hampton. Oh, the thought of romance had more than crossed her mind a time or two before, but she had always been a bit halfhearted about it. No longer. Not after the way he had danced her around her living room.

After the apple pie and coffee had been consumed, Powell gave her a polite, but slightly lingering, good-night kiss at the door and then said: "You've handed me an intriguing challenge, Laurie Lepanto. I will now be expected to turn pedestrian shelves of creamed corn and condensed tomato soup into the stuff from which romantic dreams are spun. A lesser man might be somewhat fazed by such an unusual recipe, but I can hardly wait to get at it."

Laurie smiled warmly, said good night, and practically floated back into the living room, sinking back down on the sofa. Everything was moving along splendidly in her head, when suddenly, from out of nowhere, one nagging little word popped up out of nowhere—competition.

She was proposing to let most of the other eligible widows of Second Creek in on the good thing she had just sampled for herself. Women like Renza Belford, Myrtis Troy, Novie Mims, and Denver Lee McQueen would be dancing and flirting and batting their eyelashes at Powell, playing it to the hilt. Maybe some of them would take it into their heads to invite him into their homes for meals as she had done. Just where would it all end once she had turned all those lonely hens loose on this savvy silver fox?

Laurie got up and started clearing the table, mentally chastising herself for entertaining such fears and doubts. Was she not president of the Nitwitts? Had she not reigned supreme for the better part of three consecutive two-year terms? She knew by heart all the quirks and idiosyncrasies of each and every member and could predict them like the Mississippi Delta sunrise. What did she really have to worry about?

"Get a grip, ole girl," she said outloud a bit later, talking to the stack of dishes she was rinsing in the sink. "Once you've put it all out there, just run with it. You'll be just fine. End of discussion."

When her head hit the pillow later that night, however, she felt she had been slightly premature in shutting off her internal debate. She had the distinct notion that she was getting ready to set something in motion that could not be reversed. She had reached similar junctures in her life before and had never regretted any of the decisions she had made. Second Creek solutions, the residents of the town had always called them — intriguing mixtures of instinct and bravado that ended up involving everyone, usually for the better.

Chapter Three

M R. CHOPPY was shifting his weight on a stone bench in Second Creek's Downtown Park, listening intently to Laurie's improbable proposal while Powell kibitzed nearby with a benign, hopeful expression on his face. The three of them had just finished drinking coffee and munching on sugary bear claws at the Town Square Cafe across the street. It was a lazy Sunday afternoon in mid-May, full of swirls and breezes; the summertime humidity the Delta was so famous for had not yet materialized. All the better, Laurie had imagined, to make her initial presentation to Mr. Choppy, and she eagerly awaited his response once she had finished.

"Now, Miz Lepanto, you know I have the utmost respect for you, but you don't really think this scheme'd work, do ya? I mean, this is the grocery business I'm in, and I know my store's

a down-home and comfortable kinda place to be in, but dancin'
in the aisles? You don't think that's a bit of a stretch?"

"I know it's not business as usual, Mr. Choppy, but I'm perfectly serious," she said, being careful to keep a smile on her
face. "I really believe my idea could turn things around for you,
and desperate times require desperate measures, after all." She
briefly bit her lip. "Oh, not that I think this will be viewed that
way. I simply see it as an entertaining ploy to get some of your
women customers to reacquaint themselves with your store
after unwisely flirting with that obnoxious MegaMart."

Mr. Choppy's ordinarily agreeable countenance was a network of creases, wrinkles, and squints. He looked genuinely
troubled. "You'd be askin' my bag boys to fill all those grocery
orders, and I have to tell it to you straight. Kenyatta and Jake
are both good kids, but they aren't the brightest bulbs on the
Christmas tree. They're still pretty young and raw, and they
blink out from time to time. I can see lots of potential for trouble
in doin' somethin' like this."

Powell spoke up quickly from his end of the bench. "I'm sure
Laurie would be willing to help supervise the grocery lists while
I do the dancing, wouldn't you, dear? Just think of it as a team
effort."

She nodded her head with the broadest grin she could manage. "I'd be happy to double-check all the orders as we go
along. That would keep those mistakes under control."

Mr. Choppy still looked perturbed. "I just don't know. It
seems like somethin' that could backfire so easily on me. People
bring in grocery lists all the time that look like they were written during earthquakes. Some of 'em are even worse than a

doctor's prescription. You couldn't guess what was on 'em in a million years. One time that crazy Lady Roth came in with a list she'd scrawled, and she had no idea what was on it. Well, I was the poor fool she asked to try and figure it out for her, but she stormed off when I couldn't make head nor tail of it. Needless to say, she blamed me for not being able to decipher her god-awful writin' and hasn't set foot in my store since."

"Ah yes, our dear Lady Roth," Laurie mused. "The worst nightmare of every merchant in Second Creek and vicinity."

Indeed, the eccentric and elderly socialite, who was fond of wearing outlandish silk turbans and dangling earrings the size of shrimp forks, had terrorized nearly every business in the county at least once over the past four decades. She seemed to have materialized out of thin air a month or so after a particularly violent hailstorm that had damaged the county's soybean crop quite extensively and initiated a period of grave financial difficulties for many Second Creek farmers. Financial ruin in exchange for Lady Roth. It didn't seem like a fair trade-off at the time, and still didn't, but the woman had nonetheless taken her place as part of the charm of Second Creek.

"Lady Roth is someone I'll gladly hand over to the Mega-Mart. I'd even write her a letter of recommendation," Mr. Choppy added.

"No doubt," Laurie said. "As for the penmanship issue, we'll tell everyone to print neatly. No longhand permitted."

"Well, here's somethin' else, Miz Lepanto. Where am I gonna get the music from? I don't even have an old-fashioned turntable, and we only got two lousy radio stations in this town—the one that plays Loretta Lynn and Dolly Parton and all that country music and the other that plays that hippity-hop stuff the kids listen to."

"There's a Big Band station up in Memphis we could tune in," Powell said. "All of the music they play would be appropriate. Why, just the other night, Laurie and I were dancing to their playlist."

There was more silence, and Laurie was surprised to see that Mr. Choppy's features had not softened one iota. Something seemed clearly out of whack to her. After all, only a day or so ago he had gone to the trouble to reveal his financial predicament to her. She had thought it was an appeal for help. Now he seemed reluctant to accept her assistance. Laurie began to wonder if he had already given up the Piggly Wiggly for dead, but she doggedly pressed on. "I promised you I'd run all this by my club, and that's just what I'm going to do. As I mentioned before, we don't have unlimited funds, but I'm going to propose that we use our slush fund to help you make a partial payment or two on your accounts and then advertise the Waltzing at the Piggly Wiggly Campaign to get you going again for good. Think of it as a loan, not a gift. You can pay us back whenever. We've been waiting for years for some exciting and worthwhile cause to get our juices flowing, and this one fits the bill perfectly."

Then Powell delivered the coup de grace. "The only other choice you have is to close the store and give in to the Mega-Mart. Is that what you really want to do? What about your family legacy?"

"It means a helluva lot to me, of course. Hell, it's my whole life when you come right down to it."

"Then you have everything in the world to gain by letting us help you," Powell added. "It will be our great pleasure and tons of fun to boot—cha-cha-cha and one-two-three—if you catch my drift."

Finally, Mr. Choppy seemed to be relenting. "I do catch your drift. And you'll get back to me as soon as possible on what your club says?"

"Absolutely," Laurie replied with a sense of satisfaction. "I'll be meeting with them tomorrow."

"I just wish there was some other way, Miz Lepanto. I just wish—"

"Now don't second-guess this. It will be a huge success, you'll see."

They left it at that, as Mr. Choppy excused himself, said good-bye, and made his way back to his car. Laurie and Powell remained on the bench, inching closer together in his absence, and Laurie said: "That was a lot more difficult than I thought it would be. I was sure the reason he told me about his financial problems was so I could come up with something that might help. But now, well, he was just full of resistance today."

"I think we wore him down, though."

"I hope so. He's always been a dear man, but he's also remained something of a mystery over the years."

Powell rose, indicating they should follow the gravel path around the cypress pond that was the centerpiece of the park. "In what way? He sells groceries. He butchers meat. Seems pretty cut and dried to me."

"Well, I don't want this to sound like so much gossip, but my mother used to say that the scuttlebutt on Mr. Choppy was that he never married because his heart was broken by a woman. No one ever knew who she was. Mama said lots of people over the years played that particular guessing game and always came up empty. Mama's friends always said that it probably took place during World War Two, right after that rainstorm that brought those actors to us from Hollywood."

"Yes, I've heard bits and pieces of that story around town."

"Well, Mother said that's how he got his nickname, you know. He was born Hale Dunbar Junior, but whatever happened between him and this mysterious woman most likely cost him that missing finger. The details were always kept rather hush-hush by the Dunbar family. He likes to say that his nickname refers to the fact that he does such a good job as the Piggly Wiggly's resident butcher, chopping up all those grand cuts of meat for everyone, but most people think his missing finger is the actual inspiration behind the name."

Powell took her hand in his as they walked along and said: "Did you ever have any ideas about who this woman was and what actually happened? You don't suppose there's any chance he did away with her, do you? You know—missing finger, missing person." He gave a little shudder with his shoulders.

"Oh no. That has never entered anyone's mind. Mr. Choppy is just entirely too gentle a soul. Trust me. He wouldn't be capable of anything like that. His whole life has been the Piggly Wiggly. No wife, no children to look after and take care of. It's just not like him to accept defeat so easily. I'd halfway expect him to take that meat cleaver of his to the MegaMart before calling it quits. But maybe there's something else going on with him that we just don't know about."

They walked the rest of the way around the pond in silence, and then Powell broke away and did something that surprised Laurie. He leaned down, picked up a rock, and skipped it across the water, causing a succession of ever-widening ripples atop the dark-green surface. Ripples.

"That was a very impressive throw," she said. "You almost made it to the other side. That cypress knee got in the way at the last minute."

"I like to go for the gold when I do things. I find it kind of amusing that ballroom dancing is now an Olympic sport, and you really *can* go for the gold now. If that had been the case when Ann and I were in our prime, I have no doubt that we would have been strong contenders for a medal. I would have liked to have achieved something like that. So I really don't see how I can fail to deliver for Mr. Choppy and the Piggly Wiggly."

"First things first, though. We need to get all the ladies on board tomorrow."

"Speaking of which, I definitely think I should be present when you address your club. If any of them should get cold feet, no pun intended, of course, I'll be on hand to warm them up with a dance step or two."

"You read my mind. I had every intention of inviting you to come. We could even look upon it as some sort of trial run — with the dancing and all, I mean."

He deferred with a quick bow of his head and said: "It's settled then. And you don't foresee any stick-in-the-mud among the group?"

Laurie quickly reviewed the behavior of her friends. "Well, Myrtis Troy might make a fuss about the club's slush fund. Money is her middle name, and she's always got those dollar signs in her eyes, but it's nothing I can't handle. I'm practically the president-for-life of the Nitwitts. Poppa Doc had nothing on me."

"How is it you've managed to become such a woman among women? I can't imagine anything more difficult than keeping that matronly stew from boiling over."

Laurie laughed and wagged a finger at the imagery. "You make us all sound a bit like the witches from *Macbeth*."

"Bubble, bubble, toil and . . . yes, I see what you mean."

"It's okay. You're forgiven. And probably not off the mark. Most of the members do have strong personalities. I just happen to have one that's a wee bit stronger."

Powell took a deep breath. "Comes from living in Second Creek, I guess."

Laurie smiled mischievously. "So how does this strike you? Waltzing at the Piggly Wiggly shall become all the rage between the hours of noon and two o'clock six days a week."

Powell put his arm around her shoulder as they turned off the gravel path and said: "Sounds like good, enforceable fun to me. I can't wait."

Chapter Four

$\mathcal{T}$HE VERY SHORT and pigeon-breasted Novie Mims, world traveler and purveyor extraordinaire of somniferous, vacation slide shows, was holding forth and gesticulating wildly in the midst of the Nitwitts' meeting. They were gathered in Laurie's parlor the next morning to get their initial glimpse of her Piggly Wiggly presentation. Of course, everyone present was beginning to wonder if they would ever get a word in edgewise once Novie had taken the floor.

"Let me repeat, ladies—uh, and Mr. Hampton—I do not think this Piggly Wiggly scheme would be a proper use of our club slush fund. I'm almost sure I remember we all agreed the fund was to be used for a carefree trip someday. All of us together at some lovely tropical spot, fanning ourselves with palm fronds, putting our feet up, and sipping lots and lots of happy during happy hour. And instead we are to use it for the purpose of waltzing around in the aisles of a grocery store? I think not."

The others were arranged around the room on sofas and chairs in a semi-circle, listening with intense interest and waiting to pounce when Novie came up for air.

"You mean there's actually some little spot on the face of this planet you haven't yet graced with your presence, Novie?" the full-figured Denver Lee McQueen asked, her heavily made-up face and quizzical brows the perfect illustration of sarcasm. "I'm still completely in shock that you let that man outbid you for the privilege of being the first passenger on the space station."

Novie narrowed her eyes and directed a little puff of air upward toward her graying bangs. "Hilarious, Denver Lee. Almost as hilarious as one of your madcap showings at the Second Creek Art Gallery."

Renza Belford fussed with her fox fur and lifted her classic, angular profile dramatically, giving the impression of having just caught a whiff of some unpleasant odor. "Horse apples! I don't recall any such plan for a carefree trip to the tropics, and Denver Lee is right, Novie. You've seen it all, done it all, and kept the passport office in business all by your lonesome. And, I might add, subjected us to every living second of your travels in the process with those slides of yours."

"Well, excuse me for trying to have a life outside the Home Shopping Network and Weight Watchers!"

Laurie sensed a wolfpack mentality developing. "All right, ladies. I think I can say with some authority that there was no prior general agreement about a trip. I'm quite sure I would have remembered it had we agreed to it. I read over Wittsie's notes thoroughly after every meeting, and I simply don't recall any such discussion." Then she leaned forward a bit in her favorite armchair. "Now, as for my Piggly Wiggly proposal, I believe it will turn out to be very worthwhile, not to mention fun, but there'll be no stampeding here. We'll discuss it all very thoroughly, and then we'll take a vote on it."

"And I'll be more than happy to trip the light fantastic with any of you charming ladies right after you've given this your official approval. That should get us off to an energetic and enthusiastic start," Powell added, standing in the doorway where he had been playing the part of eye candy for the matrons assembled before him.

His comments seemed to give the proceedings a discernible stir and lift, causing spindly, eternally confused Wittsie Chadwick to go off on one of her convoluted, stream-of-consciousness sequences from her perch in the corner: "We're not ready for the vote yet, though, are we? I don't see how we could be, no one's made a motion yet, have they? I don't think so, I don't see it anywhere in my notes . . . did I miss something? I've written everything down, though, I'm almost sure of it. Let's see, I could go all the way back to the beginning and check . . ."

"Calm yourself, Wittsie, dear. No, we are not ready for the vote," Laurie said with a gracious smile. She was always careful to handle the club's recording secretary with kid gloves to keep her on track. "We need to make sure that everyone is on board and all concerns have been addressed and answered before that can even take place. Now, who has another question?"

"How does Mr. Choppy feel about all this?" Myrtis Troy said. "He's a very proud man. I remember his father—he fit that self-made profile if anyone ever did. Tell us the truth now. How did he feel about a bunch of rich, widowed biddies coming to his rescue?"

Novie sucked in her breath, looking deeply offended. "Speak for yourself, Myrtis. I do not consider myself a biddy. Really, I don't know why you want to speak about us in such self-deprecating terms."

"Oh, don't be so sensitive. We are what we are. Why, this entire session this morning is nothing if not a cluckfest. All our meetings are glorified cluckfests and —"

Laurie again intervened. "Okay, that's more than enough. In answer to your question, Myrtis, I can tell you that Mr. Choppy had his reservations at first. But I think he's realized he's down to his last option. Of course, he fully intends to reimburse us as soon as he can. I told him that he should think of this as a loan, not a gift. I think he felt a little better about it when I put it that way."

"Oh, well then, we could still use the money for a trip somewhere down the road, if we're going to get it back," Novie added. Some of the others looked momentarily exasperated, but Laurie quickly changed the subject.

"If we agree to do this, we need volunteers not only to go down and dance with Powell for rehearsals but also to work on the advertising campaign. We need to come up with a catch-phrase and place a few ads in the paper, maybe even hand out circulars around the town square when the time comes. I've already had a thought I'd like to run by all of you. What about: Come to the new, improved Piggly Wiggly—where you'll waltz through your shopping? How does that strike you?"

There was a general nodding of heads, together with a

sprinkling of laughter, after which Powell said: "Of course, you could just as well fox-trot or samba through your shopping." He paused to take a bow. "I shall be at your service, ladies." There was another round of titters and giggles. "And I just this second thought of another possible catchphrase. Why not: Fill out your shopping list and your dance card. Come to the Piggly Wiggly?"

Laurie was pleased to see that Powell's suggestion had actually drawn polite applause, so she moved in for the kill. "Now, of course, we don't have to work out our ads right this minute, but we could approve the project and start divvying up the workload. We need to move quickly on this because time is definitely running out on Mr. Choppy. So, if there are no more questions and there's no further discussion, do I hear a motion from anyone to vote on the so-called Piggly Wiggly Campaign?"

"Very well, then. I'll make the motion," said Denver Lee, raising her hand after a brief silence. "Let's show some derring-do."

"I think it's more silly than anything else, but I'll second it," added Renza.

Laurie turned to Wittsie and nodded. "Now we're ready for the vote, dear."

As it turned out, the vote was unanimous, but from the way they all lined up immediately after to dance with Powell, Laurie began to suspect they might have gone along with it for that particular perk and maybe not much else. The word *competition* again briefly reared its ugly head but was soon squashed by a surge of the confidence that rarely abandoned her in daily life. She was able to watch each of her friends take a turn or two with Powell around the room without blinking an eyelash,

although Myrtis Troy—the last in line—created a minor distur-
bance during her fox-trot by calling attention to her new shoes.

"Can you guess how much I paid for them?" she said to
Powell, who looked clearly disinterested. "I bet you'll never
guess how much I gave."

"Oh, I'm not good at guessing how much women pay for
things. My wife never shared that with me."

"Well, guess what color they are, then."

He peered down quickly at the pumps, then shook his head
as they continued to dance. "Not good at the current trend in
women's colors either. Ann would tell me she was going to
order shoes from catalogs in ridiculous-sounding colors like
okra and nutmeg. Once, she even said she'd chosen something
in a shade called jojoba bean—now what the hell is that, I ask
you? And I'll be damned if I could tell what color they really
were when they arrived."

Denver Lee then spoke up loudly, pointing emphatically at
the shoes and startling everyone. "Eucharist!"

Myrtis turned her immaculately coiffed head sharply while
still following Powell's lead. "What did you say?"

"I think your new shoes are Eucharist-colored. Same shade
as communion wine," Denver Lee replied.

"Now that is downright sacrilegious, Denver Lee."

"This from someone who hasn't been to church since her
husband's funeral. When was that—seven years ago? Has your
hand ever darkened the collection plate?"

Myrtis finally broke away from Powell to stare her friend
down. "How would you know how often I go? We don't even
belong to the same church, which is just as well since I wouldn't
want to drink out of that cup you all pass around. No wonder

you cross yourselves after you take a sip. No telling what sort of germs you share. Well, I'll take my spiritual lumps in a clean, dry paper Dixie cup with plain ole soda crackers, thank you very much."

Laurie quickly stepped in to keep the peace. "Now, ladies, let's do try to be a bit more ecumenical, shall we? Actually, I have seen that color listed before in catalogs as port wine, so perhaps Denver Lee has a point. Now, Myrtis, why don't you finish your dance with Powell before the music ends?"

Myrtis appeared disgruntled at first but soon melted when Powell extended his hand and they resumed their dance.

"You know, Myrtis, I always find that discussions of religion and politics only bring people to blows," he began. "That's why I have always sought refuge on the dance floor. It's a tremendous equalizer, you know. Some of the plainest, quietest people in the world shine when they're dancing. And by the same token, some of the world's most beautiful and wealthiest—jet-setters, some might say—have absolutely no sense of grace and rhythm. Dancing brings people together and makes them feel really good about themselves when it's done right. I've always felt that it's the only true religion we have on this earth."

"How poetic you are, Powell—as smooth with your words as you are on your feet," she replied, her face suddenly aglow.

Laurie continued to observe all of it closely. She had not miscalculated with her Piggly Wiggly concept. She could easily see for herself how effective Powell was going to be if the Nitwitts were any indication.

Next up were several rounds of Bloody Marys and an assortment of finger foods, followed by the assignment of various tasks for the Piggly Wiggly project. Powell and Laurie were to collate the final candidates for advertising slogans, design the eventual ads, and press for as much media coverage as they could muster; Myrtis, obsessed as she was with figures, was put in charge of collecting ad rates for the various media outlets; Renza and Denver Lee were to cast their wide net of contacts and come up with a list of likely women to call, mail, and otherwise approach for participation in the store's new service; Novie was entrusted with getting circulars printed up; and Wittsie—dear, well-meaning, but ordinarily overextended Wittsie—came up with a brilliant suggestion all on her own, the home run of the outing.

"Well, I was just thinking . . . it's less than two weeks to the Annual Delta Floozie Contest," she began. "Maybe we should try to time this and get Mr. Choppy to have his new grand opening that same day. . . . So many more people would be in town milling around The Square, you know. It would be a whole lot easier to spread the word that way, don't you think? I mean, as long as it's this close, we might as well take advantage of it . . ."

Laurie cut her off with a gasp of surprise. "I think that's a marvelous idea, Wittsie. The Floozie Contest always starts around ten o'clock in the morning. People could walk right on over to the Piggly Wiggly for a little dancing and shopping. Maybe we could even arrange to have the winner lead a parade over to the store and then lead off with the first dance. Imagine the publicity we could get out of that. Congratulations, Wittsie, that's absolutely inspired, don't you agree, ladies?"

Wittsie blushed crimson when the others literally bombarded her with their sincere compliments, and the discussion ended on that unexpectedly high note of camaraderie with the ladies all atwitter.

"Wittsie," Denver Lee began, closing in on her with a blast of spicy Bloody Mary breath. "Did you have a few of these delightful concoctions we're all now swilling before we got here? That was a perfectly brilliant suggestion, but I have to confess that I can never even remotely come up with anything that works out in my life unless I've had a generous snootful."

"But I . . . I haven't been drinking, Denver Lee. My Bloody Mary is always the virgin variety. I call it My Bloody Shame," Wittsie replied, thoroughly flustered as usual. "The only alcohol I've touched is rinsing my mouth out this morning with Dr. Tichenor's . . . maybe I swallowed a bit by mistake. Would that have done it? I don't know . . . I didn't have anything to drink before the rest of you showed up, honestly. I'm not good at being sneaky, you know. I can't even bury the dog's heartworm pill in his food without him discovering it and spitting it out."

Denver Lee patted her friend on the shoulder with a patronizing grin. "Dear Wittsie. Never change, sweetie. Whatever would we do without you?"

Wittsie blinked several times. "Oh, thanks . . . I think."

"Denver Lee, stop picking on our Wittsie," Laurie said, moving around the room in her usual role as peacemaker.

Over in the far corner she noticed some ongoing histrionics and closed in quickly as Myrtis and Renza seemed about to come to blows with dueling celery stalks yanked from their Bloody Mary glasses. "What on earth are you two getting so hot under the collar about?"

"Oh, it's not what you think, Laurie," Myrtis replied. "We're not really mad. We're just having a difference of opinion about something."

"Yes," Renza added, adjusting her fur. "We were rather animatedly discussing our theories about Mr. Choppy's missing finger, since he was the focus of our meeting."

Powell and the others moved in quickly to join the gathering, and Laurie said: "Any conclusions? And for God's sake, girls, stop brandishing those stalks at each other like bayonets!"

Renza returned her celery to her glass and drew herself up. "Well, I was of the opinion that something monumentally dark and tragic occurred that has been skillfully covered up by the Dunbar family and perhaps even the authorities all these years. Something that was violent. Not to mention grisly and horrifying."

"I don't agree with that at all," Myrtis said. "I don't think Mr. Choppy has a vicious bone in his body."

"Well, horse apples to that," Renza added. "He has a temper. I've seen it now and then when children run through his store and knock things off shelves and spill things. His grumpy old man genes start showing up."

Then Powell spoke up decisively. "I don't think there's any doubt that Mr. Choppy is a kind and gentle man most days. I've been seriously considering another intriguing possibility."

"And what might that be, Powell?" Renza said, her demeanor the very definition of skepticism.

"Indulge me, if you will," he began, as the ladies pressed in even closer. "Perhaps this sounds overly melodramatic, but what if in fact the trauma occurred when Mr. Choppy was merely trying to escape?"

The comment elicited a roomful of silent, puzzled expressions, but Laurie finally said: "Escape from what? You mean from this mysterious woman everyone is always talking about? Is that how you meant it?"

"That's precisely how I meant it. What if the only way he could get away from her and put his life back in order was to cut off his finger?"

That brought a chorus of gasps and uncomfortable titters. Denver Lee spoke up first. "Great heavens, Powell! You mean to say that Mr. Choppy was like a wolf chewing off its foot to get out of one of those barbaric traps? What on earth would make you think of something like that? Oh, that's a positively gruesome image!"

Powell closed his eyes and nodded slowly. "It may be gruesome, but it might very well be accurate."

"Well, I've heard of cutting off your nose to spite your face, but never cutting off your finger to spite your girlfriend," Denver Lee replied. "After all it was his index finger, not his ring finger. I don't suppose we'll ever know the truth, though. I mean, all these years have passed, and Mr. Choppy has never seemed the least bit inclined to reveal to anyone what really happened. I mean, couldn't he have just gotten distracted while chopping meat and whacked himself by accident?"

Renza shuddered while patting one of her foxes absentmindedly. "After that comment, I don't think I'll ever touch link sausage again. Thanks so much for thinning out my breakfast menu, Denver Lee."

Laurie shook her head. "Well, missing finger theories or no, I think we owe Mr. Choppy and the Dunbar family the effort we're about to put forth, considering their service to the community. We're definitely doing the right thing in trying to help him keep his head above water. We can be proud of ourselves for this."

That seemed to put an end to the speculation about Mr. Choppy's nub, and after every last drop of Bloody Mary mix had been dispatched and each of the ladies glowed somewhat through their judiciously applied makeup, the meeting officially disbanded.

"AFTER OBSERVING today's confab," Powell said to Laurie after the last of the group departed, "it occurs to me that the six of you have a rather peculiar relationship. Up until Wittsie's suggestion at the end there, I was beginning to wonder if any of you even liked each other the least little bit. That was no cluckfest—it was more like a catfight." He was standing beside her at the kitchen counter helping her put the leftover ladyfingers into plastic bags.

"I know it probably looks that way at times. We do meow at each other a lot. Fortunately, we rarely scratch," she replied. "The best way I can explain it is to say to you again that we've all been brought together by our losses. Believe it or not, our very own Wittsie Chadwick actually started the club as a makeshift support group just after she lost her husband, but it got to be more than she could handle. She eventually fell back on being the secretary and let someone else take over running it."

"You, for instance?"

"Guilty. 'Ladies,' Wittsie said to us. 'I am too much of a nitwit to continue to try and run the club. I'm serious. Last night I gave a seven-course dinner party and made a complete mishmosh of the silverware. I had people trying to cut filet mignon with my best collection of letter openers.'"

They laughed together and Laurie continued: "We let her resign on one condition. That she let us name the club after her. She had been calling it the Second Creek Widows' Club, which sounds so clinical and dreary, like something in the old Kinsey Report. So I said, 'Why don't we take you at your word, dear Wittsie. We will call ourselves the Nitwitts in your honor.'"

Laurie paused and winked. "We all had a good laugh, and she went for it. Of course, that doesn't change the fact that the only thing all of us really do have in common is that we lost our husbands. That was our starting point, and over the years we've found other ways to relate, even though we sometimes do irritate each other. But it's all in the family—and a very special family at that."

Powell was nodding and smiling at the same time. "You handle that family of yours pretty well, though. You're like the referee at a boxing match. And you were pretty sure they would all go along with your plan, weren't you?"

"These women don't have a whole lot else to do. Oh, they see their children and grandchildren from time to time, and Novie isn't the only one who likes to travel, although she is the only one with a slide show addiction. Denver Lee creates and exhibits her oil paintings, even though she knows deep down that she doesn't have any real talent for it. I don't think anyone's ever bought one of them. Of course, Myrtis thinks she's impressing people with how much money her husband left her, but the truth is, she doesn't have anything else to do or talk about anymore. And Renza treats her collection of fox furs the way some people treat their pets, but when you think about it, it's a pretty low-maintenance way to put up with animals."

Powell couldn't help himself. "No care and feeding, just mothproofing."

Laurie offered a rueful smile. "At the end of the day, though, they all come home to their big, empty houses, so being a member of the Nitwitts helps break up the loneliness and makes the time go by a little faster—anything to speed up the long healing process we're all still going through."

Powell sealed the bag he had just filled and caught her gaze. "And that last part applies to you, too?"

"Essentially. I make no bones about it. To some extent I'm still very much about Roy not being around anymore."

"Well, maybe we should do something about that. What do you think?" Even before she could answer, he gently pulled her toward him and kissed her tenderly, their warm tongues intertwining.

When it was over, she felt genuinely satisfied. This kiss was different from the perfunctory ones he had been giving her over the last few months while making his entrances and exits. This one had an emotional charge that had been patently missing before, and she liked the way it kept her good and stirred up on the inside.

"I think that was very nice," she said. "Definitely a keeper."

They finished with the last of the bags and walked together back into the living room. The big band station was still working its magic, so they began dancing to "Speak Low," and then Laurie said: "I've told you a little something about my life. Now you tell me something about yours. I couldn't help but notice how often you mention your wife's name in ordinary conversation. I'm sure you loved her very much. She must have been one of a kind."

He didn't miss a beat. "Let's just say she had fascinatin' rhythm—in every sense of the word." He was wagging his eyebrows at her, and she didn't hesitate to laugh out loud.

"You have a downright devilish sense of humor, Powell Hampton. I've always liked that about you."

"Comes from trying so hard all my life not to step on people's toes. And I do mean that literally."

She wanted to make him open up even more but decided not to press at this early juncture. There was plenty of time to explore their burgeoning relationship and to discover if he was truly ready to trade in memories of his Ann for the flesh-and-blood reality of another woman.

For the time being, that kiss he had given her in the kitchen would do nicely.

Chapter Five

IN THE WEEKS following their initial approval of the
Piggly Wiggly scheme, the Nitwitts were the perfect
illustration of busy as well as busybody—burning up the phone
lines, stopping people on the street, and otherwise getting out
the word to anyone they could corner. For his part, Mr. Choppy
was in awe of their energy and persistence, so much so that he
even began to wonder if their dogged determination might
not be turning people off. On one occasion he made the mistake
of taking Denver Lee and Novie aside for a confidential chat
after they had double-teamed one of his most loyal yet fragile
customers, Addiemae Armstrong, as she was standing quietly
in the aisles, doing some comparison shopping on the price of
baked beans.

"Now, Miz Denver Lee and Miz Novie, you know I'm
delighted that you all are doin' this for me," he began, plastering

a far-too-wide smile on his face as she spoke. "But over there in the canned goods aisle, don'tcha think you mighta come on just a bit too strong with Miz Addiemae? I assume you know she has terrible arthritis, particularly in her knees, and I just don't think dancin' anywhere at anytime would be somethin' she could manage. I already have her business well in hand—why, she goes all the way back to Daddy's time. She'd never turn her back on the Piggly Wiggly or be caught dead out at that Mega-Mart. What we need to do is find us some new regulars."

Denver Lee heaved her generous bosom and stared him down. "She didn't seem to object, Mr. Choppy. And anyway, all we were doing was letting her know what was coming up shortly. What you haven't considered here is that even if she can't take advantage of Powell's prowess in the aisles, she may have friends or relatives who can. The point here is to get the word out to as many people as possible. Believe me, we know what we're doing, don't we, Novie? That's what being a Nitwitt is all about."

"Indeed, it is. Nitwitt Power. Hear us roar, as they said back in the seventies. Now, don't fret, Mr. Choppy. Promotion is the name of the game. As an experienced world traveler, I can assure you that advertising whatever little adventure you want people to sample is the key to success, even if all it amounts to—as in this case—is leaving home for a short trip to the Piggly Wiggly."

Denver Lee gave her friend a polite nudge. "Leave it up to you to work in all your trips. You are incorrigible, Novie."

"You know you really love it. You know deep down you live for my slide shows."

"Oh, sure. Just the way you've lined up for all of my paintings. Anyway, let's hurry up and finish here and then trot over to your place to stir up a Bloody Mary or two. I'm dry as a desert after a morning of talking up Powell Hampton in the aisles, delicious as he is."

"Let's make it your place. I think I'm fresh out of Absolut, and we don't want to have to resort to one of Wittsie's Bloody Shames."

"My place it is, then. Teetotaling is hardly becoming to women our age."

"You are so right. I always feel more on top of things when spirits have their wicked way with me."

Wisely, Mr. Choppy had not commented further, other than to thank them again for all their efforts, and he quietly retreated, mentally conceding the points they had made.

By the eve of the Piggly Wiggly's new grand opening, Second Creek was literally buzzing with pent-up energy. The Nitwitts had done an exemplary job of publicizing the event with their carefully crafted newspaper ads and radio spots. For seven days straight the local stations had been running the commercial Powell had recorded himself with the cooperation of the big advertising agency up in Memphis he had often employed during the heyday of his dance studio. He had chosen a lush arrangement of "Embraceable You" for the background music and delivered the copy he and Laurie had written together as if he were inviting every female along the length of the Lower Mississippi and all its tributaries into his boudoir for an evening of endless and scandalous delight.

"Ladies (pregnant pause) when was the last time you really

got to (another pregnant pause) dance?" the copy began. "I mean the old-fashioned way (yet another pregnant pause) with a man holding you in his arms like you were Cinderella at the ball. Well, that kind of memorable experience can be yours Monday through Saturday from noon to two p.m. at the Piggly Wiggly just off The Square right here in Second Creek. Bring in your shopping list—and please print legibly—to the friendly bag boys, and they will fill your order while you dance with me (herald trumpet sounds in the background) Powell Hampton, formerly of Studio Hampton in Memphis—the Mid-South's most popular source of ballroom training for well over thirty-five years. Yes, it's an exciting new way to buy your groceries—all waiting here for you at your new, improved Piggly Wiggly—where you'll now waltz through your shopping and fill out your dance card at the same time. Starts Saturday, June second at noon. Ladies (last pregnant pause) don't you dare miss the time of your life!"

The newspaper ads, along with the circulars that Novie Mims had commissioned on pretty pink stationery, contained approximately the same sentiments. The club's world traveler had also come up with an idea that was a throwback to the pre-air-conditioning era.

"I've ordered up some of those cardboard church fans—the kind all the funeral homes used to use to advertise on. I remember fanning myself with one at my grandmother's funeral when I was eleven. We can pass them out to people in the square the day of the Delta Floozie contest," Novie explained on one of her many visits to Mr. Choppy's office to keep him briefed. "It's likely as not to be pretty hot—unless it rains, God forbid—so every time they all fan themselves they'll see the Piggly Wiggly logo and be reminded of what's going on right after the contest is over. It's subtle, but it'll get the job done, believe me."

"That's a right nice touch, Miz Novie. Almost ironic, ya know. If this scheme a' yours don't work out as well as we all hope it will, I'll be throwin' a funeral of sorts for my own worn-out little grocery store."

"Nonsense, Mr. Choppy. It's not worn-out—it has character, even a patina."

"What's that? Sounds like tomato paste."

Novie laughed merrily and leaned forward in her chair. "No, you must be thinking of Contadina. Patina is a kind of veneer, an indefinable aura associated with age. The Piggly Wiggly definitely has it. Don't you dare let those negative thoughts even enter your mind. You have not had the distinct pleasure of dancing with Powell Hampton. You don't know what a thrill that is going to be for all the ladies. They'll keep coming back for more, I can practically assure you, and it will mean more business for you all the while. I tell you, we're on to something here—I just feel it in my dancing shoes."

Mr. Choppy chuckled to himself. "I'll take your word for that, Miz Novie. No need for me to be samplin' the goods. Don't think the world is ready for that image, do you?"

Novie winked at him smartly. "Oh, you're always so self-effacing, Mr. Choppy. In your own way you're just as cuddly and adorable as you can be, or at least I've always thought so. Hard work and dedication to one's family traditions are very appealing."

"Well, I never much thought about myself that way. There's nothing too glamorous about butchering meat all day."

"It's the power of the cleaver. Very macho, you know."

At which point Mr. Choppy had glanced down at his nub, looking decidedly uncomfortable, and the conversation had come to an abrupt halt.

As for the expense angle on the project, Laurie had not miscalculated. The club's rainy-day fund had been just large enough to cover all costs, including allowing Mr. Choppy to make a much-needed payment on account to Billy West Rogers and the other key food vendors in order to freshen the store's stock—and still leave the ladies with a little to play around with.

More significantly, word-of-mouth had increased to a fever pitch, with many of the women Renza and Denver Lee had contacted eventually calling up Mr. Choppy at all hours with an endless array of questions:

"Can I make a reservation? I do so despise standing in line!"

"How long do I get to dance with Powell?"

"Is it only one dance?"

"Can I bring my own tape? I don't want to dance to just anything that comes over the radio!"

"How should I dress? Is this going to be formal or casual? I'm not sure I have a thing to wear."

"Should I ring up Powell Hampton first and discuss my needs with him?"

That last one had given Mr. Choppy considerable pause, if not a sense of outright alarm, causing him to give Laurie a call and say to her: "Do you think by any chance that the woman means by that what I think she means? Oh, my goodness, Miz Lepanto, I think we may have opened up a big ole can a' worms wigglin' their sassy tails."

But Laurie had managed to calm him down, reminding him

of the standard-issue response they had agreed to give everyone who pressed them too much: "First come, first served—drop on by right after the new Miss Delta Floozie is crowned in the town square." Of course, they had also privately agreed to extend the hours that first day if demand far exceeded expectations—a dilemma devoutly to be wished.

So now it had come down to a dress rehearsal, so to speak, of the Piggly Wiggly's new service the evening before the big day. Mr. Choppy, Powell, Laurie, and all the other Nitwitts had gathered around one of the checkout counters right after the customary nine o'clock closing to iron out any bugs in the process. The two bag boys, Kenyatta Warner and Jake Andersen, were also on hand—the former rolling his eyes while rap music was surging through his headphones and the latter chewing gum nervously while picking at one of the more persistent zits on his ruddy, adolescent face. Mr. Choppy's most dependable and experienced cashier, Lucy Faye Stiers, a plump and gregarious middle-aged woman who always wore a hairnet and a denture-induced smile, completed the cast of characters.

"Please take off your headphones, Kenyatta," Mr. Choppy said. "I need you back on this planet while I'm goin' over this stuff." The boy immediately slipped them down around his shoulders and prepared to receive his marching orders. "You and Jake will work with Miz Lepanto on the grocery lists. She'll go over each one as the ladies come in and make sure everything is clear before you start to fill up one a' the shopping carts. You'll take turns on the orders, and we'll obviously do 'em one at a time while Mr. Hampton dances around with the ladies. Oh, and any questions you got about various cuts a' meat, you obviously bring straight to me."

He hardly needed to have uttered his last statement. Even many of the people who had fallen for the so-called charms of the MegaMart still dropped by the Piggly Wiggly when they wanted filets or other premium cuts of meat for their special-occasion dinners and other elaborate affairs. In fact, Mr. Choppy had never relinquished his apron to anyone else in the store, much less hired anyone new to take his place once he had inherited the business outright from his father years ago. But that particular skill by itself obviously wasn't going to be enough to keep him in business much longer.

Kenyatta looked comfortable with the instructions his boss had just given him, but Jake seemed to be puzzled about something, shaking his unruly mop of carrot-orange hair.

"What's the trouble, son?" Mr. Choppy said.

"I was just wonderin' 'bout the brand names, sir," the boy replied. "Are they gonna tell us which brand of soap and cereal and ice cream and stuff like that they want us to find for 'em? Know what I mean, sir?"

Mr. Choppy made a slit of his mouth and narrowed his eyes. "Good point." Then he turned to Laurie. "We need to make sure all the ladies have written down that kinda specific information on their lists before we let one a' the boys go hunt and peck for things all over the store. It'll be an unholy mess if we get the wrong brand of whatever it is. If there's one thing I know about the grocery business, it's that people are fiercely loyal to their brands. You can't pry 'em loose from the ones they grew up with."

"I've already thought of that little angle," Laurie added. "Don't worry, we'll get this down to a science in no time, won't we, boys?"

The two of them simultaneously answered with a "yes, ma'am," and at last the moment had arrived for an actual trial run. The ladies had drawn straws for the order in which they would dance with Powell. Renza had won the privilege of going first. While the other members looked on chattering and mumbling excitedly among themselves, everything was set in motion when Mr. Choppy started his stopwatch and shouted: "Go!"

Since so many women had raised objections over the phone about not having control over the music, they decided to replace the radio with a CD player, and Renza had brought along her copy of "Moonlight Serenade" for her spin down the canned goods aisle. Powell quickly went into action, taking her in his arms while being especially careful not to disturb the arrangement of tiny fox-face lookouts around her shoulders.

"You and your furry little friends look perfectly stunning tonight," he told her as they sashayed about alongside shelves stacked with peas and carrots, Niblets and sliced green beans, all of which Mr. Choppy had placed on sale for the Grand Opening. Indeed, Renza had dressed up for the occasion in a silver-sequined outfit far more appropriate for a Second Creek Little Theater production of *Auntie Mame* than a trip to the grocery store, and her salt-and-pepper hair showed evidence of a visit to the beauty parlor earlier in the day. Completing her well-coordinated ensemble was an expensive string of pearls she had thrown on to keep all the little foxes looking particularly spiffy.

"Oh, horse apples, Powell. I'm modestly presentable, I suppose," she replied, looking up into his eyes. "But if I seem to have an extra sparkle in my eye, it's because 'Moonlight Serenade' has always transported me to another time and place. The

song makes these cans of vegetables all but disappear as mysteriously as Glenn Miller did."

"Glenn Miller made cans of vegetables disappear?" he
replied with a deliberate friskiness in his voice. "And here all
this time I thought he just played a mean trombone and conjured up arrangements to die for." He frowned ever so slightly.
"Maybe that wasn't the most judicious choice of words considering his denouement."

The joke seemed to catch Renza off-guard, and she puffed
herself up, thrusting forward every one of her fox faces in all
their mute splendor. "Now, you know good and well what I
meant."

"Indeed I do. So tell me—and I mean this with all due respect to that wonderful musician—exactly where do you think
Glenn Miller actually went that fateful day?"

She turned her head to the side momentarily, her lips pursed
thoughtfully. "Since you asked, I would have to say that my
best guess would be the recycle bin. Or maybe he's even here
among us now. Maybe the unusual weather we have all the time
is just the vehicle to transport us to and fro—heavenly music of
sorts, jarring though it may be at times."

Powell looked dumbstruck. "What an idea! Meteorological
orchestration. And who, pray tell, would the conductor be?"

Renza's forehead wrinkled. "If I knew the answer to that,
Powell Hampton, I don't believe I would be here—in the
moment, so to speak. Good heavens, we've gotten so serious
and philosophical. I'm here to dance and be swept off my
feet. Shall we lower the level of the dialogue and settle for the
merely mundane and a touch of the traditional male-female
hormonal?"

"I'd be more than delighted to do so," he replied, throwing his head back with a hearty laugh.

At which point they effortlessly slow-danced into the realm of chili—with and without beans—Sloppy Joe sauce, canned corned beef, and Vienna sausage.

Meanwhile, Laurie, Lucy Faye, and Jake were going over Renza's list one last time before the boy began filling the order, after which Mr. Choppy turned to him and said: "Just remember, Jake, we'd prefer it if the orders were ready about the same time the customers finish their dancin'."

And with that unequivocal directive from his boss, Jake was off to the races, pushing the cart with a great deal of urgency toward the produce section. Laurie tried to keep pace but found herself more or less eating his dust.

"Jake, I think you can slow down just a tad. This isn't NASCAR, you know," she cried out, waving her hands to flag him down.

"Yes, ma'am," he replied, allowing her to catch up with him. Then he sought her advice as he approached the first item on his list—one pound of fresh tomatoes. "Suppose whoever it is don't like the ones I pick? I mean, I see these ladies pickin' over the produce all the time, and some a' the tomatoes or cucumbers or whatever I wouldn't even take the time to wash off are the ones they end up choosin'. I can't read what's goin' on in their heads."

Laurie smiled and patted him on the arm. "Don't you worry about a thing, son. I can show you a trick or two. I was practically born in the produce section of this very store, you know. You just use your common sense. No, better yet—use your stomach sense. Pick the ones you'd want your mother to cut up for the bacon, lettuce, and tomato sandwiches she fixes you for lunch. You like BLT's, don't you?"

He nodded enthusiastically, causing a few locks of his orange hair to fall down into his eyes.

"Well, then, if they still feel firm and yet look ripe enough to eat, they'll probably be absolutely fine with the customer. You don't have to overthink this. Just trust your instincts, and you'll do just fine."

The boy broke out in a grateful grin and began weighing the likeliest candidates on the nearby produce scale. "This idd'n as bad as I thought it was gonna be, Miz Lepanto. Thanks a lot."

Laurie winked as Jake slipped the tomatoes into a big plastic bag, and they moved on to the dairy case from which Renza had asked them to extract a pint of Mississippi Valley Farms cultured buttermilk — the only name brand Mr. Choppy carried, in fact — so that particular task was a snap.

"You're doing just great, son," Laurie said as Jake quickly located a carton, even though she neglected to add that she was beginning to feel like they were on some kind of culinary scavenger hunt.

On the other side of the store, Powell and Renza had come to the end of the canned goods aisle and were just beginning to start back up — approximately halfway through the strains of "Moonlight Serenade" — when Renza said: "Oh, don't you think we could dance back along a different aisle?"

Powell looked puzzled. "Have a hankering to ogle the paper towels and toilet paper around the corner, do you?"

She laughed heartily. "It does sound so pedestrian when you put it that way."

"There's a practical consideration, though. We'd be dancing

farther away from the music. Unless, of course, we ask Mr. Choppy or someone else to follow us around in minstrel fashion with the CD player."

"Oh, I like that idea. Let's do try it."

So Kenyatta was quickly pressed into service to walk behind the slow-dancing couple as the dreamy, time-honored final chorus of "Moonlight Serenade" played, even though the booming beat from his ever-present headphones was adding a decidedly funky, knee-bending strut to his step. It was a contrast that would have startled Glenn Miller, himself, from his outpost in the spiritual recycle bin, where he was, no doubt, arranging and orchestrating heavenly hits with his sheet music and trombone.

By the time Powell and Renza had reached the aluminum foil and Saran Wrap, "Moonlight Serenade" had come to its magnificent conclusion, but Laurie and Jake were still three items shy of completing Renza's list. The two tasks did not end anywhere close together, and everyone gathered around the checkout counter to discuss how to fine-tune the process. Powell spoke up first, suggesting that they either repeat the music or go on to another song until the order was ready.

"I think we ladies would like that better," Renza proclaimed, batting her eyelashes. "More time to dance with you, of course. More time to be outrageously flirtatious and ply our charms."

Mr. Choppy was brandishing his stopwatch over his head. "The song was only three and a half minutes long, but it took Jake and Miz Lepanto nearly six minutes to find everything on the list."

"Wait a second," Laurie added. "This is beginning to remind me of that TV game show where the contestants race around the supermarket against the clock. I think we ought to relax a bit about this. Think of it this way. People end up waiting in line at the checkout counter all the time. So what if they have to wait a minute or two for their groceries after Powell has swept them off their feet? This doesn't have to be an exact science. We don't want to make the ladies feel like they're on an assembly line. It's the customized and personalized aspect of this that I think we want to emphasize."

Mr. Choppy admitted: "I guess we were gettin' a little carried away. I'll put the stopwatch away this time. This isn't a swim meet."

The second run-through featured Powell and Denver Lee doing a very energetic cha-cha to a jazzed-up rendition she had found of "Night and Day," while Laurie began her supervision of Kenyatta and the new list.

"I just adore Cole Porter, don't you?" said Denver Lee, moving in sync with Powell as seductively as her extra poundage and flowery muu-muu would allow. "It's the most sophisticated music in the world, in my opinion. They just don't write tunes like that anymore. What do you think?"

Powell arched his eyebrows, looking supremely smug. "I think the beat, beat, beat of the tom-tom goes on. I think I get no kick from cocaine. But I get a kick out of you. I think night and day, you are the one. I've got you under my skin. Shall I go on?"

The man was clearly in his element, Laurie reflected, demonstrating why he remained such a fantasy for many of the older women in Second Creek. He had smooth words with smooth moves—a killer combination.

"Oh, do go on, Powell."

"Shall I speak in French?"

"Yes, yes, yes!" Denver Lee exclaimed, clearly enthralled. For a moment, she felt as if the pounds that hugged her matronly frame had melted away to accommodate the schoolgirlish ardor that had overtaken her.

"Je crois que vous êtes une bell femme!"

"Be still my heart," said Denver Lee, heaving her bosom to the beat. "You are the Maurice Chevalier of canned goods."

"Mais oui, madam! Bien sur!"

Finally, their choreographed romance came to an end. This time, the groceries were ready a couple of minutes ahead of the dancing finale, but Laurie was quick to proclaim the go-round an anomaly. "Denver Lee, everything you've written down on your list was in the produce section." She paused and then rattled it all off. "Grapes, grapefruit, pineapple, pears, peaches, plums, apples, avocados, apricots, lemons, limes, lettuce, blueberries, blackberries, and beets. Kenyatta and I camped out there and didn't have to move anywhere else, and what's with all this alliteration—are these secret patterns in produce or something?"

Denver Lee clasped her hands together and sucked in air. "Ah, I think you may be close to deciphering my brilliant new artistic concept."

Laurie—not to mention everyone else in the store—had clearly drawn a blank, and there was a simultaneous and emphatic shaking of heads.

"Haven't got it yet? Let me explain. You see, I think the trouble with my paintings so far is that they've all been such random collections of still life. No rhyme or reason to them. But the other day as I was checking out the latest Sue Grafton novel at the library, I thought to myself, 'If this woman can write mysteries according to the letters of the alphabet, I can do oil paintings the same way. So I'm going to do a bunch of sketches in alphabetized fruit and vegetable groupings, then work up the paintings from those. You know, all the 'A' produce together, then the 'B' produce, then the 'G,' the 'L,' and finally the 'P.' Obviously, I can't do some of the letters—definitely not 'X' and probably not 'Z'—unless I wanted to try a painting with nothing but different types of zucchini, though I'm not sure there are different types. Still and all, I think this may be the breakthrough I've needed, and I decided to use this occasion to get the items all at once for the sketches."

Novie was predictably the first to react with skepticism. She snatched the list from Laurie and scanned it quickly. "Denver Lee, some of these fruits and vegetables or whatever you want to call them are not going to look very good forced next to each other. Lemons, limes, and lettuce, for God's sake? A painting with nothing but grapes and grapefruit? Don't you realize you'll have nothing but yellow and green coming out the wazoo? It completely disregards proportion and color. People are going to think you've got some kind of food fetish."

"I most certainly do not have a foot fetish!"

"I said food fetish. Go have your hearing checked, you silly fool!"

"Oh, well, that's a bit different. But what makes you such an art expert? You may have seen a famous painting or two, but none of it has apparently rubbed off on your slide composition. Honestly, Novie, you couldn't frame a fig!"

Once again, Laurie refereed. "All right, ladies. We are not here to debate the complexities of art and photography. We are here to prepare for tomorrow's opening, so let's move on." Then she turned to address Kenyatta. "Now, because I can definitely assure you Mrs. McQueen's shopping list was not typical of what we'll encounter, I think you should handle the next list as well, son."

And yet another Nitwitts' fire had been momentarily doused.

The third take on the set, so to speak, turned out to be the charm. Powell led Novie in a slightly scaled-down version of a Viennese waltz to "Falling in Love with Love." He had to be careful with his more dramatic turns to avoid knocking cans and boxes off the shelves—and, in fact, one box of Quaker Instant Grits was felled—but it was nonetheless choreography nearly as impressive as Yul Brynner's 'Shall We Dance?' sequence with Deborah Kerr from *The King and I*. To top it all off, Kenyatta and Laurie pulled up to the counter with the shopping cart within a few seconds of the last four bars.

"Oh, man, this was tha bomb!" Kenyatta announced, giving Jake a crisp high-five and grinning proudly.

For her part, Novie was breathless, claiming she hadn't had such a workout since climbing the steps of the Temples at Abu Simbel in the middle of a sandstorm to take her customary slide show photos.

"New this fall—the windstorm collection," a nearby Denver Lee added somewhat under her breath.

There was only one other incident that caused a minor problem, and that came after Wittsie's fox-trot to that old Johnny Mercer standby "Goody, Goody." A crimson-faced Jake pushed her loaded shopping cart to the checkout counter where Lucy Faye awaited, and then he quietly slinked off, whispering something in Kenyatta's ear.

Laurie took Wittsie aside for a discreet conference while her groceries were being rung up. "Wittsie, I know for a fact you're well past sixty if you're a day. Why on earth are you still buying huge boxes of Kotex? Poor Jake was embarrassed to death. He could barely look me in the eye the rest of the way."

"Oh, Laurie, it wasn't for me," she began, sounding both flustered and apologetic at the same time. "It was for my grand-daughter, Meagan, who's visiting me right now. Oh, I didn't even think about that nice boy. I wondered why he looked so uncomfortable a few moments ago, but with his ruddy coloring and all, I wasn't really sure something was wrong—redheads do tend to look kinda raw and uncooked, you know. Maybe that's a weird way of describing it, but I'm almost sure I've never seen a redhead with a decent tan. I had a redheaded friend once who got burned so bad she had blisters on her back the size of walnuts. Do you think I ought to say something to the boy? No, that would call attention to it even more, wouldn't it?"

"It would, indeed. Better just forget about it. Anyway, it's something the young man would have encountered sooner or later. He'll be very lucky if that's the worst thing he's ever embarrassed about."

A few minutes later Mr. Choppy gathered everyone around him and said: "Well, Mr. Hampton, Miz Lepanto, and ladies of the Nitwitts, do you think we're ready to open our dancin' doors to the general public?"

"No doubt in my mind," Laurie replied.

Powell backed her up quickly. "There at the end, I think we got it exactly right, don't you, ladies?"

The group enthusiastically agreed, and then Mr. Choppy glanced at his watch. "It's nearly ten o'clock. I think we all need to go home and get a good night's sleep for the big day to-morrow. Thanks, folks—one and all. It was . . . what was that thing you said a while back, Kenyatta? Somethin' about an explosion?"

The boy beamed, struck a hip-hop pose with his arms and legs, pursed his lips, and finally leaned in to his employer. "Word was . . . tha bomb, Mr. Choppy. You just wait till tomor-row. It's gonna be tha bomb!"

Chapter Six

OR ALL ITS quirkiness and sleepy southern pace, The Square of Second Creek had an almost Mediterranean look and feel to it—two- and three-story brick and lacework-balconied shops on all four sides, and a massive white-columned courthouse with a terra-cotta roof. The four short streets comprising The Square had been closed to traffic more than forty years ago, creating one of Mississippi's earliest and most popular pedestrian malls, and the only blight on the ensemble was the empty storefronts caused by the infamous MegaMart.

The Honorable Floyce Hammontree, who had been Second Creek's mayor more than twice as long as Laurie Lepanto had been president of the Nitwitts, regretted the economic erosion around the venerable Square, but the sales tax revenue derived from the shopping center on the Bypass was more than making up for those particular losses. Known for his trademark pencil mustache; dark, bushy eyebrows; and seersucker suits, Mr. Floyce, as the electorate had come to call him over the past two decades, had meticulously avoided contemplating the long-term impact of the MegaMart on the downtown district. Instead, he consoled himself with the notion that as long as lively events such as the Annual Delta Floozie Contest could be held throughout the pedestrian mall, Second Creek had nothing to fear. Once they had a taste of The Square and all its many charms, he reasoned, people would continue to come back for more.

No one had ever quite figured out where Mr. Floyce's people were from. He had always claimed to be from someplace in southeast Mississippi, but when pressed further on the matter, he had never bothered to pinpoint the exact location. On the heels of a devastating storm, he had mysteriously managed to get elected to a position of trust in Second Creek, as if he had cast a spell over the entire populace, much as Oberon had caused Titania to fall in love with a mere mortal disguised as a jackass.

"You know," Mr. Floyce was saying to his secretary, a few hours before the Floozie Contest was about to begin. "Being the master of ceremonies of this over-the-top competition is just about my favorite mayoral duty. Why, I'd choose my Bert Parks turn any day over whipping up the city budget or approving raises or fighting with the councilmen or any of the rest of it. Politics can be such a down and dirty business. Of course, that goes no further than this room."

They were seated across from each other in his pretentious, plaque-adorned office, and wizened little Minnie Forbes took notes on the little pad she was never without, carrying it around with her as if it were a purse.

"No, no, Minnie, dear. You don't have to write that down. I was just rambling on out loud."

"Yes, sir, I understand," she replied, adjusting her bifocals.

"Everything I'm saying to you now is, well, off the record."

"Of course, sir."

He fidgeted in his chair a bit and then leaned forward with a determined glint in his eye. "I have to confess that my traditional opening monologue is a great way to feature my talent as a stand-up comic. I guess that all really started when the wife and I took an anniversary trip to Vegas way back when. There are days when I think how nice it would be to be Wayne Newton or somebody like that."

Minnie nodded respectfully. "Oh, I've always loved Wayne Newton, and I enjoy all the jokes you tell around the office. I often repeat them to my husband at home, and he passes them on to the boys at the catfish plant."

"Thank you, Minnie," he replied, clearing his throat. "I've also always fancied myself as a crooner of tunes in a Vic Damone-y or Steve Lawrence-y or even a vintage Frank Sinatra-ish sort of way."

"Well, I like the little song you composed for the Floozie Contest, and I think you have a very nice voice. Everyone around the office seems to think so, too. I've heard them say so at the watercooler and in the lounge."

"Ah, yes—'She's a Doozie, She's a Floozie.' It is an amusing little ditty. And funny you should mention it. Just between the two of us, there may soon be some commercial potential for my song and perhaps a new career waiting in the wings for me.

Specifically, the MegaMart may be interested in distributing and selling my CD. Now, wouldn't that be a hoot? My song available to people wherever there's a MegaMart, and I don't have to tell you that there's one in practically every little town in all fifty states."

"Oh, how exciting! What a tremendous opportunity for you!"

"But you never heard me say anything about that, right? Mum's the word."

"Of course, Mr. Floyce. You know you can trust me. I'm your biggest fan."

Mr. Floyce preened. If only everyone were as appreciative as Minnie.

A COUPLE OF HOURS later Mr. Floyce surveyed the crowd from his perch on the makeshift podium, mentally estimating the number of contestants who had entered this year. He turned to Minnie, who stood next to him, jealously guarding the beautiful crystal Miss Delta Floozie trophy:

"Thirty-three lined up over there this year, Minnie. That'd be an all-time high, wouldn't it? I'm pretty sure we've never had this many before."

Minnie tilted her head, first one way, then the other, and reviewed the extensive notes she had written down on her pad. "You're right, Mr. Floyce. Last year we had twenty-nine, and that was a record then, so this will, indeed, be the most ever. Why, soon we'll have as many as Miss America does."

His Honor was pleased. The event was becoming more and more popular all the time, and this year they would be getting television coverage from WHBQ in Memphis, thanks to Laurie

Lepanto. She had come to his office and informed him of her fund-raising scheme for Mr. Choppy's store and even solicited his help in coordinating the Floozie Contest with the debut of waltzing at the Piggly Wiggly.

At first Mr. Floyce was skeptical. "It sounds a bit like organized chaos to me, Miz Lepanto. We have enough problems every year with crowd control as it is."

Indeed, the June affair had grown into Second Creek's largest tourist event. Women of all ages competed by dressing up in seedy feather boas and tacky sequined gowns, and the winner did not have to be a teenager, or even in the undersixty demographic.

Laurie had remained undaunted. "It can't get any worse than it was the year my cousin, Miss Kittykate, won on her eightieth birthday. I'm sure you remember all the uproar that caused. But your officers handled it all beautifully."

"You have a point there," Mr. Floyce replied. Then his face darkened. "And didn't Miss Kittykate up and die the very next day?"

"Unfortunately, yes."

"Too much excitement?"

"Too much booze and no sleep," Laurie added. "We found out later that she'd stayed up all night celebrating with a gallon of Madeira and then went out at sunrise and rolled all the lawns in her neighborhood. Even got up on a stepladder and draped the toilet paper over the branches just like it was tinsel on a Christmas tree."

Mr. Floyce had struggled to keep a straight face. "Well, I can see the upside to your parade idea, Miz Lepanto. I suppose it would give the losers a chance to keep on struttin' their stuff. It would take just a little of the sting outta not having the trophy for the mantel, I do believe."

"Then we can count on you to go the extra mile for us on this?"

"You certainly can. The more publicity, the better for Second Creek. And may I say that I've heard that radio spot for the Piggly Wiggly that Mr. Powell Hampton produced. You've got most of our Second Creekers all stirred up about this. It'll be interesting to see how it all works out."

And then they had shaken on it.

Yes, Mr. Floyce was indeed pleased. All signs were pointing to the most successful Floozie Contest ever, and who knew? Maybe WHBQ would even capture some of his opening monologue and broadcast it across the Mid-South. Some producer somewhere might see it and offer him a gig at some comedy club and he could bill himself as the Mayor of Comedy and eventually get on Jay Leno or David Letterman and then get a TV series based on his comedy stylings like Tim Allen had done and then he would make movies like that guy Jim Varney who had made up that Ernest character and it would all just be too grand and glorious for words and then—

"Mr. Floyce," Minnie spoke up, interrupting his reverie. "It's time to introduce the judges and get things started."

His Honor came down to earth. "Why, yes, thank you, Minnie. You know me. Always projecting things in my head." He leaned down and gave her a wink. "But I have a feeling some great precedents are going to be set today here in Second Creek. Perhaps history will be made, and we'll be a part of it."

. . .

THE FIRST MINUTE or so of Mr. Floyce's monologue seemed
to be falling flat, and he couldn't imagine why. He had stayed
up practically all night rehearsing the thing, driving his wife, Jo
Nelle, crazy, so he knew it couldn't possibly be a matter of timing. And the material—why, he was certain it was some of his
best. What was wrong with these people? Too many out-of-
towners and not enough Second Creekers, perhaps? Maybe it
was the heat and humidity. Most of the crowd seemed far more
involved with those cardboard fans the ladies of the Nitwitts
had handed out than they were with listening to and truly
appreciating his witticisms. Those Nitwitts were a tedious
bunch to deal with at times.

"You're a good-looking group out there," he continued, trying his best to put their paltry early responses behind him. "So
glad you chose to paddle up Second Creek today. Of course,
that's better than bein' up Second Creek without a paddle!"

He paused for the payoff. There were a few uncomfortable-
sounding titters. Maybe even a groan or two. He steeled himself
and forged ahead.

"Well, looks like we have a record number of contestants
this morning for our annual event. I would tell all you ladies in
the competition how lovely you look, but I know you're no
ladies. And the most unladylike among you will be our winner."

He waited to see if that line did any better, but the audience
of restless children and their irritable parents trying to keep
them in line apparently had no idea what to do with it. He
began to sweat profusely and fidget with his notes, debating

whether or not to crumple them up and move on to the actual competition, but he was keeping a sharp eye out for that TV camera from Memphis and elected to continue.

"Winning the Miss Delta Floozie Contest can mean you've hit the big time. Why, everybody will be talkin' about you. The trouble is, they'll all be talkin' about you behind your back!"

He perked up a bit when a more sizable laugh floated up to the podium. Maybe these folks weren't such duds after all. "Not only that, you won't have to spend a fortune on your wardrobe because no one'll care what you look like with your clothes on. Just one of the tricks of the trade, I guess."

The naughty humor brought forth as many gasps as it did giggles. Well, at least he had their attention now. "All things considered, though, bein' a floozie's not as bad a profession as you might think. It does have its rewards. I guess y'all know the old joke about Florence the floozie who went back home to her high school reunion and ran into one of her old girlfriends? No? Well, it seems her girlfriend asked her real cattylike, 'What are you up to now, Flo?' And Florence answered back just as tart and smart-aleck and catty: 'Oh, about a hundred dollars an hour!'"

Mr. Floyce was in heaven as the crowd finally got with the program and rewarded him with his biggest laugh yet. Damn, where was that TV camera? Wouldn't you know they'd be late just when he was getting the audience all warmed up? Then, out of the corner of his eye, he saw Minnie Forbes pointing to her watch, and he knew he had exhausted all the time allotted to his monologue. Damn, and damn again! Wasn't he ever going to get his big break?

. . .

THE PRELIMINARY ROUND had gone swimmingly. Lots of wiggling and mugging and posturing among the thirty-three contestants, but the field had just been narrowed down to five finalists, and Laurie was pleased that no one who had truly impressed her had been left out.

"Who's your favorite?" she whispered to Powell, who was sitting next to her. They were both a bit uncomfortable in the folding chairs the town fathers had positioned around the square for the audience, but the anticipation of what lay ahead at the Piggly Wiggly was keeping them focused and their minds off their sore rear ends.

"I like Miss Bella DeBall and her Old South theme," he whispered back. "It's just deliriously tacky."

"No, no, no. My money's on Miss Emerald Greene. Very original stuff she trotted out. For some reason I think she's going to be the winner. There's something about her that's very special, something I can't quite put my finger on."

One of the most endearing and amusing traditions of the Floozie Contest was the requirement that each contestant assign to herself an over-the-top alias and develop that image through dialogue and costuming over the course of the competition. Miss Bella DeBall, for example, had positioned herself as a somewhat over-the-hill and ridiculously melodramatic Scarlett O'Hara type.

"I had to sell the plantation for taxes," she had explained in well-rehearsed, histrionic fashion during her preliminary-round monologue on the podium. "And now I've taken to the streets to make ends meet with just this remnant of my former grand existence draping my body." Which remnant, by the way, consisted of a skimpy halter top and pink silk hot pants underneath the ribs of a hoopskirt that covered absolutely nothing. She ended her presentation with a caveat that had brought the house down: "Better not even think of tryin' to pay me in anything other than Confederate money, boys!"

Another finalist, Miss Catfishnet Stocking, had cleverly combined one of the Delta's most profitable industries — catfish farming — with the attire of choice for many a streetwalker — fishnet hosiery. Her costume featured a cartoonish headdress with a papier-mâché catfish, and she had showcased her gorgeous, fishnet-clad gams in a killer leather mini-skirt. "The catfish is a bottom-feeder — cruisin' around down there in the mud. I've been known to fool around in the mud — that's my bottom line. And here's another: care to mud-wrestle with me, boys? Why don'tcha come on down and see me sometime? You'll need a real big hook to catch me!"

Then there was the exotic Miss Juana Goodtime, who wore a red-hot, off-the-shoulder blouse; a bright yellow skirt slit up the leg; and carried around a maraca in each hand to punctuate her every remark — a Hispanic drumroll of sorts. Between that and the high-pitched, birdlike noises she constantly made, she managed to come off like a down-home cross between Charro and Carmen Miranda.

"Hey, hombres," her monologue had begun. "You wanna good time, try this hot tamale — Señorita Juana Goodtime. I shake my maracas for you, si? You like jalapeños? You try this hot pepper, hombre? You like it spicy, you like it the South American way, si? I got what you need, señor!"

In stark contrast was Pretty Woman, Too, who had chosen to

imitate Julia Roberts's streetwalker-turned-Cinderella character. Fortuitously, or perhaps more deliberately, the contestant had emphasized her physical similarities to the star—she was tall with a generous smile and had long, silky legs, set off perfectly by the black leather hip boots she wore. The same pageboy-style blond wig completed the illusion, as did the opening monologue.

"You see this, boys?" she had proclaimed, brandishing an enormous wad of play money in front of her. "You're gonna want to spend this kinda money for an entire week with me. Why, I'll follow you around anywhere, and we'll take bubble baths in the Jacuzzi together and eat strawberries on the carpet and go to the horse races to smooth out steaming divots— anything you want to do. You can even take me out to dinner, and I promise I won't eat the garnish or throw the snails across the room this time. Hey, baby, don't be afraid to scale the heights—I'm your Pretty Woman, Too, and worth every single penny! Whaddaya say, is it a done deal or what?"

Laurie's favorite, Miss Emerald Greene, made perhaps the most striking and indelible impression of them all. With her skin-tight, low-cut, sequined gown; spiked heels; and wig—all of those in the exact same shade of billious green—plus her matching green eye shadow, lipstick, nail polish, emerald ear-rings, and other costume jewelry accessories, she looked like someone Dorothy and her friends might have encountered had they wandered into the low-rent district of the Emerald City. Appropriately, her monologue did not disappoint.

"Hello, all you scarecrows, tin men, and cowardly lions out there. It's not a brain or a heart or some courage you need. It's a little hanky-panky, courtesy of Miss Emerald Greene of Oz. One of the best times Miss Emerald Greene ever had was with a Munchkin, so after a visit with Miss Emerald Greene, you get a free all-day sucker, courtesy the Lollipop Guild. I have an endless supply from those precious little dudes—we just take it out in trade, you see."

Laurie had felt then that Miss Emerald Greene had come up with the most original and flamboyant concept and continued to stick by her prediction that she would be the eventual winner and, therefore, the first to dance with Powell at the Piggly Wiggly.

Then it was time for the final posing, after which the judges would render their decision. The five finalists took their turns on the podium, each of them batting their eyelashes, pouting their lips, and giving a provocative series of come-hither looks to the audience below. The applause and cheering was generous for all of them, but Miss Emerald Greene and Pretty Woman, Too, seemed to have a slight edge over the others.

Finally, the competition phase was over. Minnie retrieved a slip of paper from one of the judges and handed it over to Mr. Floyce, who stood behind the microphone with a smirk, milking the moment for all it was worth. "Ladies and gentlemen, the judges have reached their decision. As mayor of Second Creek, let me congratulate all of the contestants on a very creative and spirited contest this year, and let me also say that I believe any lamppost throughout the great state of Mississippi would be proud to have any one of you leanin' up against it."

Mr. Floyce waited for the modest laughter to subside and then began in earnest. "Fourth runner-up is . . . Miss Catfishnet Stocking!"

Miss Catfishnet Stocking plastered the gamest smile she could manage on her face, blew a kiss to the audience, and accepted the bouquet of flowers Minnie handed her. Then she moved aside for Mr. Floyce's next announcement.

"Third runner-up . . . Miss Juana Goodtime!"

That produced one last vigorous shaking of maracas from Miss Juana Goodtime, who bowed out gracefully.

"Our second runner-up is . . . Miss Bella DeBall!"

Laurie turned to Powell and patted him sympathetically on the leg. "You weren't that far off, though."

"Well, I'm pulling for your girl now that mine's out of the running."

The unbridled murmuring of the audience and the tension it was producing had reached its zenith as the two survivors huddled together holding hands, and Mr. Floyce was clearly taking his own sweet time revealing the winner.

"First runner-up," he said at last. "Pretty Woman, Too! The winner of this year's Miss Delta Floozie Contest is Miss Emerald Greene!"

The audience evidently agreed with the decision, rising to its feet to cheer boisterously and applaud loudly, while the ecstatic victor accepted her trophy and prominently displayed it high above her head as if she had just won the World Series.

"Congratulations," Powell said to Laurie in the midst of all the noise. "You really nailed it!"

After the commotion had died down somewhat, Miss Emerald Greene stepped to the mike to make her acceptance speech in front of the sea of smiling faces below. "I'd like to thank my parents, of course. Particularly my mother. Without her expert cosmetic guidance and outlandish fashion sense, I could never have got myself up like this. And, of course, everyone would agree that I owe a debt to the Wizard, himself, without whose inspiration I could never have come up with the idea for Miss Emerald Greene. Thank you, one and all, and remember to always follow your own yellow brick road of dreams."

There was another appreciative round of applause as Miss Emerald Greene took her final bows while Mr. Floyce stepped up for the pièce de résistance — the climactic performance of his masterpiece — "She's a Doozie, She's a Floozie." Minnie quickly punched up the music on the CD player she had brought along, and Mr. Floyce, whose voice wasn't actually half bad for the boondocks, started in with gusto:

> *"She's a doozie, she's a floozie,*
> *And at times she even looks a little woozy;*
> *She's a winner, and a sinner,*
> *Though we have to say we won't hold that agin her;*
> *Now it's true she is a lady of the night —*
> *But that doesn't mean she's not a welcome sight;*
> *She's a doozie, she's a floozie,*
> *And we have to say we're just a little choosy;*
> *She's a beauty, a rooty-tooty,*
> *And we like the way she shakes her little booty;*
> *She's a doozie, just a floozie,*
> *But we're thankful that she chose to come our way, hey!"*

It seemed that so many people had become so familiar with the catchy little tune that a number were actually singing along now, leaving Mr. Floyce with the perfect opportunity to pitch his latest moneymaking scheme as soon as the applause had died down. "Ladies and gentlemen, for those of you who'd like to own a copy of 'She's a Doozie, She's a Floozie,' I have CDs for sale at a reasonable price. If you're interested, just give my secretary, Minnie Forbes, a call at my office anytime, and she'll make sure you get one. They could become collector's items one day, you know."

After the buzz from his last statement died down, Laurie and Powell approached the podium, and Mr. Floyce remembered that there was another important announcement to make.

"And now, ladies and gentlemen, we have a special treat this year for all of you. Some of you may already know that Mr. Choppy's Piggly Wiggly just off The Square is introducing an exciting new idea—dancing in the aisles while you shop. One of our most prominent citizens, Mr. Powell Hampton, formerly of Studio Hampton, will do the honors for any of you interested ladies. To christen this new service, we are going to ask our new Miss Delta Floozie to lead us in a little parade over to the Piggly Wiggly, and she will be the first to dance with Mr. Hampton. Meanwhile, for those of you who have two left feet, remember our many food vendor tents around The Square. There's plenty of lemonade and popcorn and hot dogs and hamburgers and peanuts and I don't know what all else, so keep on having a good time, eat and drink up, and thanks for coming to Second Creek this weekend for the Annual Miss Delta Floozie Contest!"

It took a while to organize the parade properly, but with the help of the Second Creek Police Department, it got done. At the head of the line, of course, was Mr. Floyce, escorting the new Miss Delta Floozie. The unlikely couple were followed in turn by the other four finalists, Laurie and Powell, the rest of the Nitwitts, who had had a nip or two for courage, more of the contestants, and finally an assortment of ordinary female citizens whose curiosity had gotten the better of them.

Chapter Seven

M<small>R. CHOPPY WAS</small> somewhat overwhelmed by the revved-up spillover from the Floozie Contest. He was a virtual stuck record, cornering people right and left: "Glad to see you, folks! Hasn't been this much traffic in the store since those straight-line winds took the finger right off the Presbyterian Church. Remember that? People were lined up all the way out to The Square for the free food Daddy was givin' away. No sir, not since then!"

"Well, I've been doing an impromptu survey of sorts," Laurie said, taking him aside at one point. "And about half the customers—the women, of course—said they came in to try the dancing in the aisles, and the other half just came in to gawk at the goings-on. But both groups said they'd do a bit of shopping while they were here, so I think we're going to accomplish our mission."

"Sure hope so, Miz Lepanto."

"And see over there, Mr. Choppy?" she continued, pointing to a television crew. "WHBQ has set up shop for Powell's first dance. Imagine all the attention you're going to get when this gets broadcast up in Memphis. All the cable systems in this part of Mississippi carry the Memphis stations, too. You couldn't ask for better publicity."

They both glanced at the throng of people gathering around the camera and crew, and Laurie couldn't help but giggle. "There's never a shortage of people who can resist making fools of themselves, especially in small towns. They wave like a pack of kindergarten children whenever a television camera appears."

"You're right about that. This is everything I'd hoped for and more. And so far the boys are handling the pressure just fine, I'm happy to say. Lucy Faye, too." He hesitated, suddenly setting his mouth in a grim slash. "But if you don't mind me sayin' so, Miz Lepanto, I'm a little bit nervous about doin' that interview with the TV folks. I've never done one, ya know."

She took his hand and patted it gently. "You just be your regular self. Don't worry. If you get tongue-tied or something, they'll do it over and over until it comes out right. Kind of like takes in a movie scene. They're not going to let anything inappropriate go out over the air."

Powell and Mr. Floyce approached them with a preening Miss Delta Floozie in tow, and Powell said: "Our winner here has selected 'You Don't Know Me' for the slow dance we're going to do."

"Oh, I've loved that little number since I was a teenager," Laurie replied. "Guess I dated myself pretty good there, didn't I?"

The former Miss Emerald Greene daintily wrinkled up her nose. "My studied opinion is that 'You Don't Know Me' is one of the great honky-tonk, sad songs of all time. It's right up there with 'Crazy' by Patsy Cline. I think it stirs and percolates all the female juices." Then she sang a few quick bars a cappella.

"You have a very impressive voice," Powell added. "Very full and rich—almost Mermanesque."

"Why, thank you, Mr. Hampton. I'm almost positive no one's ever compared me to The Merm. That's a first for me."

"I'm surprised. You even look like her just a little bit. The younger Ethel Merman, I mean. The one that took New York by storm."

Then she handed him a CD. "I brought you the classic Ray Charles version with all the strings in the background for our dance—a little soul for our soles, if you don't mind a little dancing humor. I can remember playing that record until I wore out the grooves, thinking about all the boys I had crushes on when I was just a wee adolescent thing. Oh, I would think to myself, if only the boy of my dreams really could get to know me. What a surprise package he'd find."

There were a few smirks and giggles, and then the TV reporter, who had previously introduced himself to everyone as Ronnie Leyton of the "Eye on the Mid-South" program, moved in with his crew to pin lavaliere mikes on the dancing couple, as well as Mr. Floyce and Mr. Choppy. "We'd like to get a few comments from all of you before we get started," he explained.

The crew quickly white-balanced the camera to eliminate any possibility of green faces, the reporter did his intro, and then the media-savvy Mr. Floyce was up first. "As the mayor of Second Creek I'm sure I speak for all our citizens when I say that this new dance-while-you-shop feature now being offered by our downtown Piggly Wiggly is yet another reason to visit us here on our quaint and charmin' little town square. We just wound up our Annual Delta Floozie Contest, of course, and that event just grows larger and larger every year. It's just one more reason for you tourists out there to find out what Second Creek is all about. Why, sometimes I think we're the best-kept little secret in Mississippi . . ."

From the copious notes in his hand, it looked like Mr. Floyce had fashioned a filibuster-length speech in the grand manner of Deep South politicians, but the reporter seemed to anticipate the maneuver and cut him off without hesitation. "Thank you very much, Mayor Hammontree. Now, if you don't mind, I need you to stay right where you are while we set up the over-the-shoulder of me."

"But I wasn't through," Mr. Floyce insisted, looking thoroughly exasperated.

"We're on a tight production schedule, sir. Sorry," Ronnie Leyton answered.

Mr. Floyce looked a bit disappointed that his moment was over but quietly obeyed as the reporter breezed through his B-roll shots and then moved on to Mr. Choppy, who was by now sweating profusely and mopping his brow with a piece of Kleenex.

Laurie rushed to his aid, taking him aside and whispering in his ear. "Just relax, Mr. Choppy, you're not on trial here. Picture yourself having one of your ordinary friendly conversations with one of your customers. That's just a harmless TV reporter over there, not Lady Roth on the rampage. Just keep that in mind. You've survived Lady Roth. Everything else is a piece of cake."

She had chosen the perfect words to put him at ease, and Mr. Choppy's familiar smile returned. "Okay, Mr. Leyton, I'm through with my pep talk now," he said, dabbing his forehead with the Kleenex one last time.

The reporter gave him a thumbs-up and posed the first question. "Tell us a little bit about the history of the Second Creek Piggly Wiggly, sir. For instance, how long ago did it first open for business?"

Mr. Choppy took a deep breath and bravely faced the camera. "Well, my daddy, Mr. Hale Dunbar, started it up in the Roaring Twenties. We were the first franchise market in Second Creek, and by the time I was born during the Depression, the Piggly Wiggly was the place to go and visit with your friends while you shopped. You could even leave 'em messages on our big cork bulletin boards over near the front door. That's been our ongoing tradition for decades."

"Do you recall a particularly memorable message?"

Mr. Choppy's face lit up almost immediately. "Sure do. It was the time Mr. Hunter Goodlett proposed to his pretty little girlfriend on the bulletin board. Tacked up a piece a' paper that said, 'Miss Mary Fred Sharpe, will you marry me, please ma'am?' Mr. Hunter had an eye for the ladies, all right, but he was painful shy, you see. And the next day he came by to check, but she hadn't seen it yet. I started to give her a call to let her know she had a message, but Daddy said, 'No, I got a better idea!' And his idea was that anyone who came in to shop could bet on when Miss Mary Fred would finally see Mr. Hunter's message and answer back. You had to predict the day, the hour, and the minute she would tack up her reply and whether she'd say yes or no, and the one who came closest to gettin' all that right was gonna win a shoppin' cart fulla free groceries. I tell you, my daddy had a knack for gettin' people into the store."

As Mr. Choppy paused to chuckle softly under his breath, it was obvious he had all but forgotten about his early bout with nerves. "Funny thing was, it took Miss Mary Fred so long to come by and see the message that practically everybody in town knew about the proposal before she did. But finally she saw it and replied."

"Let me guess. She said yes."

"Sure did. And believe it or not, somebody guessed it down to the minute. I believe Daddy was so impressed he doubled the amount of free groceries. Oh, and Mr. and Miz Hunter Goodlett are still goin' strong."

That brought the interview to an abrupt but successful conclusion, and while Ronnie Leyton and his crew once again set up for the B-roll, Laurie enthusiastically took Mr. Choppy aside.

"You were brilliant. I'd forgotten all about that big Hunter and Mary Fred to-do."

She suddenly realized that her tendency to preside over things had appointed her director of this little mini-drama by default. Though Ronnie Leyton was handling his crew with admirable efficiency, she was handling the cast of characters — one by one, it seemed — and Powell was next in line to receive her words of advice.

"I think you should keep a low profile and let our Miss Delta Floozie have her fifteen minutes of fame all by herself."

"Exactly what my gentlemanly code of manners suggested I

should do," he replied. "My moment to shine will come when we start dancing together."

"This is a dream come true for me," Miss Delta Floozie was saying once Powell had graciously deferred to her during their interview. "This isn't my first time at the rodeo, you know. I had entered before but never managed to make the finals. So I went back to the drawing board, and this year, as Miss Emerald Greene, I found the right formula and obviously struck a responsive chord with the judges, and because of that I get to slow-dance with Mr. Powell Hampton right here in the Second Creek Piggly Wiggly. Now, I ask you outright, how many of you girls get to say that?"

Then it was time to move the proceedings to the canned goods aisle, and everyone began to press in noisily around the tuna fish and the pink salmon in an attempt to get a front-row spot for the forthcoming soiree.

"My God!" Laurie exclaimed, turning to Ronnie Leyton. "This is almost as bad as one of those rock concerts. I think we need to do a little crowd control to keep this from getting out of hand, don't you?"

So the TV crew began directing traffic, assigning the overflow to surrounding aisles, while Laurie intervened to soothe all the ruffled feathers. "Ladies and gentlemen, I'm sure that Miss Delta Floozie and Mr. Hampton will put in an appearance along all of the aisles, so whether you're waiting for them near the A-1 steak sauce or over by the Green Giant peas, you won't miss the important action."

Then the music started playing, and the Ray Charles version of "You Don't Know Me" was as deliciously lush and dependably slow-paced as it had always been, enabling the couple to live up to Laurie's promise. At least three different aisles of onlookers and bystanders were treated to a ballroom clinic on the art of the sensuous slow-dance—the kind most often favored by illicit lovers and newlyweds and teenagers with crushes. There was appreciative applause all along the route. Two straws, malt shop, romantic—bordering on corny—some might have called it.

"Why, I felt just like I was at the junior-senior prom, sir," Miss Delta Floozie said, curtsying before her partner as the song ended and the onlookers offered one last cheer of approval.

Powell bowed low in gentlemanly fashion in return. "And I thank you for the dance, my dear. True, the lights were a little on the bright and fluorescent side, and we were missing that romantic waterfall made out of paper streamers, but all in all, I think our 'Evening at the Piggly Wiggly' was something to press in our scrapbook of memories."

What happened next would be talked about for some time to come in and around Second Creek, Memphis, and the rest of the Mid-South. It happened so fast, in fact, that Ronnie Leyton and his crew still had their camera rolling, and the entire flabbergasting sequence was captured on tape, much to the everlasting chagrin of Mr. Floyce.

Miss Delta Floozie ripped off her green wig with one hand—exposing her manly crew cut underneath—pulled a pair of silicone falsies from her cleavage with the other hand, laughed in what could only be termed a conspiratorial manner, and finally proclaimed loudly in a voice one full octave below the one she had been using: "Hi, there, Second Creek and all you folks out there in TV land. Good-bye to Miss Emerald

Greene, and a good old-fashioned southern hush-my-mouth howdy-do from Mr. Gary Greene, Esquire, winner of this year's Miss Delta Floozie Contest!"

Everyone who had witnessed the unexpected reversal of gender first hand, including Laurie, stood rooted to the floor, eyes bugged out in disbelief. It was Powell, however, who finally shattered the astonished silence.

"I'll be damned," he said, but he sounded more amused than offended. "I've danced with plenty of women in my time, and I swear I couldn't tell you weren't, well, the genuine article. For that alone I'd say you definitely deserved to win the award."

"Oh, I had a little padding here and there to help with the smoke and mirrors. Also enough warpaint on to put all the female televangelists in the world to shame. I went all out to win this time. Even slammed down Slim-Fast for a solid month and lost ten pounds in all the right places. Of course, then I had to sort of build them back up with a little padding. It was practically an engineering project when all was said and done."

Mr. Floyce stepped up, his face as pink as the tomatoes ripening over in the produce bin. "Excuse me, Mister Gary Greene, but you do realize you've made a mockery of the Delta Floozie Contest, don't you? You've won the crown under false pretenses! And I do emphasize the word *false!*"

The young man playfully dangled the falsies he was still holding. "Are you referring to these, Mister Mayor?"

A number of people in the crowd started laughing, causing Mr. Floyce to glare in their general direction before resuming the confrontation. "This is no joking matter. This contest is supposed to be for women only. We obviously can't allow you to keep the crown under these circumstances. We'll just have to give it to the first runner-up. Where's Pretty Woman, Too?"

Gary snickered and put his wig back on, though it was slightly askew. "You're gonna give the crown to Howard?"

"Who the hell is Howard?"

Pretty Woman, Too—hip boots, blond wig, and all—immediately pushed her way through the crowd. "I'm Howard, and I'll be with you in a New York minute," she began. But just as she reached Mr. Floyce, off came the wig and down a register plummeted the voice. "Yazzuh, that's me, Howard Richard Westerfield, at your beck and call."

"Howard and I had a bet with each other and some of our friends that one of us could definitely win the Floozie Contest this year, and, what the hey, we finished one-two," Gary continued to explain. "Pretty damned good, huh? We had no idea we'd both do as well as we did."

"Good God!" Mr. Floyce exclaimed, grabbing at his chest. "This isn't one of those ludicrous drag contests. We aren't New Orleans! Second Creek is supposed to be a family-friendly place. Next thing you know, we'll have MTV wanting to come here."

Gary gave him a devilish wink. "Don't worry. Most of your contestants every year are women, but I can tell you that some of us boys have been seriously trying to win it for quite a long time now. And there's nothing in the rules that says you have to be a woman. I know because we went over them several times with a fine-tooth comb. All you have to do is make up a character and stick with it, and that's exactly what Howard and I did. I'm sure it would surprise you to find out just how many men have entered the contest over the years. Since they all lost, though, none of them ever felt it was worth it to go public. That changed as of today, of course."

By now Laurie had gathered her scattered wits and resumed her directorial duties. She tapped Mr. Floyce on the arm for a discreet one-on-one. "You do know the camera is still rolling, don't you? I suggest you stop worrying about who you're going to give the title to and get together with Mr. Leyton about what he will and will not put on the air."

For the record, Laurie couldn't remember when she had seen such a look of panic on the man's face, but the Honorable Floyce Hammontree was nothing if not a quick study. He instantly launched into damage control mode.

"May I invite you and your crew back to my office on the square to discuss a few things, Mr. Leyton?"

"Just briefly, Mayor. We have that schedule to keep. I'm expected back in Memphis to put this together."

And at that point, the camera was finally shut off, and Mr. Choppy stepped up. "Well, folks, we hope you liked our little floor show today, complete with a twist. Hey, what can I say? That's show business. But don't forget your shoppin' now. We've got plenty of items on sale throughout the store, and for you ladies who've come in to dance, Powell Hampton will be at your service until two o'clock. Thanks for comin' to the Piggly Wiggly, and if you need anything or have any questions, please call on me or any of our friendly staff. As my daddy used to say, 'We know who you and your people are, and that's why we want your business!'"

Laurie whispered in his ear. "Way to turn those lemons into lemonade, Mr. Choppy!"

.   .   .

LAURIE WAS RELIEVED when things began to settle into a routine over the next couple of hours. Powell was getting quite a workout from all the ladies, none of whom had apparently been deterred in the least by his flawless performance with a drag queen. It all meant, of course, that Mr. Choppy and the Piggly Wiggly were definitely raking in the money, and by two-fifteen it was apparent that the store was going to have to extend the dancing hours—at least for this one occasion—until three o'clock.

"Don't ever remember takin' in this much at one time," Lucy Faye was telling her boss just as three finally rolled around. "Think we can keep up at this pace, Mr. Choppy? There just ain't that many people in Second Creek and nearby. Why, I'd almost be willin' to bet we've had near as many people in here today as they have regulars out at the MegaMart."

He shook his head while scanning the backed-up lines at the other two registers. "Oh, I doubt we can keep this up. This kind of grand-opening excitement never lasts too long. But it has given us a temporary shot in the arm."

Jake pulled up with the groceries of Powell's current partner—a Mrs. Imogene Wyatt, who had come all the way from nearby Greenwood with a pink silk rose pinned in her big, blond, country-singer hair—but Laurie, who was trailing the cart, had a bad case of the giggles about something and kept covering her mouth to keep from bursting into outright laughter.

"What's so funny?" Mr. Choppy said, while helping Jake unload the groceries onto the conveyor belt.

"Something Jake told me a few minutes ago. He said he knew without a doubt that Miss Emerald Greene was a man as soon as we started working on her shopping list. Why don't you tell it, Jake?"

"That Miss Emerald Greene's list was mighty peculiar for a woman. I mean, she wanted Right Guard—that's what me and all my buddies use under our arms, you know—and she wrote down Gillette Disposable Razors—not them pretty pink Lady Gillette ones—she meant the man's razors, and then she wanted some Aqua Velva aftershave and some shaving cream, but she wrote down 'for sensitive beards' next to it, you see what I mean? Then when she . . . I mean, he . . . took off her wig—I mean, his wig . . . it all made sense. I figured somethin' was up, ya know."

Mr. Choppy patted the boy on the shoulder and leaned in confidentially. "Yep, that was a fine bit a' detective work you did there, son."

"A new supply of razors and all that other paraphernalia makes sense to me," Laurie giggled. "I'm sure she . . . I mean, he . . . was fresh out after getting ready for the contest. A heavy five o'clock shadow would probably have been a dead giveaway to the judges." Laurie glanced down at her watch. "Meanwhile, I think I'd better go check on Powell and see if his feet are still attached to his body, poor fellow. This has been every bit the marathon we'd hoped for. Didn't I tell you it was going to be a huge success, Mr. Choppy?"

He nodded, briefly flashing a smile her way, but for some reason she got the distinct impression that his heart wasn't really in it.

.   .   .

AROUND TEN O'CLOCK that night, Mr. Choppy sank down on
the edge of his bed and blew out a whole chestful of pent-up air.
"Lord, help me get through all this with grace," he said out loud
while glancing prayerfully at the ceiling.

Yes, the store had taken in a healthy amount of money today.
And yes, the publicity was invaluable, probably postponing for
a little longer the day the MegaMart would be able to count the
Piggly Wiggly among its commercial victims. Mr. Floyce had
been unable to talk the Memphis TV crew out of discarding the
footage of Gary Greene's, aka Miss Emerald's, unexpected revelation, and therefore the piece was going to appear shortly as a
segment of the popular "Eye on the Mid-South" program.
Despite His Honor's assurances to the contrary, Mr. Choppy
knew there was no way such lighthearted coverage would
end up doing anything more than reinforcing Second Creek's
already-eccentric reputation. But really, that was nothing to
worry about. The town could certainly handle a few more gawk-
ing tourists.

Nonetheless, the last few weeks had been very difficult for
him to endure. From the moment Laurie Lepanto had pressed
him for the details of that Hollywood troupe's appearance during the war, he had struggled to keep the memories of that tor-
mented period of his life from rising to the surface. He knew the
entire town was still curious about what had happened way
back then, but he and his family had been careful to keep them
all in the dark as much as possible.

Mr. Choppy reached over and picked up the framed picture
on his nightstand. It was not of the much-rumored ladyfriend, it

was of him—Hale Dunbar Jr.—as a young man of sixteen. He shook his head. It was now virtually impossible for him to believe he had once looked like that, but he had been a rather striking lad back then. A full head of curly brown hair, the sunken, rawboned cheeks of a boy on the verge of manhood. The smile on his face an expectant one, the sort of smile teen-agers trot out with regularity because they believe the entire world is theirs for the taking. Indeed, there was nothing Hale Dunbar Jr. believed he could not have or try for back then.

Bits and pieces of the past bubbled up.

Some Hollywood studio—maybe Paramount, maybe MGM—had sent a troupe out all over the country to help sell war bonds, and a few of those actors had gotten sidetracked down South. Their Studebaker had broken down in Second Creek on the way to some Big Band shindig at the Peabody Hotel up in Memphis. They had come into the Piggly Wiggly out of a driving rain to buy something to eat while their car was being repaired at the garage down the street.

Hale Dunbar Jr. had stars in his eyes at the outset, even though all of them turned out to be B-movie players. Two of them—Shirley Ann Turner and Jack Westman—told him they had just gotten small parts in something called *The Line Forms in Rio*, stopping short of admitting they were just glorified extras. Nonetheless, Hale was in the presence of the honest-to-goodness Hollywood that he had always worshipped.

But it was the trio of pretty singing sisters who stole the show that night.

"We're the Andrew Sisters," one of them announced casu-ally as Hale Jr. stood nearby.

"Whooee!" Hale's father had shouted, winking at his son. "I

cain't believe I've got Patti, Maxine, and LaVerne Andrews right here in my little store!"

Another sister quickly chimed in. "No, you misunderstand, sir. Everyone makes the same mistake. We're not the Andrews Sisters, we're the A-N-D-R-E-W Sisters. We're Pearl, Peggy, and Polly Andrew. We're not even real good look-alikes, but we do know all their songs."

Everyone in the store had flocked to the sisters like chickens after feed. The requests began to pile up.

"You want us to sing right here in the aisles?" Pearl Andrew, the oldest sister, had said, looking incredulous.

"Why, sure!" Hale Dunbar replied. "Dance, too, if you want. We're havin' one of our Second Creek thundergushers out there. We never know what brings 'em on, but I can promise ya it won't let up anytime soon, so why not liven up my store a little while ya wait?"

The sisters gave in and immediately went into action, doing the jitterbug and other dances with some of the men over by the butcher's counter so they could get in line and take a number. They also managed to work up passable a cappella renditions of "Don't Sit Under the Apple Tree," "Boogie Woogie Bugle Boy," and "Bei Mir Bist Du Schoen," to the delight of the crowd. The Piggly Wiggly was transformed into an impromptu Hollywood Canteen for one improbable evening, and Hale Jr. took part, drinking it all up like manna from heaven.

He fell in love overnight, as so many young men do. He was a goner with stars in his eyes from the start.

She had dangled it all before him, she was to become his means to the main chance, and he was going to have it all—the secret life he had always wanted, a life far removed from Second Creek, Mississippi.

Mr. Choppy put down the picture, walked over to his dresser, and looked at himself in the mirror. Seventy-one years old now and not only filled-out, but paunchy and balding. But there were still traces around the eyes of that sixteen-year-old boy. He sometimes wondered how he had managed to preserve that hopeful spark. Maybe it was because he had gotten a lot of the bitterness and rage out of his system the night he had gone to the store after hours and taken the meat cleaver to every piece of packaged animal flesh in sight.

Not long after, the gossipy, behind-the-scenes, whisper-filled legend of Mr. Choppy and the *Mysterious Woman* was born.

With every passing year, however, it was getting more and more difficult for him to remember her face. He had no picture of her, just his fading memories of the way she had looked and moved and laughed and made love to him during that brief, hectic watershed period of his life. He knew Laurie and the others couldn't have guessed the many details of the true source of his secret, all-day discomfort. He was just going to have to steel himself for what lay ahead—a prolonged period of sleeplessness as he tossed and turned with the replays of what had happened so long ago. Either that or he would manage to fall asleep and have disturbing dreams about her. The worst were the ones where the woman who seemed to have it all had come through for him and he had soared to unbelievable heights and the world was still at his feet and—

"Enough, you old fool!" he shouted, defiantly making a fist of his maimed hand in the mirror. Then he marched into the bathroom to brush his teeth and prepare for bed. His one modest consolation was that he was still in business with his family's cherished Piggly Wiggly to occupy much of his time—at least for the time being—keeping his broken dreams at arm's length.

LAURIE AND POWELL sat in her kitchen sipping wine and soaking their feet together in a big bucket filled with warm water and Epsom salts. The long day had taken a lot out of them both, but they were somehow finding the energy to carry on a genuine, full-fledged flirtation.

"You are one smooth operator," she said, gently rubbing her big toe along the top of his arch. "You didn't even blink when Gary Greene tore off his wig. Some men I know would have been very upset. If it had been Mr. Floyce dancing, there might have been a blow or two landed. Maybe even gunfire, God forbid. There's always been something about him that doesn't quite add up."

"Floyce Hammontree is a typical pompous politician on the prowl for the ideal photo op. I found it especially amusing that he accused Mr. Greene of making a mockery of the Floozie Contest. How can you make a mockery of something that's already a parody? I mean, a parade of streetwalkers vying for best in show? Woof, woof! That's about as camp as you can get."

"Amen," she answered, laughing brightly.

"I have to admit I was startled at first. But you run across all kinds in the ballroom trade. Ann and I once attended a very elaborate drag ballroom competition in Paris—the Folies-Brassiere." He paused for a hearty chuckle. "Some of the male participants looked and moved exactly like women—and vice versa. Why, you couldn't even tell in conversation with them up close. Well, maybe if you got really, really close up, which you could hardly do without appearing impolite. I have to give Mr. Greene credit for a job well done. Same for his friend, Howard."

Laurie paused for a moment. There he was drifting back to Ann again. Somehow he always found a way to work her into the conversation. Maybe he meant absolutely nothing by it—after all, once in a while she had made a reference to Roy in his presence. On the plus side, he had become increasingly affectionate with her. More lingering kisses. Prolonged handholding. An unexpected touch or caress that gave her the good kind of goose bumps. So she really had no cause for complaint. Then, a delayed insight crashed in on her, producing the sunniest of her smiles.

"Oh, I get it!" she said, then breaking out into conspicuous laughter. "'You Don't Know Me.' I get it now!"

Powell looked at her sideways. "What are you talking about?"

"The song Miss Emerald Greene, or rather Gary chose for your dance: 'You Don't Know Me.'"

Then Powell suddenly got it, too. "Oh, yeah. A nice little touch of irony, there, from a clever girl—I mean, guy. It was really rather a bit of a code song, wasn't it?"

"Yes, it was. Anyhow, I don't know why Mr. Floyce got so bent out of shape. I thought everyone at least suspected that a man or two had slipped into the Floozie Contest before. You know how word of mouth is in this town."

"You have to remember that Floyce Hammontree lives in his

own special world. God knows what really goes on in that head of his. I am justifiably proud of the fact that the first time I cast a vote in Second Creek after moving here, it was against that man and his endless banter. Somewhere along the way I think he definitely missed his calling, and it's way past time for him to retire."

Laurie decided to forge ahead, taking advantage of the gentle glow of amusement. "Speaking of retiring, I'd be more than happy to have you stay the night here." She added an exclamation point of sorts by playing footsie with him beneath the surface of their soothing footbath.

"You like my devilish sense of humor, and I like your directness," he replied. "Well, let me put you at ease. Yes, I'd very much like to stay here with you tonight. Absolutely no dancing, though. We'll have to think of . . . something else." Then he leaned over and gave her one of those kisses she liked so much. Warm, reassuring, lingering. She had to catch her breath after it was over.

They retired to the bedroom, and she turned out the lights as they undressed, the only illumination streaming in from the bathroom door, which was ajar. It afforded them both some measure of modesty.

"It's been a few years," he told her, laying his long bones down beside her. "I trust I haven't forgotten anything."

The remark put her at ease, and she responded in kind. "Same here, but my instincts tell me we'll be just fine."

Then he propped himself up on his side, leaning into her, and they kissed warmly once again. He moved down to her breasts and her nipples, and it was quite clear to her that indeed he had not forgotten how to stoke a woman's fire. He was steady, patient, tender—everything she had hoped he would be. Soon, they were well into the throes of making love, beginning a new chapter in their emotional lives.

Afterward, they clung to each other as their pulses wound down, and she was the first to speak.

"That was wonderful, Powell. To be honest, I wondered if I would ever be able to make love to anyone again." Their limbs still entwined, she could feel the impact of her statement moving through him.

"I know just what you mean."

Then she realized that what she had said had far more meaning for him than for herself. "Oh, Powell," she began. "Look who I'm talking to. I hope you don't think I was being insensitive."

He kissed her lightly on the forehead. "Nonsense. You don't have to walk on eggshells around me."

Whatever else they were feeling, they left unsaid for the time being, falling asleep in each other's arms.

Chapter Eight

*P*OWELL WAS SITTING at Laurie's breakfast table with his face buried in the morning paper. She was standing at the stove, brewing coffee and scrambling eggs and trying her best not to project too far into the future.

No, this man was not Roy and never would be, solid and predictable the way Roy was—but he was someone she was already prepared to accept and enjoy as her new companion—and husband if it came to that. He was as skilled in bed as he was on the dance floor, and the rhythms he had shown her the night before had left her breathless and satisfied. She was now officially out of the back porch deep freeze and smack dab in the middle of the world of the thawed and warm-blooded again.

"Bad news," Powell said, suddenly peering at her over the top of the paper.

She momentarily put down her slotted spoon. "Oh, no. Who died?"

"Not someone. A building. Another one doomed to destruction by the likes of the MegaMart."

"You don't mean Piggly Wiggly, do you? Not after all the trouble we've gone to."

He said no, then invited her over with a tilt of his head and pointed to the front-page article. "The Grande Theater. It's been condemned, and they'll start razing it this Saturday, it looks like."

Laurie scanned the photo of the now somewhat derelict art-deco building. The Grande had been the town's pipeline to Hollywood for over seventy years, but the pedestrian, cookie-cutter fourplex next to the MegaMart had caused it to go dark for good a few years back. Since then, as the article indicated, it had gone downhill at an alarming pace, with an assortment of vandals and countless flocks of roosting pigeons hastening its demise. The roof had collapsed. And now, this final, ignominious blow.

"Oh, I could just spit on Floyce Hammontree!" she exclaimed. "All that talk he did during his last election campaign about how he was going to do everything he could to save the Grande. Oh, it could be a museum, or a restaurant, it could be used for staging the Floozie Contest, it could be practically anything."

Powell nodded. "I've heard rumors that somebody wants to put in a parking lot or some tacky quick-oil-change business on the site. They must have greased his sweaty palm but good."

"Yes, I've heard those rumors myself." Laurie hurried back

over to the stove. "You know what? I have half a notion to round up the Nitwitts and we'll all march over to his office and at least give him a piece of our minds. Six angry socialites with nothing but time on their hands. That ought to put the fear of God into him."

"Go for it."

"I don't suppose it'll do much good, though."

"Hey, no harm in trying."

"No, there's not. And we Nitwitts are damned good at stirring things up."

"None better in my book."

She noisily tapped the slotted spoon on the edge of the skillet a few times. "I think I will then. It's something that needs to be said and done. In fact, I think I'll start calling everybody up right this minute and see what we can organize. Gritty gentility does the trick every time."

"Nothing like wealthy women on the warpath. Remind me never to get on the bad side of you Nitwitts," he concluded, giving her a peck on the cheek.

HIS HONOR WAS hemming and hawing in the presence of the Nitwitts. They had gathered in a specially arranged meeting at the mayor's office on Saturday morning. Minnie Forbes fussed in the background, frantically taking notes.

"Uh, ladies, there are, uh, health hazards and an exhausting array of city ordinances to consider in regards to the Grande. Uh, the place is completely overrun with pigeons, which are dirty, filthy birds and well-known carriers of various diseases. Have any of you ever heard of histoplasmosis? It's a very serious lung disease that you can catch by inhaling pigeon feathers, if I'm not mistaken. I cannot risk the health of our population by allowing such a festering sore to remain in our downtown area."

Laurie drew herself up with all the authority she could muster. "Festering sore? Aren't you being a bit dramatic? Besides, all those pigeons can be exterminated with a little effort. Wouldn't that be less expensive than demolishing the entire building? Aren't we throwing the baby out with the bathwater here?"

Mr. Floyce looked almost indignant. "I guess you don't realize that the roof caved in because of all the pigeon doo-doo on top of it. Why, you'd, uh, have to replace the entire roof, which would entail a partial demolition anyway. That would substantially affect the integrity of the building. There are practical considerations you ladies clearly haven't thought about, well-meaning as you may be in this regard."

"Whatever happened to your campaign promise about adaptive use of the building? You do recall that you made such a promise, don't you? Or was that just so much rhetoric to get votes?"

"Yes, I did mention that during my last campaign, Miz Lepanto, but that was before I realized what truly terrible shape the building was in. This is not as simple as it looks. You can't just will somethin' into usefulness. And the Grande has outlived its usefulness, I'm afraid. Only the pigeons find it useful these days. That's a fact. As I said, it's become nothin' more than a saggin' pit of pigeon poop and filthy feathers."

Novie Mims closed her eyes and shook her head emphatically, wagging a stubby, bejeweled finger in his general direction. "How astoundingly and awesomely alliterative of you, Mr. Floyce. But I disagree. I offer one word in rebuttal—tourism."

"I'm well aware of our tourism potential, Miz Mims," he replied, barely able to keep the hostility out of his voice.

"Well, then, you are missing a golden opportunity for more of it by not restoring the Grande to its former splendor. Why, we could have Hollywood film revivals and other events related to the performing arts in there. We could have Mississippi actors and writers perform and read their works in there. We could invite Morgan Freeman or John Grisham or Gerald McRainey—people like that. They're devoted Mississippians through and through. I above anyone else in Second Creek understand the value of tourism. I've been to practically every country in the free world and some not-so-free, and I have the slides to prove it."

All the other Nitwitts exchanged knowing glances and rolled their eyes. "Yes, Miz Mims, I have attended one or two of your slide shows at the Rotary Club. The one with all the ocean shots from the back of your many cruise ships was, uh, especially riveting."

"We are not here to discuss Novie's slide shows," Laurie added. "We are here to save the Grande. I do think, however, that Novie makes a valid point about an adaptive use for the theater, Mr. Floyce. Don't you think we could make every effort to contact some of the organizations that offer grants to preserve worthy landmarks? Have you bothered looking into any of that?"

Mr. Floyce looked acutely uncomfortable and shifted his

weight behind his desk. "Ladies, we just don't have time to save every saggin' roof and broken-out window in this town. There are major priorities that demand my, uh, our constant attention. Industry to attract. Salaries to pay. Roads to pave."

"Ah, yes, the Great Pungent God of Asphalt," Laurie returned. "My late husband, Roy, once told me that the secret to being a successful politician here in the Deep South was to pave as many roads as possible. Convert somebody's gravel washboard to smooth asphalt, and you have a loyal voter for life."

Mr. Floyce cleared his throat with a great deal of authority. "Paving county roads is an entirely worthy goal and a judicious use of taxpayers' money. Getting people back and forth from their homes to their work is completely laudable and necessary."

"Then perhaps you'll admit you're more concerned with selling CDs of your Floozie Contest song than with the welfare of this city. Or that the concept of zoning is completely alien to you," Laurie added, pulling no punches. "Roy also said that the only use you had for zoning was in a basketball game."

Mr. Floyce frowned. "I had no idea Roy Lepanto was such a detractor of mine. He apparently had no intention of ever saying any of that to my face."

"Let's just say he had your number, Mr. Floyce. He was in the insurance game, as you might remember, so he was very good with figures."

"And, uh, what is that supposed to mean, dear lady?"

Laurie moved in for the kill. "The scuttlebutt around town is that one of those oil change/self-serve gas station combinations wants the site of the Grande. Now I wonder whose coffers were filled to allow that little zoning atrocity? Second Creek is not just Anytown, USA. It's a very special place that needs special considerations, which you don't seem willing to provide."

"I respect your passion in this matter, but I'm not going to dignify that with a response, Miz Lepanto. You are not an elected official, and you do not understand all the responsibilities that go with this job. I appreciate your input, but I think our meeting should be adjourned at this point."

Mr. Floyce then smiled his best politician's smile, shot up from his desk, and gestured to a by now flustered Minnie to show them the door. "Thank you all for comin' and expressin' your opinions, ladies. As always, it was delightful to hear from you. It's this sort of feedback we count on to do the job we are capable of doin' for the community. The door to my office is always open to you."

In the corridor outside, Laurie was livid. "I feel like a naughty child who's been sent to her room for mouthing off to her parents. Mr. Floyce has the whole routine down perfectly."

"Has what routine down perfectly?" Novie said, as they all huddled together.

"The art of saying things that mean absolutely nothing but nonetheless keep people moving along the assembly line."

There was a general nodding of heads, and then Laurie glanced at her watch. It was almost eleven o'clock and the hour of the Grande's destruction was at hand. "Okay," she continued. "I know we didn't even come close to saving the Grande, and I guess we all knew we'd get nowhere with Mr. Floyce, but I propose that we all at least go down there and bear witness to this heinous act. Do I have a show of hands?"

There were no dissenters, and the Nitwitts headed out of

City Hall, marching like well-dressed and perfectly coiffed war-
riors on their way to paying their last respects to that fascinating concoction of bricks and mortar that had memorably
entertained several generations of Second Creekers with the
best Hollywood had to offer.

THE NITWITTS ARRIVED at the demolition scene to discover a
sprinkling of other citizens waiting for them, perhaps none
more surprising than Mr. Choppy.

"Who's holding down the fort right now?" Laurie asked as
he approached her on foot, slightly out of breath.

"Oh, I think the Piggly Wiggly can survive for a few minutes
without me. I just had to come and pay my respects, though."

"That's just what we're up to. Although I have to admit, I
don't think we'll wait around for the last brick to fall. It's a bit
toasty standing out here in these clothes in the middle of June,"
she replied, fanning her face with her hand. "We Nitwitts are
generally dressed to the teeth, I'm afraid."

Novie Mims mimicked her gesture and said: "The last time I
was this uncomfortable was in Belize when the ceiling fan
burned out in my hotel room. It was like walking around inside
a greenhouse with a blanket draped over you. Just no relief,
unless you dared to go down to the beach where everyone was
jiggling around naked as jaybirds."

Soon, the demolition crew began to go to work with their
drills and hammers and other paraphernalia. This was no massive fatal blow with a wrecking ball swinging from a crane. No,
this was a delicate and painstaking dismantling of the building
piece by piece because the bricks and stone blocks had been

sold to a subdivision contractor, or so the newspaper had announced.

Laurie grimaced as the workmen on scaffolding began digging out the course of bricks just below the roofline. "It's like watching a dentist pull someone's teeth one by one. I don't know how much more of this I can stand."

Indeed, Renza Belford had already turned on her heels and headed for her car while baby talking to the fur around her shoulders. "All this heat and sun is hard on my handsome little babies, isn't it? We don't like that mean Mister Oxidation, do we? Well, don't you worry. Mama's gonna take you all home right this very minute and put all of you back in the nice dark closet again. Yes, she is." And then she blissfully rounded the corner, sparing her friends the rest of her precious soliloquy.

Gradually, the combination of the prickly heat and the brick-by-brick boredom of the demolition depleted the Nitwitts. They headed home to consume their chilled toddies and prop their feet up now that it was after the marginally respectable hour of twelve. The crowd gradually thinned out until only Laurie and Mr. Choppy were left.

"Such a shame that no one could find a use for this grand ole lady," Laurie began. "They just don't make buildings like this anymore."

Mr. Choppy was shaking his head. "Instant grits."

"What?"

"Somethin' Daddy said to me years and years ago. Guess he saw this trend comin'. He pointed out that lotsa foods we've been sellin' for a long time were goin' over to the instant concept. People just couldn't wait around for things anymore. Five or ten minutes was too long now. Everything had to be ready in an instant. Seems like business in general has gone that way, too."

"You're so right. It seems that more and more we're being pressed to become just like any other average nameless town."

Mr. Choppy had a distant, pensive look on his face. "Spoken like a true native Second Creeker, Miz Lepanto. And you're right, that theater across the street was not just a grand ole lady, she was one helluva Hollywood broad with a lotta unforgettable memories for a lotta people who bought a ticket to sit inside her. She didn't take guff off no one."

"I didn't know you were such a big fan of the Grande."

"Oh, yeah. My daddy and mama used to take me to the movies every Sunday afternoon from the time I was a little boy. Saw *Gone With the Wind* and *The Wizard of Oz* there when they finally came to Second Creek. Then when I got a little older and could go by myself, I'd use most of my weekly allowance to buy a ticket and some popcorn so I could stare up at that magical screen and go all over the world in my mind and imagine it was me up there on the screen falling in love with beauties like Miss Ava Gardner. It was—" He came to an abrupt halt, almost as if an invisible hand had been placed over his mouth.

"It was what?" Laurie said, breaking the awkward silence.

"I don't know what I was gonna say next. My mind was wanderin' all over the place, I guess. Just got a little carried away."

Laurie studied him carefully and read between the lines. He was clearly holding something back. As they turned and headed down the street together, she caught a glimpse of something surprising. Pristine, poignant, and completely surprising. It was a single tear, coursing down his left cheek.

. . .

A FEW MINUTES LATER, Laurie and Mr. Choppy walked into the front door of the Piggly Wiggly to find Powell posing by the bulletin boards in what was either a costume or a disguise.

"You sorta remind me of Abraham Lincoln in that getup," Laurie said, giving his fake beard, top hat, and tails the once-over.

"Good. Old Abe is exactly who I'm supposed to be today."

Laurie circled him one last time, thoroughly amused, and said: "So, what's the plan, Abe? Are we going to recite the Gettysburg Address over the intercom or what? Attention shoppers—fourscore and seven years ago, there were unbeatable bargains in aisle five?"

"That's a clever idea, but no, what we are actually going to do is try and slow-dance with Mary Todd Lincoln."

Laurie gave him a bewildered glance, and curiosity finally got the better of Mr. Choppy. "Come again, Mr. Hampton?"

"You may find this hard to believe, but I received a letter from Lady Roth the other day," he explained. "She said she had read all about my dancing, and it was enough to persuade her to give the Piggly Wiggly another try—"

Mr. Choppy interrupted. "Her and her handwritin' from hell."

"Be that as it may, she said she would be willing to come down and shop, provided I would dress up like Abraham Lincoln. She would, of course, put in an appearance around noon as Mary Todd Lincoln and provide some very special music for the occasion—'The Battle Hymn of the Republic.'"

Laurie reviewed the complete picture in her head and could barely suppress her laughter. "So the deal is that you've agreed to slow-dance as Abraham Lincoln to the 'Battle Hymn of the Republic' with Lady Roth dressed up as Mary Todd Lincoln, right?"

"That's the extent of it. I'm not sure I've ever seen anybody do anything but march and salute to that Yankee anthem. It's a rather unwieldly vehicle."

"Well, I appreciate what you're doin' for the store, Mr. Hampton, but in this particular case, you got a lot more guts than I do," said Mr. Choppy, who then cast an anxious glance in Laurie's direction. "Miz Lepanto, would you mind bein' especially careful when you go over her shoppin' list? If it looks anything like the last one, Mary Todd Lincoln is gonna go away without any groceries."

"Don't worry," Powell explained. "I made Lady Roth promise to type her list, or I wouldn't agree to the deal."

Laurie was greatly relieved. "I have to admit I'm really fascinated by this entire scenario. I don't think I've ever seen Lady Roth without one of those turbans wound around her head, and if I remember my history correctly, Mary Todd Lincoln definitely did not fancy them. So we all may be getting a glimpse of Lady Roth's hair for the first time ever. Hey, for all we know, she could be bald under there. Some elderly women do get that way, you know."

Then they all began watching the clock, waiting with some trepidation for Lady Roth's entrance. She arrived alone promptly at noon in full 1860s drag—off-white crinoline hoopskirt, rustling petticoats, pantaloons, and all. What appeared to be a towering brunette wig, replete with fussy ringlets, adorned her head, and she carried a delicate, blue silk fan in her right hand, no doubt to keep from being overcome by the vapors.

Laurie could not resist, whispering to Powell out of the side of her mouth. "She reminds me more of Marie Antoinette's grandmother than Mary Todd Lincoln."

"On the other hand, you have to admit she does look somewhat mental. That's realistic, at least."

Mr. Choppy stepped up and offered his hand. "Welcome to the Piggly Wiggly, Lady Roth. We are delighted to have you back. We hope you'll have a very satisfactory shoppin' and dancin' experience with us today."

The very wrinkled Lady Roth appeared to be offended, withdrawing her hand immediately, and launched into one of her less-than-lucid monologues in that pretentious British accent of hers. "Today you will please address me as Mrs. Lincoln. You have no idea what I have been through as First Lady. My countrymen will never know how I have suffered, how many sacrifices I have made for the common good. So many things that happened were not my fault. They were beyond my control. Tell them, Mr. President."

Powell was slow on the uptake and had to be elbowed subtly by Laurie. "Oh . . . yes. Well, as the president I can vouch for the fact that what she says is absolutely true. In my humble opinion she is, uh, our most misunderstood First Lady."

Lady Roth gave him a reverential nod. "Thank you, Mr. President. And now, dear Abe, if you will reach down into my cleavage and retrieve the CD I have brought for our dance today . . ."

Powell narrowed his eyes. "You want me to reach down where to get what?"

"Oh, very well, then," she replied, retrieving the item herself and then handing it over. "Here it is. Shall we get started?"

A few of the people shopping in the store had gradually drifted over and gathered around to witness the impromptu costume drama, although Laurie and Kenyatta went right to work on Lady Roth's shopping list. When "The Battle Hymn of the Republic" was punched up on the CD player, however, the size of the audience nearly doubled.

The sight of Powell laboring mightily to slow-dance to such unsuitable music with a leaden Lady Roth in tow began to resonate like a *Saturday Night Live* skit. A mischievous cluster of shoppers started trailing the couple, playfully imitating their stiff, uninspired choreography. Lady Roth, however, appeared to remain unfazed.

"These people are trying to persecute me as usual, Mr. President. But I shall rise above it in a manner befitting a First Lady. You would expect nothing less of me. No, the nation would expect nothing less of me. All the finger pointing and sniggering in the world cannot deter me from my mission as First Lady."

Powell played along masterfully. "How right you are, my dear. Let's just ignore them and discuss matters of greater interest to Second Creek—I mean, the nation. We are here, after all, to serve their interests."

"No, no. You were right the first time. I'm completely bored with the nation. The people are so unappreciative of the little things. I don't know why Dolley Madison bothered to save the silver. Or was it the china? Whatever, I prefer to concentrate on Second Creek now. Have you heard they're tearing down the Grande Theater?"

Powell sighed. "Ah, would that they had chosen the Ford Theater first! As Monty Hall once may have said, 'Stay away from curtain number three!'"

Lady Roth tapped him smartly on the cheek with her fan. "You and your fatalism, Mr. President. I don't know what I'm going to do with you. It's gotten so I simply cannot take you anywhere—you and your deadly sense of humor."

"That may be the case, my dear, but I don't know when I've had a more interesting dancing partner."

At which point His truth stopped marching on and thankfully came to a halt in the CD player, causing the onlookers to respond with a healthy round of applause and simultaneous cheers.

Mr. Choppy broke through the crowd and led the way to the checkout counter where Laurie and Kenyatta had taken great pains with Lady Roth's typed shopping list. Powell's directive had no doubt saved the day, and there were no mistakes. Everything had worked out perfectly.

"Well, I think everything is in order, Mr. Choppy," Lady Roth said after thoroughly inspecting her bags. "I will return next week, but not as Mary Todd Lincoln. I want to be Bonnie, and Mr. Hampton will be Clyde. I would like to do the Charleston over by the Blue Bell ice cream so I can stick my head inside those frosty doors should I get overheated. After all, the Charleston does take a lot out of a girl. Poo poo pee do." She turned to Powell, batting her eyelashes and coquettishly working that fan again. "Do you think that would be possible, you marvelously tall thing, you?"

"Oh, I don't see why not. I'm sure we can work something out. I shall remain at your beck and call, dear lady."

And with that, Lady Roth made her exit while Mr. Choppy himself did the honors and carried her bags out into the parking lot.

Laurie laughed as Powell removed the top hat and beard and exhaled dramatically. "I doubt the real Abe Lincoln had to endure anything that onerous," he told her. "Lady Roth has all the flexibility of one of those cast-iron lawn jockeys. It was like hauling around an anvil!"

"That tiny little thing?"

"She may be tiny, but she handles like a Sherman tank. Who knows, she may have even had part of a transmission underneath that hoopskirt." Powell took out his handkerchief and sopped up the sweat that had beaded up along his jawline beneath his beard. "By the way, I'm just curious. What did that paragon of peculiarities bother to order from the Piggly Wiggly today?"

"You won't believe it. Three limes. A box of strawberries. Saltines. A Mason jar. Scotch tape. A can of ripe olives. A tin of sardines. One sixty-watt lightbulb—Mr. Choppy let us break up a package just for her because she absolutely insisted she didn't want or need two. A roll of aluminum foil. And get this: one blueberry. Mr. Choppy also granted us permission to sell her a single blueberry. Now I say that's truly bending over backwards for someone's business. What do you say?"

"I say: what in hell does anybody do with one blueberry?"

Laurie thought for a moment and then grinned slyly. "That is known only to God . . . and possibly Mary Todd Lincoln."

Chapter Nine

ONNIE LEYTON'S second creek segment took the "Eye
on the Mid-South" program by storm, and Piggly
Wiggly publicity began to gather a modest momentum. Feature
writers at the Jackson *Clarion-Ledger,* Memphis *Commercial
Appeal,* and Little Rock *Arkansas Democrat-Gazette* got wind of
the dancing gimmick and soon found their way to the unimpos-
ing little store just off the town square to interview Mr. Choppy,
Mr. Floyce, Powell Hampton, and, in some cases, even Laurie,
the bag boys, and Lucy Faye Stiers. A couple of other regional
TV stations got in on the act, and everyday shopping suddenly
became a celebrity event. Even the run-of-the-mill citizens of
Second Creek began to acquire their fifteen minutes of fame,
and some few had even acquired something approaching the
big head over the attention.

"I seen you last night on TV, Lucy Faye," her gum-chewing friend and contemporary Doris Tynes told her the next day. Doris had come in to thump a big, ripe watermelon and round up a package of frankfurters and some buns for a family back-yard barbecue. "You sure looked different to me, though. Did they put a lotta that TV makeup on ya or what? Somethin' about you just caught the light a certain way, I swear."

Lucy Faye preened and whistled through her teeth gleefully, pointing to her head. "You got you a good eye there, Doris. It was my hairnet. I fixed it up real fancy. Got a real bright gold glow to it even now, as you can see. My daughter says she thinks it could even become one a' them fashion trends."

"I'll be," Doris replied, examining it closely while tugging at her faded, floral-print housedress. "I could of swore you had dyed your hair. Not that I would've holded that against you."

"Well, I just dyed the hairnet is all. Hollywood, here I come, I guess. Now, whaddaya say about that?"

"I say don't quit your day job, girl."

The two women nudged one another and laughed so hard that Lucy Faye even emitted a little snort, enjoying the good-natured ribbing at her expense.

Kenyatta and Jake, too, were pumped by the publicity, but there was a downside. One or two of their high school friends were always hanging around the parking lot just in case another camera crew showed up. They spent most of their time after school waving or talking to their girlfriends on their cell phones, occasionally coming in to buy candy and gum. One of Kenyatta's best buds, a roundball prodigy named Ahmad Morris, was particularly persistent.

"Hey, Kenyatta, you think that TV crew gone show up in here today?" he would ask over and over, with a basketball always tucked snugly under his arm.

And Kenyatta would have to break away from his bag-boy duties for a moment to give him the same report. "Ain't heard Mr. Choppy say nothin' 'bout it. Why you keep buggin' me all the time?"

"Cuz maybe I could make a few a' my best moves on camera, know wha' I'm sayin'? Maybe some college coach out there see me on TV and axe our coach 'bout me. You got to be seen to make noise."

"You thinkin' 'bout a scholarship?"

"That's what I'm talkin' 'bout."

"Damn, Ahmad, if you as good as you think, you don't need no appearance at the Piggly Wiggly to get a college coach interested. You need to get you a life away from up in here. I know you can see I got work to do for Mr. Choppy. Must be nice to hang loose all the time and not have to work."

Nonetheless, Ahmad took Kenyatta's constant guff and doggedly kept returning in hopes of being discovered as the next NCAA legend.

In the month following the Floozie Contest, a fairly steady trickle of normally introverted women emerged from the local woodwork to sample the new service, and it wasn't long before Laurie and Mr. Choppy had to get together for their first meeting in his office to evaluate the effectiveness of the ploy and examine the financial bottom line.

"It's real clear to me that many of these ladies have been showin' up just for the dancin'," Mr. Choppy began, as the two of them poured over sheets and scraps of paper strewn haphazardly across his desk. "They're obviously doin' most of their grocery shoppin' elsewhere, 'cause they keep handin' over these paltry lists you see here to you and the bag boys—just a few random items to satisfy the dancin' requirements but nothin' that a convenience store couldn't handle. I hate to say it, but I suspect that big ole MegaMart is still gettin' the lion's share of their business. In a way we're almost back to square one, except that the clock's still tickin' away on my little store's shelf life."

"In other words we're getting closer and closer to the expiration date."

"You said it."

Laurie carefully thumbed through a stack of vaguely familiar items and shook her head. "I'm afraid your figures don't lie. These do not represent a week's worth of groceries for a growing family."

"It's showin' up on the ledger, too. I tell ya, Miz Lepanto, sometimes I just hate bein' right about things. I told Lucy Faye that the store would prob'ly not hold on to the level of business we brought in during all that grand-opening hoopla. The novelty wore off real quick, and I'm still barely breakin' even, despite everything."

"It's too soon to give up, though, don't you think? Those articles in the Memphis and Jackson papers could have a positive effect down the line. You don't want to discount word of mouth. Sometimes it takes awhile for that sort of thing to really kick in, so I wouldn't be too discouraged yet."

Mr. Choppy gave her a look that suggested an odd blend of stoicism and determination. "Oh, I'm not givin' up by any means yet. I just thought you and the wonderful ladies of the Nitwitts ought to know that it's nip and tuck here at the checkout counters, and I'm not tellin' you 'cause I want you all to go out and beat the bushes any more'n you have already. God knows, you've all done your part, and as for Mr. Hampton, well, what can I say? He's just been a prince about it all."

"Yes, he has," Laurie replied. "He's been booked solid during his daily two-hour stints, as you well know, and he has the sore feet to prove it. I've been giving him soothing foot baths nearly every night at my place. They say the way to a man's heart is through his stomach, and I don't do half bad in that department, if I do say so myself, but lately, I've been taking an alternate route through his tired feet." She began laughing slyly, as if some private joke had just been revealed to her. "All by herself, of course, our Lady Roth has literally kept him on his toes with her decidedly peculiar requests. Or character parts, shall we say?"

"Ain't it the truth? Lady Roth's a hoot and a holler. She was as good as her word after that first go-round as Mary Todd Lincoln. Let's see, next she was Bonnie to Mr. Hampton's Clyde, and that was a sight to see, huh?"

Laurie continued her muted giggling. "It was one of the most painful things I've ever had to watch—that slow as molasses Charleston she did, trying to cross her knees like that with her bad arthritis. I could see Powell grimacing to every beat, but she didn't miss a one. If nothing else, she's game."

"That she is. And then the next week she showed up carryin' that basket of violets as Eliza Doolittle, right?"

"You got it. When they sashayed down the aisle to 'I Could Have Danced All Night,' I actually thought Lady Roth looked halfway graceful. Powell told me afterward she did a credible Cockney accent all the time she was talking to him. She does have a knack for staying in character. She's really quite an actress when you come right down to it."

Mr. Choppy enjoyed a belly laugh. "I overheard her callin' him guv'nuh at one point, I believe."

"And he kept telling her to enunciate properly and stop sounding like a gutter snipe. They both did it up right."

"I wonder if she went to the video store and checked out *My Fair Lady* or somethin' to bone up," Mr. Choppy mused. "That's what I woudda done."

"She definitely throws her heart and soul into these outings."

"Yeah, and she really comes up with people you wouldn't ordinarily think about. Like when she was Mamie Eisenhower with her hair combed down in those bangs and all, and Mr. Hampton put on that skullcap to look like ole President Dwight. Some of the regulars couldn't figure out who he was supposed to be. I believe somebody even came up to me and asked me if he was Yul Brynner."

"I don't think I'd ever get Eisenhower confused with the King of Siam," Laurie replied in bemused fashion. "Even if both of them were a big deal at the same time in the fifties."

"Me, neither, Miz Lepanto. I always really liked Ike, though. One of our best presidents, I think. As for the fifties, they were heady times here at the Piggly Wiggly. My daddy really had it goin' back then." Then Mr. Choppy sat back a bit in his chair, suddenly growing serious. "But what I didn't understand was how even all those floor show–type outings didn't help business more'n they did. We had all the regulars who started to come in just to find out when Lady Roth was gonna make her next appearance. Take Mr. Blake Isaacs in particular, the CPA from down the street. He'd take off his lunch hour just to be here to watch Mr. Hampton and Lady Roth in their latest roles. But he never bought anything more'n a stick a' gum while he was here. He wanted to be entertained, but he didn't want to buy too much in the way of groceries. Shoot, maybe I shoudda charged admission to Lady Roth's performances."

"I thought all those Lady Roth regulars were a promising omen at the time," Laurie added. "Especially when they started showing up with those placards to rate her performances. I thought to myself we had really rustled up some new customers."

"She got perfect tens from that bunch when she was Priscilla Presley. I got a big kick outta Mr. Hampton in that greasy-lookin' black wig, doin' all that pelvis action to 'You Ain't Nothin' but a Hound Dog.' But you know what? It just hasn't increased business that much. In fact, it's even kinda cluttered up the aisles at times for the real shoppers."

Laurie quickly reviewed his figures once again and shot him a pained expression. "I'm so sorry, Mr. Choppy. I never envisioned this would actually backfire a bit. Is this your round-about way of telling me we ought to stop the dancing in the aisles? I'm sure you know that Powell and I wouldn't dream of doing anything to make things harder for you. Just say the magic word, and we'll stop doing what we're doing."

Before he had a chance to answer her, Jake suddenly appeared in the doorway, slouching down with his unkempt, rusty hair in his eyes and looking a bit intimidated. "Excuse me, Mr. Choppy, but there's this real strange girl with long, stringy hair that wants to talk to you about somethin'. She's up front near the checkout counters. Miz Lucy Faye asked her what she wanted, but all she'd say was that she wanted to talk to the owner, 'cause she had a surefire way to help the store out."

Mr. Choppy eyed him sharply. "Son, I'm conductin' some important business here with Miz Lepanto. Is she solicitin' somethin' or other?"

"What's that mean?" the boy replied, his face a perfect adolescent blank.

"Son, are they teachin' you anything in school these days?"

The boy looked even more dumbstruck. "Pardon, sir?"

"Never mind, Mr. Choppy. Please. Go tend to it," Laurie added, breaking in. "It might mean some extra business somehow or other."

Mr. Choppy rose from his chair authoritatively and said: "All right. But you come along with me, Miz Lepanto. Two heads are always better'n one."

The three of them headed together to the front of the store where they encountered a sad-faced, very thin, young woman in a granny dress who quickly pressed a business card into Mr. Choppy's palm as soon as he approached.

"And what can I do for you today, Miss, uh, Me-Me From Memphis, is it?" he said, glancing down briefly at her card.

She drew back with an agitated expression. "No, not Miss Me-Me From Memphis. Just Me-Me From Memphis. There's no Miss printed up on my card."

Mr. Choppy was struggling to maintain his customary poise, noting that the woman would not look him directly in the eye. "Okay, Me-Me From Memphis, it is."

"I was hoping you would allow me to demonstrate my performance art for you, and perhaps you might like it well enough to feature me on a regular basis the way you do Mr. Powell Hampton, for whom I have the utmost appreciation and admiration. I read all about him in the *Commercial Appeal,* of course, and I figured that if something as unusual as that was going on down here, why then, I might just fit in myself."

Mr. Choppy's intuition told him to say no, but there was that pressing matter of the volume of dancing far outstripping the volume of shopping. On the outside chance that she might be able to help him balance that better, he decided to take Laurie's suggestion and hear her out. "When would you like to set up this demonstration or whatever it is that you'd like to perform for us, ma'am?"

"Oh, no, I'm not ma'am, I'm just . . . Me-Me From Memphis. It's very important that I promote my identity as a performance artist. So many of us tend to sail off the edge of the earth into anonymity, and it's because we don't emphasize enough who we really are. So, please, no ma'am, no Miss, just plain ole little Me-Me From Memphis."

"I think I got that part straight . . . you're Me-Me From Memphis. But back to my question: when would you like to show me whatever it is you're gonna show me? I'm really a very busy man, and I don't have all day."

"How about right now?" she replied, momentarily pulling the curtain of hair away from her face. "I don't really need any setup time. I just need to buy something from you here in the store, and we're on our way. I'd like to keep it a surprise for now, but believe me, you're going to absolutely adore what I do. It will bring even more customers into your store than you're drawing now, and it won't cost you a thing. I rely strictly on tips from my audience."

Mr. Choppy dismissed Jake and took Laurie aside for a discreet consultation. "Whaddaya think? Am I lettin' myself in for some more grief here?"

"Well, she is a bit drab and undernourished-looking, but she doesn't look like a terrorist, if that's what you're asking me. I say we give her a chance to show what she's got. What can it possibly hurt?"

They broke huddle, and Mr. Choppy said: "Okay, Me-Me From Memphis. You have our undivided attention."

"Well, first of all, I'll need to buy a carton of milk from you," she explained. "Which way to the dairy case?"

Mr. Choppy pointed toward it, and they all headed in that direction.

"Of course, I prefer whole milk to skim, or even one percent," the young woman added on the way. "So much more substantial for my original, artistic purposes, as you will soon discover with delight."

He nodded apprehensively. "We have all the percentages here in our store—regular, two, one, and fat-free."

"I would have expected nothing less," she replied as they reached the selection of dairy products. Then she leaned down and grabbed her pint of milk. "My dear ole southern grandmother used to call this sweet milk, and I can definitely agree with that sentiment. There's nothing so dear to my heart as old-fashioned sweet milk. Yum, yum!"

Then they all headed back to the checkout counter, where Lucy Faye dutifully scanned the purchase, accepted her money, and doled out her change. Kenyatta started to put the milk in a bag, but Me-Me From Memphis wrested it from him politely. "That's okay. Don't bother, young man. I need that right this very minute." She quickly surveyed the store and pointed in the general direction of the produce bin. "Over there is just the right spot, I think. Let's go over there where most of the shoppers are at the moment. We need an audience to appreciate what I am about to do. That way you can gauge the effect I will have on your regular shoppers. I just know you'll be impressed."

Mr. Choppy and Laurie followed along, both with a mild sense of foreboding, and soon they were standing beside the tomatoes; red, green, orange, and yellow bell peppers; and sweet Vidalia onions. Five people were in the vicinity, poking, prodding, and picking through with relish, but all activity came to an abrupt halt when Me-Me From Memphis suddenly and loudly unveiled her act.

"Umm, umm, umm!" she began, opening the spout and drinking directly from the carton. "Sweet milk! So very, very delicious and nutritious! Nothing better in the whole wide world than sweet, sweet, milk, is there, folks? Does the entire world not adore its sweet, sweet milk? Better yet, does the slow-witted, ever-grazing, cud-chewing cow even imagine what a wondrous liquid it squirts from its swollen udders? Oh, squirt, squirt—squirt for the masses! Cutting across all social classes!"

The surprised shoppers were now exchanging puzzled glances. Then Me-Me From Memphis dropped the carton on the linoleum floor with a thud and dramatically framed her face with her hands like a damsel in pronounced distress or the late but enormously celebrated Judy Garland in the midst of a climactic finale at a Carnegie Hall concert.

"Oh, no! Not my precious sweet milk! Oh, see how it flows

out onto the ground and, oh, how that stabs me in my beating heart! What hideous waste is this! What shameful, horrid waste!"

"Kenyatta!" Mr. Choppy shouted, turning around quickly. "Got a cleanup in the produce aisle!"

But Me-Me From Memphis protested vehemently. "No, no, no, Mr. Choppy. You don't understand. I'm not through yet. You'll spoil my act. You just have to hang on and be a bit more patient!"

Kenyatta trotted over with a mop, ready to make short work of the mess, but Mr. Choppy played traffic cop and put his hand up. "Hold on, son. Looks like we're gonna have to wait a little longer to see where she's goin' with this."

Me-Me From Memphis gave him an appreciative nod and resumed her routine. "Is there a sadder sight in the whole wide world than what we are witnessing right here at this very moment? Oh, sweet milk spilt! Oh, sweet milk lost! And all that calcium, tempest tossed!" Then, the tears started flowing. Genuine tears streaming down her cheeks and her voice quavering with emotion as if she had just been informed of a death in the family. "What can I say? What can I do? This sweet whole milk is lost to you! Lost to the world and to its teeth. Lost to its bones, so hang the wreath! Oh, sad, sad, milk! Sad, sad, spilt milk!" There was an overwhelming silence as Me-Me From Memphis, still wracked with sobs, then took the liberty of a bow.

Mr. Choppy's face was a virtual mask of disdain. "Is that it?"

"Oh, yes. That's it. Finis. The end. My command performance of 'Crying Over Spilt Milk.'"

A wave of recognition in the form of hushed oohs and ahhs spread throughout the small band of bystanders, and there was even an apprehensive hint of applause.

"S'okay if I clean it up now, Mr. Choppy?" said Kenyatta with a skeptical frown and a profound shaking of his head.

Me-Me From Memphis pointed to the spreading puddle about the same time Mr. Choppy nodded. "Perhaps you can understand now why I won't use skim milk," she explained. "It's just too thin—doesn't show up on the floor nearly as well. An artist must pay attention to that sort of detail, and I can attest to the fact that I spilled many a carton before I hit upon just the right consistency, just the right flow. It makes all the difference between pedestrian and bravura, if you will allow me."

Mr. Choppy shot Laurie a sideways glance, trying desperately to search for the words that would avoid hurting the young woman's feelings. In the end he decided there was no way around it, and he settled for blunt. "We appreciate you droppin' by today, but maybe your act would be better suited to someplace like the MegaMart. They're a lot better at spills over there than we are, what with their PA system and all."

Me-Me From Memphis tilted her head to the side. "So the answer is no?"

"Afraid so. But thanks for thinkin' of us, though."

Me-Me From Memphis immediately dried her tears on cue, shrugged her shoulders, and shuffled off without so much as a word, disturbingly emotionless and unmoved by his dismissive reaction.

"Please come with me back to my office, Miz Lepanto," Mr. Choppy finally said as the performance artist exited the front door.

Once there, he rummaged through his desk drawers while Laurie looked on patiently in silence. It took him awhile, but he eventually pulled out a Magic Marker, a pair of scissors, and some posterboard. Then he went to work creating a handwritten sign that he taped to the front door. ABSOLUTELY NO PERFORMANCE ART ALLOWED IN STORE—it read, drawing little more than blank stares from the vast majority of his customers.

"Bravo, Mr. Choppy," Laurie observed. "I guess this whole thing has gotten a bit out of hand."

He gave her his most generous smile. "Don't you worry about it, Miz Lepanto. You tell Mr. Hampton that as long as he's willin' to help me out with that wonderful dancin' of his, I'll keep holdin' down the fort and see if we can still manage to turn this thing around. I was taught to always fight things through to the end."

"Will do."

"But I've had second thoughts about your Nitwitts. Maybe we better soft-pedal the financial ledger to your ladies for right now. Wouldn't want 'em to get discouraged after all their hard work. And as you say, it could still work out."

Laurie agreed to keep the ongoing business difficulties hush-hush for the time being and headed home to prepare yet another soothing foot bath and rub for her valiant Powell's talented but aching feet.

LADY ROTH WANDERED into the Piggly Wiggly twenty minutes later unannounced, uncostumed, and well past regular dancing hours, presumably to pick up a few odds and ends—with a definite emphasis on odds.

"What is the meaning of that sign on your door, Mr. Choppy?" she said, tracking him down near the meat counter where he was wrapping up an order for three filets that someone had phoned in for a last-minute company dinner. "The one forbidding performance art, I mean. Are you possibly referring to me? Do you wish me to stop coming to dance with Mr. Hampton? Is that your intent?"

Mr. Choppy quickly turned things over in his head. "Oh, absolutely not, Lady Roth. That sign has nothin' to do with you."

She adjusted her turban and gave him a haughty stare. "Are you not enjoying my performances then? Do you not consider them art? I put a great deal of thought and planning into the characters I portray, and I thought you looked forward to my appearances as well. My perception was that the entire store enjoyed them. I am thinking particularly of that rowdy but appreciative contingent that holds up those cards like they were Olympic judges or something. Do you wish those people to stop coming to your store as well?"

Mr. Choppy could see that he had a problem on his hands. Perhaps a cup of coffee or tea with a little sweet talk on the side would be in order, so he hastily issued the invitation.

Lady Roth took her time, working the various muscles of her wrinkled face while debating. "Very well, then. We shall discuss this further over a bit of refreshment at the Tea Room. And don't let me forget to return and pick up three flashlight batteries and some mint-flavored toothpicks."

"No problem," he replied, thankful she hadn't said three toothpicks and some mint-flavored flashlight batteries.

THE SECOND CREEK Victorian Tea Room was in between the
lunch and dinner crowds, so Mr. Choppy was able to get a table
for two quite easily. The restaurant was the sort of pricey place
partial to ferns, potted palms, and stained-glass windows,
its menu catering mostly to society matrons and upscale busi-
nesspeople, and it had become one of the culinary mainstays
of the town over the past thirty years or so—holding its own so
far with the newer franchise restaurants out on the Bypass.
Lady Roth appeared to be pleased with the cozy corner table
they had been given and settled back in her chair to survey
the room.

"I don't know those two women over there across the way.
Of course, they look like they've wrapped plain ole fabric bolts
around their midriffs," she said with dripping disdain. "No,
don't turn around, Mr. Choppy. That would not be polite. I
merely wanted to point out that I have no earthly idea who they
are. That is all to the good. Should they have extraordinary
hearing like dogs and pick up any of what I have to say to you,
it won't matter in the least. If I don't know them, they can't possibly be anybody."

"I admire your logic, Lady Roth. Very unique and to the
point."

A sunny young blond waitress in a white apron stepped up
to take their orders. Lady Roth quickly opted for an Irish coffee, while Mr. Choppy stuck with sweet tea, but not before
catching up on his manners with their waitress.

"You're Polly and Gardner Ralston's daughter, aren't you?"

The girl flashed a winning, toothy grin and said: "Why, yessir, I am. I'm Lizbut Ann Ralston."

"Yeah, I thought so. You're all grown up now, but I still recognized you. I can remember when your mama used to wheel you around the store in one of my grocery carts. She'd buy you a box of animal crackers to keep your hands off all the stuff on the shelves. Where are you now?"

"I'm a junior at Ole Miss. Hope to enter the Miss America Pageant and eventually end up in New York. I'd like to think I could do something on Broadway."

Mr. Choppy nodded approvingly. "Well, you went to the right place for the trainin', honey. There've been three Miss Americas already from Ole Miss. Good luck to ya. Maybe you'll be the next Mary Ann Mobley. Or Lynda Lee Mead. They won back to back, you know, and from the same sorority at Ole Miss to boot. Everybody said they'd never give it to two Mississippi girls back to back, but they did."

"Oh, yes, I know." And with that, Lizbut Ann blushed a bit, thanked him, turned on her heels, and went to fetch their drink orders.

"I noticed you are teetotaling," said Lady Roth, eyeing him skeptically as she resumed the conversation. "I know sweet tea is de rigueur for southern consumption in the middle of the day, particularly in the summertime, but couldn't you break down and get a little greased up with me? I really don't care for drinking alone, you know. It's entirely too desperate and calculating-looking for a lady to do so."

"Got a few more hours at the store till we close. I'll have my little toddy when I'm safely at home tonight. Don't want to fall asleep during store hours. I know how to get through my long days, and drinking on the job doesn't cut it for me."

"Ah, yes! That last one before bedtime does hit the spot." She looked around the room one last time as if she were a spy of some kind and then leaned in. "I am going to tell you something I have never told anyone, Mr. Choppy. Did you know I am related to Sarah Bernhardt, the well-known and highly celebrated actress?"

Mr. Choppy thought it wise to proceed cautiously and continued to kiss up. "As well as British royalty?"

"Oh, that was on my father's side. His father was the Duke of Langenhangen or Llewellynhangen or something multi-syllabic and impossibly Welsh who was fifth in line to the throne. But so many people would have had to die or be plotted against in order for him to inherit it that he decided to come to America and take his chances. But my aunt on my mother's side was married to Sarah Bernhardt's first cousin. Or was it my first cousin on my mother's side who was married to Sarah Bernhard's aunt? I can't remember, but you get the picture. I never like being bothered much with genealogical details."

Mr. Choppy tried to do the family tree in his head but gave up quickly. "Well, you've got all kinds of famous branches, looks like. Quite a sturdy tree, I'd imagine."

"Indeed. And that is why I have always fancied myself an actress. When I was a young girl, I wanted to go on the stage and live up to such an illustrious thespian heritage. I wanted to change my name to Vocifera P. Forest. I thought that had such an intense, yet pastoral, quality. But my parents did not approve at all. Oh, it wasn't particularly the name, although they thought it was ridiculous and made me sound like I was a species of fern."

"Lady Roth, you're far more delicate and exotic than any fern could ever be," Mr. Choppy interjected.

"Perhaps so. But my parents felt that acting was very far beneath someone of my lineage. I might as well go off and join the circus and shovel elephant dung. Instead, I would get married to the proper gentleman—Heath Vanderlith Roth, as it turned out—try saying that fast three or four times, I know I amused myself no end over the years doing just that—and I would live happily ever after as all good little patrician girls do."

"And didja?"

"Did I what?"

"Live happily ever after?"

"I was smothered in southern comfort. Not the liqueur, although I do fancy a snootful from time to time, but the other kind of comfort that comes with marrying well in the Deep South."

"And that's a bad thing?"

She was about to answer when Lizbut Ann arrived with their drinks. Lady Roth stirred the frothy layer of whipped cream into her coffee and waited for it to cool, while Mr. Choppy squeezed lemon into his glass of iced tea.

"It wasn't what I expected," Lady Roth continued after a spell. "I thought having all those creature comforts might make up for not doing what I really wanted to do. But it didn't. It made me feel like I had been paid off to take no chances in life. In some ways, you know, that's a lot worse than trying and failing." She paused to touch her turban with her index finger. "Would you like to know why I wear these all the time?"

He nodded his head, genuinely fascinated.

"It has nothing to do with bad hair days. I simply do not have those. No, indeed. It's to make myself memorable. If I couldn't be Vocifera P. Forest, at least I could be Lady Roth. Do you remember Miss Kittykate and her antics? I'm not exactly sure what she originally set out to accomplish in her life, but this was the place where she could be memorable there at the end. Do you understand at all what I'm saying?"

Mr. Choppy didn't answer right away, taking a sip of his tea and then intently catching her gaze. "I understand more than you'll ever know, Lady Roth, and I have this nub on my right hand to prove it."

"Ah, well, we won't pursue that right now, I think. We're all entitled to our little trade secrets," she replied, blowing on her coffee a couple of times. "But what you must understand about me is what an outlet these dancing sessions have been for me. I view them as far more than just dancing around the market for lack of anything better to do. I'm having the time of my life, and I don't give a damn who thinks I'm an old fool. And don't think I'm not aware of what some people are saying about me behind my back and all the whispering in the aisles that goes on."

"I certainly don't think that about you. A lot of your regular admirers don't think that, and that sign I put up was not meant for you. I had an actual performance artist from Memphis come down and audition for me today, and let's just say it turned out to be one big mess. You don't even want to know, but at least now I know what performance art is. Biggest buncha bull I've ever witnessed in my life."

Lady Roth laughed and finally sampled her coffee daintily. "I have no idea what you're talking about, but, oh, how I adore

Irish coffee in the middle of the day. Middle of the night, too, for that matter. It's downright boorish to pay attention to the hour when you're indulging in any sort of distilled spirits. And this is just how I like this particular indulgence—very, very long on the Irish."

"Glad to hear it. Anyway, Lady Roth, you're welcome to come and dance as whoever you please as long as we're open. I hope you're clear on that. We value your presence and your business at the Piggly Wiggly, even if all you ever need is some flashlight batteries and mint-flavored toothpicks."

Lady Roth looked startled. "Did I say mint? I meant cinnamon."

"Got those. And the plain ones, too."

Mr. Choppy hesitated for a moment, then decided to press on. "Lady Roth, I've got somethin' I've always wanted to ask you. It's about that ice storm just before you came to town—the one that wiped out our soybean crop that year. You do remember that, don't you?"

"Of course I remember. It was quite the devastating event," she replied, after absentmindedly adjusting her turban. "Nonetheless, a great actress always likes to make a grand entrance."

"You don't think that storm really was whipped up just for you? Like: 'Ta da! Here she comes?'"

"Absolutely. I'm sure what I'm about to say is totally unprovable, but in my opinion—and that of several other people around these parts since everyone seems to discuss it all the time—that's what the weather is really for. We tend to think of it as something entirely apart from us, imposed upon us without our will. But in a way, we invite it with all our tantrums and wishes and expectations—even our cumulative prayers. And it listens to us and wakes us all up, lulls us to sleep, keeps us on our toes, shows us the way to go, as well as the things to avoid. All of those things and more. It teaches us valuable life lessons. Can you possibly doubt it?"

Mr. Choppy had an impish grin on his face. "Looking back on my life here in Second Creek, Lady Roth, I really can't deny that. Thanks for the reminder."

RONNIE LEYTON was not only the most aggressive reporter in the Memphis television market, he was the most ambitious as well. The station had received so many complimentary letters, phone calls, and e-mails about his Second Creek piece that he decided it was going to be his ticket to the big time. He had his sights set on either CNN or Headline News as the next step to broadcast stardom. It made no difference to him that they were the same outfit; he was certain it was going to happen for him this time around.

Then, almost as if he had willed it into existence, an e-mail arrived from his mole in Atlanta, a college fraternity brother named Mark Starnes who was working off and on behind the scenes as a CNN publicist. Mark had been keeping an eye out for Ronnie's best interests over there for the longest time.

"Dude," the e-mail began, "that opening for correspondent you've been hoping for has finally reared its head. Don't delay. Get your ass into gear pronto. And don't let anyone know I leaked this to you in advance. Later, Mark."

Ronnie shot back a cyber-reply: "Mucho thanks. I owe you big-time, Mark. Dinner and drinks on me if I get the gig."

He lost no time in taking the crucial first step—posting his résumé on the CNN website and updating his audition tape with the Piggly Wiggly footage. He wanted to be ready with his best stuff at a moment's notice.

When the operations director at CNN e-mailed him back within a day to send his tape along, Ronnie's confidence soared, and Mark received the following update: "Yo, Mark! Can you believe it? They say they're interested. The tape is already in the mails. I got a feeling this is gonna happen for me! Later, Ronnie."

And when the same director e-mailed him again a few days later that they really liked what they had seen, Piggly Wiggly piece and all, and wanted to interview him personally, he boarded a Delta flight to Atlanta late one evening with the heady conviction that he was not going to return to Memphis without that job. But he found himself in need of a little liquid courage once they had reached cruising altitude. Fortunately, the leggy flight attendant had parked the beverage cart beside him and his seatmate—a fidgety, elderly lady who reminded him of his grandmother.

"And what would you like to drink, sir?"

"Bourbon on the rocks. Two of them for good measure, I think. I'm in that kind of mood tonight."

She went to work efficiently, accepting his money and handing him two tiny bottles of liquor, an ice-filled plastic glass, and his seatmate a soft drink before moving on down the aisle.

He made relatively short work of his booze, eventually exposing him to comment from the observant grandmotherly type nearby. "I must say, you don't mess around there with those toddies, do you, young man?"

The impact of the whiskey was almost instantaneous, seeing

as how he had consumed them on a largely empty stomach. Ronnie impishly wagged his brows at her. "Got a big job interview coming up tomorrow. I'm pretty sure I'm gonna get it, but I'm trying to mellow out anyway. No use stressing out in advance."

The woman seemed unusually energized by his remark and said: "Ooh, what kind of work do you do?"

He leaned in, lowering his voice. "I'm hoping to become the next correspondent at CNN in Atlanta."

"How exciting for you. Well, I certainly hope you get it. You seem like such a nice, clean-cut, conservative young man. They need more of your type over there. My husband, George, has been saying for years that they have way too many Communists working there right now. He says they've obviously infiltrated the whole place. You know, they're terribly biased at all these networks when you come right down to it."

His big dose of booze induced easy laughter. "Ah, yes. Those sneaky Communists. They're everywhere, aren't they? Well, it's always been my dream to become the best, most objective, most professional electronic journalist in the business. No agendas to press or sneak by the public—just doing the very best job I can reporting the facts in an insightful manner."

"Good for you, young man. With that attitude, I'll just bet you anything you'll get the position, too, and those Communists will be on the run."

"Hey, and if I get the job, I'll make a point to sneak you a secret signal when I'm on the air. Like maybe I'll nod a couple of times at the end of my assignment, and you'll know that that means I'm saying hello to you."

The woman bristled with excitement. "Ooh, just like Carol

Burnett did when she pulled her earlobe all the time. I can't wait. They'd better hire you!"

Her words blended perfectly with the buzz moving throughout his bloodstream. Ronnie was on cloud nine for the remainder of the flight, which got in much later than he would have preferred.

Though he slept somewhat restlessly, things got off to a promising start at CNN Headquarters the next morning, where he sailed effortlessly through the employment mind games and tests that awaited him.

"Where would you like to be ten years from now, Mr. Leyton? Do you see yourself still working for CNN, or do you regard us as a stepping-stone to the other networks? In short, will you be satisfied with cable exposure?"

Ronnie assured his expressionless, gray power tie interviewer that cable had always been his goal because that was the wave of the future.

Then: "Do you respect the difference between true journalistic reporting and editorializing on the air, however subtle the techniques?"

To which he responded: "Objectivity in reporting is my mantra. Period."

In the end the decision-makers liked his intelligence, boyish good-looks, and crisp, no-nonsense delivery. It did not take them long to make their final decision, and Ronnie Leyton suddenly found himself with his dream job as a CNN correspondent, with an eventual shot at anchor if he did his homework and played by the rules.

Before he had even left the corner office of his future supervisor, he received his first assignment.

"You blew the other finalists out of the water with that Second Creek Piggly Wiggly piece, Ronnie," his mentor began. "Just the sort of offbeat story we like to put in rotation from time to time with the hard news. We'd like you to redo it for us. No female impersonator stuff this time, though. Just a good angle on the story behind the dancing. How soon can you get settled in and put something together?"

"Yesterday!" he replied, barely able to restrain himself. "Seriously, I'll get back to my contacts even before I get home tonight. I'll have it in the can for you by the end of the week — guaranteed."

Ronnie was smiling in the taxi all the way back to his hotel room on Peachtree Street, where he sank down on the edge of the bed and gave his buddy Mark a call to set up a celebratory dinner. Then he pulled out his address book to look up the number of the Piggly Wiggly. It would be just a few minutes before two o'clock back in Second Creek, so he knew he would be able to reach both Mr. Choppy and Powell Hampton with one highly efficient call.

God, was he good! He had finally made it out of local to the big time, and he was going to waste no time impressing the hell out of the CNN heavy hitters.

Ronnie got through right away to Mr. Choppy, who at first couldn't quite believe he was being contacted long distance by an official CNN correspondent, let alone one who wanted to go national with waltzing in the grocery store.

"Hey, it's just me. I haven't changed one bit, Mr. Choppy," he continued. "I'm the same guy who covered your opening-day dancing with my Memphis TV crew. I've just kicked it up a notch, that's all."

Then Ronnie went into greater detail about his ideas for the assignment, and Mr. Choppy said: "To tell you the truth, this couldn't come at a better time. I can use all the publicity I can get. You got carte blanche here, Mr. Leyton, and any magic you got in your camera, please work it."

"Great. Now, how about letting me speak to Mr. Hampton, if he's wound up his dancing for the day?" Ronnie added. "Maybe he's got some additional angles that would help put this thing over the top."

"ARE YOU DECENT?" said Novie Mims, ringing up her fellow Nitwitt Myrtis Troy at approximately eight-thirty one evening. "If not, put some clothes on right this minute, and I'll come pick you up."

"Novie? Have you dispensed with a simple hello these days?"

"Oh, never mind that. Put some clothes on. We have to drive over to the Piggly Wiggly right now."

Myrtis gave an exasperated sigh through the receiver. "What in hell for? At this time of night? Are you in your cups?"

"No, I'm not. I'm disgustingly sober. But I just got a call from Mr. Choppy about ten minutes ago. He says there's a big emergency at the store, and he wants all of us Nitwitts there as soon as possible. He wanted me to spread the word to everyone except Laurie. She was not to be told anything, he said."

Myrtis sucked in a breath of air. "But Laurie is our president. Why not her? What in hell is going on?"

"He didn't say specifically. He just said we needed to be

there. Now I assured him I'd come pick you up, so go and put some clothes on and I'll be right on over, and don't make a big to-do out of this."

"But I don't like the way you drive."

"You're one to talk. Last week when we went up to Memphis to go shopping at the outlet mall, you ran that stop sign, and do you remember what you said to me?"

"What? Did you write it down in your diary?"

Novie made a disapproving clucking sound. "When you ran that sign, and I pointed it out to you, all you could say was, 'Oh, is this my week to drive?' Like you weren't even the one at the wheel. I absolutely insist that you let me pick you up and drive us down there."

There was an awkward silence. "Novie, you know damned good and well that women our age need advance notice to venture out in public. As it happens, I've been lying around watching a bit of TV, and I have recliner hair at the moment—the back of my hairdo is all pressed up against the headrest."

"Then go put on one of your wigs. No one will ever be the wiser. You must have fifty thousand of them."

"But this is just so absurd. Is there a fire? Why is Mr. Choppy being so mysterious about this? Is he having a heart attack or something?"

This time it was Novie who expelled impatient air. "Oh, for God's sake, Myrtis, he's asked us to meet him at the Piggly Wiggly, not the emergency room. He assured me this was very important and that it was essential we all be there. I've already roused Denver Lee, Wittsie, and Renza, and they're all coming together in Renza's car, so the least you can do is throw on something, make yourself presentable, and get with the plan."

"Even if I have no earthly idea what the plan is? And why is Laurie, of all people, being kept in the dark about this?"

"Well, I suppose we'll find all that out when we get there. Meanwhile, we don't have time to play guessing games."

Myrtis was mumbling something under her breath and tailed off incoherently.

"What are you complaining about now?" Novie said.

"I was saying to myself that I can't believe all the others went along with this at this time of night."

"Well, to tell you the truth, Myrtis, I'm practically hoarse trying to convince all of you to get off your royal rear-ends and out of your respective mansions. I'm the only one with a true sense of adventure. But if it's any incentive, I've mixed up a batch of my special Bloody Marys for us to nip out of teeny, tiny Dixie cups while we're standing around the Piggly Wiggly."

At that, Myrtis finally hung up and hurried over to her walk-in closet to pick out a suitable late-night emergency ensemble. This was followed by a very lengthy and energetic cursing session while she began fussing with her flattened hair in the bathroom mirror.

"Well, damn!" she exclaimed, seeing that the situation was beyond hopeless. "A wig it'll have to be tonight."

LAURIE HAD COME to the conclusion that something was definitely up. Powell had been toying with the delicious dinner she had prepared for them, pushing the lemon-pepper catfish and homemade cole slaw around his plate while "They Can't Take That Away From Me" played in the background. His he-man appetite seemed to have deserted him completely, and she was beginning to wonder if he might not be coming down with something.

"Aren't you feeling well tonight?" she said finally. "Maybe I should take your temperature or at least feel your forehead. You've never come over here, sat down at my table, and picked at your food that way."

Powell suddenly looked as if he had been caught off-guard, quickly stabbed a piece of fish with his fork and popped it into his mouth, chewing vigorously. "No, I'm just fine, and I certainly didn't mean to ignore your wonderful cuisine. You know I think it's the best in Second Creek." Then he helped himself to a mouthful of the cole slaw. "There, that's better, huh?"

Laurie folded her arms and looked at him askance. "Is something bothering you? You've seemed preoccupied all evening, even when we were dancing. You weren't by any chance thinking of Ann, were you?"

He looked genuinely surprised and put down his fork. "Now what would make you say that? The truth is, she was the last thing on my mind."

"Don't get upset, and please don't take this the wrong way, Powell, but I guess sometimes I get a little jealous of her—all those wonderful years the two of you had together and the memories she gave you. From where I'm sitting, it's very hard to compete with a perfect memory. I hope I'm not out of line here, but I just had to say that."

He picked up his water glass and took a sip. Then he reached over and held her hand. "I can see how you might get that impression. And you're absolutely right—I do have lots of wonderful memories of her, and they're always going to be very important to me. You're also right about the fact that I have been distracted tonight and it has affected my appetite, but not for the reason you think. I had hoped to handle this as smoothly as I handle most women on the dance floor, but it seems I've fallen a little short." He glanced down at his watch. "It's ten minutes to nine. You had no way of knowing this, but I've been waiting all night for nine o'clock to roll around. There's some place I want to take you, and something I want to show you. Then you'll understand everything. Are you game?"

"Well, I suppose I'll have to be. I'm certainly intrigued by all this mysterious behavior. Will that do?"

"You bet. Here, I'll help you clear the table and put things up, and then we'll go for a little spin in my car."

Five minutes later they were cruising in and around the downtown area, but Laurie still had no idea what he was up to or where they were going. "Are we there yet?" she said, fascinated with his inscrutable expression.

"Almost. But I want you to close your eyes—and keep them closed until I tell you to open them."

Laurie complied and said: "This had better be good, Powell Hampton. The last time I was told to close my eyes like this, it was to swing at a piñata at my sweet sixteen party. I trust I am going for the goodies here."

"I promise you, you will be."

When it was time for Laurie to open her eyes, however, her first reaction was extreme disappointment. There they were in the parking lot of the Piggly Wiggly, and it was mostly deserted because it was just after nine—closing time. The lights were still on in the store, and she could see Mr. Choppy, Jake, Kenyatta, and the cashiers moving around and talking and sweeping up and otherwise looking like they were getting ready to go home. Then, somewhat in the background, she spotted the rest of the Nitwitts huddled together off to one side, some of them drinking out of little paper cups.

"What's everyone doing here, Powell? This is what you wanted me to see? What's next? Getting up early to see Mr. Choppy opening for business?"

"Don't be so quick to judge. Just trust me on this. I want you to get out of the car and close your eyes again. Then I'm going to honk the horn, take you by the hand, and we're going to go in. That's when the fun begins."

After a few minutes that seemed more like an eternity, Laurie opened her eyes on command to an unexpected sight. The lights inside the Piggly Wiggly had been turned off, replaced by scores of flickering candles and a sparkler here and there. The only other source of illumination was the spot from Ronnie Leyton's camera crew.

"What is all this?" Laurie said, straining to make everything out. "Mr. Choppy? Ladies? Anyone?"

No one answered her question, but somewhere out there in the semi-darkness, someone punched up music. It was "Dancing in the Dark," and Powell took Laurie into his arms and began whirling her around the floor to the applause of the Nitwitts and the store employees standing by. Ronnie Leyton and his crew followed behind at a tactful distance, taping their every move for at least one full minute.

"You are dancing as divinely as ever, sir," Laurie said. "But please tell me what's going on. And how did you ever rouse all the girls at this time of night? Once they take off their faces at the end of the day, it's virtually impossible to get them to budge from their fortresses, I assure you."

As if on cue, the lights went back up just as Powell began his explanation. "Mr. Choppy and I worked it all out after Ronnie Leyton told us he wanted to do another Piggly Wiggly segment as his first assignment for CNN. Seems our man from Memphis will be moving on shortly to Atlanta."

"Ah, good for him. But I'm sure the 'Dancing in the Dark' part was your idea. It has your inimitable touch."

"Yes, it was. And so was this," he replied, bringing their dancing to a halt in order to reach into his pocket and pull out a small black box.

She took it from him and opened it gingerly, her eyes widening in disbelief. "Oh, Powell!"

It was a princess cut diamond, bordered by small sapphires on either side. Laurie took a moment to draw in a deep breath and slip the ring on her finger.

"I searched high and low for this beauty, leaving no stone unturned, so to speak. Went all the way up to Memphis to scout around. Finally, I found something that really does you justice. I think the diamond matches your sparkling smile, and the sapphires bring out those bright blue eyes of yours."

"Powell Hampton, you are an impetuous devil!"

"Then I take it you'll marry me?"

Despite the fact that everyone in the store had gathered around to eavesdrop, Laurie was not in the least self-conscious when she answered emphatically: "Oh, yes, I'll marry you. Whenever you say, wherever you say!"

Everyone applauded, particularly the Nitwitts, who led the way with their oohs and ahhs and gasps of appreciation.

"Good heavens, Laurie, you've struck the motherlode!" Renza exclaimed, taking Laurie's hand to examine the ring more closely.

Novie turned to Powell and beamed. "You've outdone yourself, sir!"

"Why, thank you, ladies!" Then he leaned down to give Laurie his very best kiss—the one intended to seal the deal—followed by a lengthy hug.

Mr. Choppy stepped up next. "Speaking of whenever and wherever, Mr. Hampton and I had a crazy idea, but we didn't want to go ahead without your approval. We were wonderin' how you would feel about having the marriage ceremony here in the Piggly Wiggly. Maybe a different way of walkin' down the aisle, huh? I mean, we could decorate it up real fancy for you. I promise you won't be disappointed."

Laurie took her eyes off the ring just long enough for a brief chuckle. "What can I say? I'm a lapsed, blue-stocking Presbyterian who was nearly born in the produce section of this store. Why shouldn't I be married here, too?"

"And I'm a lapsed Whiskeypalian," Powell added. "Therefore, I think we should go out and find ourselves a plain ole Justice of the Peace to hitch us, don't you?"

Mr. Choppy nodded enthusiastically. "Ole Bob Yates will do it up right for ya, I guarantee."

"Oh, and you know what else would be a hoot?" Laurie said, turning to her beloved, grinning Nitwitts. "I'd love to have all you girls as my matrons of honor right here with me. Wouldn't that be fun? What do you say? Are you crazy enough to go along with me on this?"

Laurie was inundated by her friends, who temporarily laid aside their mini–Bloody Marys and took turns hugging her and kissing her on the cheek, each one trying to outdo the other with her congratulations. It was Denver Lee who won that particular contest:

"You've given new meaning to the phrase 'shopping for a husband,' I think. Cheers, ole girl."

Then Ronnie Leyton added a final note. "That would make an even better piece than this one. Unfortunately, I am on a deadline, and we got some great stuff tonight, so we'll just wish you the best and leave it at that."

"When is this going to be broadcast?" Powell asked.

"Not sure, but I'll keep you posted. Shouldn't be too far off. I'm sure CNN wants to strike while the iron is hot."

"Meanwhile, how about an encore of 'Dancing in the Dark?'" Laurie said, gazing up into Powell's eyes. Denver Lee lumbered over and rewound the cassette, and they began a reprise around the store with the lights down low and the smoke from the sparklers slowly curling upwards to the rafters.

"Now that I've got this under my belt," he told her, twitching his nose at the sparklers' gunpowdery odor, "my bad case of nerves has disappeared, and I'm starting to get my appetite back. In fact, I'm starving to death. Think you could warm up those leftovers when we get back to your house?"

"Not a problem in the least. And not only that, I have the perfect thing in mind for our dessert."

He drew her closer to him as they continued to dance.

"Ah, yes," Myrtis quipped to Novie, both of them filled to

the brim with their Bloody Marys. "This was definitely worth putting a wig on for."

MR. CHOPPY was sitting at his office desk going over the store figures one last time. It was almost ten-thirty, and he had asked Laurie and Powell to hang around after the last of his employees and the Nitwitts had finally gone home.

"My coffers tell me that we basically have the few weeks until your wedding, folks," he told them as they sat across from him with intent expressions on their faces. "Maybe Mr. Leyton's TV story will help turn things around, but if it don't, I may have no other choice than to finally shut down the store. Put another way, your marriage could be the last official act of the Second Creek Piggly Wiggly."

"Oh, that's just too depressing to consider," Laurie replied. "Seems no matter what we do, we can't get your little store out of crisis mode."

Mr. Choppy hesitated, looking somewhat disconsolate. "We could be out of crisis mode soon enough, Miz Lepanto. This won't be no messy, prolonged goin'-outta-business sale either. Just an off-the-wall wedding of two good friends as our last hurrah and then no more Piggly Wiggly."

"Maybe it won't come to that," Powell added. "Having this publicized on CNN could make a huge difference. It'll be seen all over the country. You couldn't have asked for a better opportunity to promote yourself."

"Maybe so." But Mr. Choppy hardly sounded convinced. "I've been thinkin' about all this long and hard, you know. If it comes to closin' my doors, my employees won't have a problem findin' other jobs around town, but I keep wonderin' what I'm gonna do with myself without this little store to run. There's that old sayin' about people dyin' soon after they retire because they just don't have anything to do anymore. I don't wanna be one of those statistics. I don't think I'm near ready to be an obit."

Laurie rose and moved to his side, putting her hand on his shoulder. "It'll all work out the way it's supposed to, Mr. Choppy. Don't lose heart."

"I'll do my best, Miz Lepanto. I'll do my best."

A few minutes later he bade them good night and watched them head through the store hand in hand to the parking lot.

Mr. Choppy returned to his desk, closed his ledger, and sighed. How had Lady Roth put it again? Oh, yes, Second Creek was a place for people who had wanted to be memorable but hadn't quite made it. That was Hale Dunbar Jr. to a tee. Waiting around these last few weeks to see if indeed this was going to be the end would be a trial and a test of his emotional endurance, but at least he would go out knowing he had made two of his favorite people very happy. That seemed to be the theme of his life—on the outside looking in, nose pressed to the glass and watching others act out their dreams.

When he walked out of the store after locking up, the night sky seemed to be up to something. There were clouds swirling around in a peculiar cauldronlike effect. Not exactly threatening because there was no thunder and no lightning, but nonetheless something was being stirred up.

He stood perfectly still for a while watching whatever it was percolate far above him. It had completely blotted out the stars.

He didn't recall a storm of any kind predicted in the forecast, but that hardly mattered.

For the time being, the thought of Laurie and Powell's wedding was something to hang on to. A glimmer of light and hope for the malaise into which he had sunk.

Part Two

Chapter Ten

IN THE WELL-HEELED Chicago suburb of Lake Forest, Illinois, Peter Lyons's widow—Gaylie Girl to her intimate social circle—was gazing out the picture window of the den in her elegant, two-story Tudor mansion. She was dressed in an orange terry-cloth robe with fuzzy bedroom slippers on her feet. The sky outside was gray and oppressive. It was four-thirty in the afternoon, and the weather had been acting most peculiar all day. Periods of rain had alternated with outbreaks of sunshine, and then there had been a ten-minute, violent eruption of hail, sending big balls of white ice bouncing to earth and beating down her delicate summer flowers. It was peculiar as hell. She was practically addicted to the Weather Channel, but nothing even remotely like that had been forecast for the Chicago metropolitan area. Whatever the case, Mrs. Lyons intended to put it out of her mind with her third snort of sherry.

She moved to her recliner, snatched up the remote from a nearby end table, and began to surf the channels of her big-screen TV. Just then her secretary, a plump, eternally cheerful young woman named Harriet Mills padded across the room with the day's mail.

"Anything of interest, Harriet?"

"Just bills it looks like," she replied, placing the stack of envelopes on the nearby polished plantation writing desk. "Were you expecting something?"

"Actually, no. It's just that I'm so bored this afternoon. As if that's a big news flash for you," Gaylie Girl added, continuing to surf with her remote. "Nothing but these silly clubs and museum fund-raisers. Ha! They always write about me in the social columns, but I never receive so much as a postcard from my children."

"Now, it's not that bad. Didn't you get a card from your granddaughter, Mary Ann, last month?"

Gaylie Girl shrugged. "She's eleven. They were down at Disney World. Her mother probably made her write that to stay on my good side. I have no illusions about my family. Of course, it's all Peter's fault. He should never have left them all their own individual fortunes. Had it been my will, I would have arranged it so none of them got their hands on a penny until they were all at least sixty-five, maybe even seventy. He should have foreseen they would all go hog wild. I know I saw it coming for damned sure."

"Oh, I'm sure you'll hear from some of them soon, Mrs. Lyons. Sometimes when you travel in these foreign countries, you just don't have the right postage and don't always know where to mail things. I remember I had a devil of a time mailing letters when I took my junior year abroad."

"You don't have to make excuses for them, Harriet. Peter spoiled them all just like he spoiled me. That's what I loved about him so much, of course. He was generous to a fault with the money he made. I knew what kind of bargain I was striking when I married him."

Gaylie Girl muted the remote and sank back in her recliner while a quick review of her lifelong good fortune flashed before her. Fifty-odd years ago she had managed to ensnare handsome Peter Lyons, heir to the Lyons Insole Fortune of Chicago—"You need the heart and sole of a Lyons to keep in step!" and "Take a walk with a Lyons and stay on the prowl!"—thus assuring herself of permanent security, privilege, and conspicuous consumption. But while Peter's feet were always pampered, his heart had not fared nearly as well, succumbing to angina almost a decade ago. All the money in the world couldn't make up for his absence. He had obsessed over his Gaylie Girl, treating her like royalty—"my queen of sole," he had called her affectionately—and spoiling her for anyone else. What else could possibly be said about a man who had clung to his sense of humor even on his deathbed in the hospital?

"Don't worry, Gaylie Girl," he had told her in broken whispers in intensive care when the end was near. "You'll . . . easily find someone else to walk in . . . my shoes. After all . . . you've got . . . a few million to choose from."

She had kissed him on the cheek, and the next instant he was headed for that sole factory in the sky—his favorite nickname for the heaven he believed awaited him for being the best little insole maker in the world. To his way of thinking, not even Dr. Scholl's, his chief competition, had worked harder at it or done it better. And in tribute to his memory and the incomparable lifestyle he had provided her, she had decided to pretty much go it alone for whatever time she had left.

"I do not want to be set up," she told her inner circle of friends whenever they mentioned a romantic prospect to her. "Just leave me with my money and my memories. I don't have the time and energy to start over that way."

The remote had landed on CNN, but she was totally uninterested in the news. Instead, she downed the last of her sherry and sighed. "I got the strangest feeling a few moments ago looking out at all that weather. It reminded me of something that happened a very long time ago. Isn't that the silliest thing?"

Harriet took a seat in an armchair, looking perplexed. "No, not really."

"I'm the sort of person who remembers what the weather was like on all of the important days of her life. My wedding day, for instance. It was one of those traditional June weddings, but the sky was dark and threatening right up to the very moment of the ceremony. Peter did our wedding up first class — my family had no money at all so he staged the whole thing — but everyone was constantly worried about getting into the church before the heavens opened up. It's funny. I remember that terrible threat of rain as much or more than I remember the ceremony."

Harriet was nodding pensively. "I see what you're getting at —"

Gaylie Girl suddenly held up her hand and shushed her,

freezing Harriet in midsentence and clicking the sound back on. "I need to hear this. I can't believe it!"

On her big-screen TV a handsome young reporter standing beside a stocky older man in front of a Piggly Wiggly somewhere, was doing his intro while the graphic—HALE DUNBAR JR., SECOND CREEK STORE OWNER—was superimposed across the bottom of the screen. ". . . and the current owner of the Piggly Wiggly—Hale Dunbar Jr.—is the second generation of the Dunbar family to run the store," he was saying. "Tell us about this very unusual service you've been offering lately to the ladies of your community, Mr. Dunbar."

Gaylie Girl scooted forward to the edge of her chair as the man began to speak. Of course it was him. It had to be him. She did not think the years had been particularly kind, but it was nevertheless the same man. Something, some quality, was still there, around his eyes mostly. There was only one small town in Mississippi called Second Creek. And surely only one Piggly Wiggly doing business there. There was simply no doubt about it. God help her, it was him.

"Well, we have a former ballroom dance instructor, Mr. Powell Hampton, who dances with the ladies from noon to two o'clock while they do their shoppin'. Or rather, we do their shoppin' for 'em. It takes a little extra effort on the part of our employees, but mostly it all comes out in the wash together."

"And have many ladies taken advantage of this opportunity? I can see how it would be quite popular."

"Yes, indeedy, it is. Quite a few of the ladies have come in. Some come to waltz, some to fox-trot, anything goes—we even had one lady doin' the Charleston with Mr. Hampton.

Everyone has a real good time, and it takes a little of the drudgery outta shoppin'. Now, some stores rely on coupons and such. We, on the other hand, just rely on a little charm and choreography. It's not your usual shoppin' trip."

Next there was footage of a couple whirling around the darkened store with candles flickering and sparklers sizzling and smoking in the background and the reporter said: "Tell us what's going on here, Mr. Dunbar."

"Well, believe it or not, this was the occasion our dance instructor, Mr. Hampton, used to propose marriage to his ladyfriend recently. As you can see, we had candles and sparklers and all the lights off for a little while to set the right romantic mood, and maybe you can tell that the music playin' is 'Dancing in the Dark.'"

"And did Mr. Hampton's ladyfriend accept his proposal?"

"She sure did. And we're even gonna have their wedding right here in the store for good measure. Just a small, simple ceremony, but it'll be somethin' to remember for many years to come."

Then came the close. "And there you have it. The remarkable story of the little grocery store in the Mississippi Delta that fills out your dance card, sweeps you off your feet, and even arranges for you to say your 'I do's,' if you're so inclined. In Second Creek, Mississippi, I'm Ronnie Leyton reporting."

Gaylie Girl turned off the set. The remote fell out of her hand to the floor. "No!" she said as Harriet scampered to retrieve it for her. "Let it stay right where it is. I may stomp the damned thing into a thousand little pieces before too long—the miserable, foul, stinking device. Why the hell couldn't the battery have been on the fritz today or something?"

Harriet's perpetual grin faded quickly. "I don't understand."

"I just can't believe it. How many news stories do you suppose that CNN channel puts on every day? Hundreds, I'm sure. And I have to tune in to that one. Can you believe the nasty, stinking luck?"

Harriet sat down, folded her hands primly in her lap and cleared her throat. "Would you like to talk about it, Mrs. Lyons? I'll be more than happy to listen. You know me and my proverbial ear. I'm here for you."

Gaylie Girl was turning everything over in her head. She had never told anyone—not even her Peter—about what had happened way back then. She had been nothing but an idiot child. Oh, her cousin Polly Andrew, who had been in on it with her in the very beginning, knew some of the details, but not the most awful part.

Over the years she had dealt with the guilt by immersing herself in Peter's wealth. That, and pretending that it really wasn't all that big of a deal. But she knew she had done something very wrong and hurtful, and that perhaps she would have to account for it when she met her Maker. For now, she was not inclined to share very much with Harriet.

"Suffice it to say that it has to do with one of the worst indiscretions of my very distant youth. I think I'm going to leave it at that. Except . . ."

Here was that chance for atonement, even though she knew the odds had always been phenomenally against her.

"Except I would like you to inquire about first-class flights to Memphis, Tennessee. Also, suites at the Peabody Hotel. I'll need a rental car once I've arrived. And none of those horrid compacts that they apparently design for hamsters. I must have plenty of room to stretch my legs. Oh, and make sure the damned thing has cruise control, too. I cannot abide cars without cruise control."

"I understand. And when will you be traveling?"

She reviewed her upcoming schedule in her head. There was that Lake Forest Library Board meeting where the agenda was going to be a heated discussion of whether or not to put filters on the library's computers to prevent curious teenagers from surfing the Internet for porn, but she could easily give her proxy for that. She was going to tell her good friend Linda Markham to cast a no vote on her behalf. Gaylie Girl did not believe in censorship in any form. Never had. She had always been somewhat on the fast track herself. But other than that contentious business, there was nothing she couldn't postpone or even safely ignore, and there was for damned sure no one who would miss her.

"Let's say next weekend. Flying out Friday, coming back Sunday. Get back to me as soon as you can."

"I'll get right to it," Harriet replied, heading immediately to her office and leaving her employer alone with her thoughts.

She had often wondered what had become of him, and now she knew. He had never gotten out of Second Creek. Never even gotten out of that store. And maybe, just maybe, she had been responsible for keeping him there. She and Polly should have known better, but those were heady times. They were also desperate times because of the war—so many people saying that the Nazis and the Japs might just win and take everything over and there would be no tomorrow, so better live for today. Better spread your legs wide and kiss the boys and make them cry before they fell on the battlefields. Let 'em spill a little seed before they spilled their precious blood.

Her cousins—Peggy, Pearl, and Polly Andrew—were touring the country and singing up a storm just like they were the real Andrews Sisters, and she had managed to tag along with them for the ride. But God Almighty, nineteen-year-olds could be so mean and cruel and stupid! If there had been some way to take it all back, she gladly would have.

She rose from the recliner and walked over to the gold-leaf mirror beside the plantation desk. She looked pretty damned good for a woman of seventy-four. Of course, her great wealth had a lot to do with that. She had had herself nipped and tucked and peeled and pounded over the decades to preserve the good looks she had been born with, trimming a good fifteen years off her age. She had always wanted to look good for Peter, and she had—streaked hair perfectly coiffed, thighs always firm and toned, breasts reasonably perky, makeup always impeccably applied. She had been the quintessential trophy wife for a powerful Fortune 500 CEO.

But now there was no one to look good for—at least not in any way that counted. Her big brass bed was always cold on that side. Her nights, a marathon of groping around for the dependable warmth that was no longer there, and she just wasn't the type to settle for an empty-headed escort who doubled as a sexual athlete. Not at this settled stage of her life. She had come to think of herself as emotionally set in bronze, as fixed as an old statue in a Chicago park.

"Never forget that he gave you that name, you dreadful little Gaylie Girl," she whispered to the mirror, almost expecting it to talk back to her and tell her that, in this instance, she had been the one who was the meanest of them all.

For the "he" she was referring to was not her beloved husband, Peter. She meant him . . . Hale Dunbar Jr. He had given her that nickname freely and innocently, and she had been emotionally unwilling to let go of it. It had somehow summed her up, he had managed to isolate her essence with his sixteen-year-old naïveté, and she had kept it for her own, insisting that Peter and her friends use it all the time. What a great irony in that, and what a tremendous shock it would have been to her social circle and Peter himself had she ever revealed its source!

She took a deep breath, feeling the sherry circulating throughout her system. Rapid-fire thudding sounds from outside quickly brought her out of her contemplation. More hail. More ice bouncing around like a shower of Ping-Pong balls. Destructive, yet strangely beautiful. Noisy, yet undeniably fascinating. And the bottom line was, it had definitely gotten her attention.

Harriet came rushing into the room, obviously alarmed by the weather. "I had to shut off my computer," she explained. "It's not a good idea to have it on in the middle of storms like this. Of course, I have a surge protector, but there's no use taking any chances. You never know what kind of damage these storms can do."

Gaylie Girl moved back to her recliner and collapsed. "I wish I could shut off my mind as easily as you can shut off your computer."

Chapter Eleven

LAURIE WAS in the midst of treating her five matrons of honor to a cozy summer luncheon at the Victorian Tea Room just down the street from the Piggly Wiggly. The big round table for six she had reserved for them beneath a white, whirring ceiling fan and flanked by potted palms seemed the picture of typical Nitwittian interaction at first. Much of the opening dialogue centered around ordering and very little else, but even that wandered off the politeness plantation before too much time had passed.

"I have no intention of ordering today's special which is the cream of broccoli soup," Denver Lee announced while perusing her laminated menu. "I'll have gas right up until Laurie's wedding day if I do."

"It's a karmic transference of sorts," Novie was quick to add from her perch across the table. "It's all those indigestible vegetable paintings you've been doing lately. What goes around, comes around."

"Well, I think I'll have the chicken gumbo," Renza replied. "Nothing indigestible about that. It's their best dish."

That set off a flurry of gumbo orders, and then there was a surprising lull in the conversation. Laurie took full advantage of it and said: "Girls, I know I told you all that this luncheon was for the purpose of ironing out some of my wedding details, and that's partially true. A bit later, I do want to discuss our outfits for the ceremony and that sort of thing, but there is something else we need to address, and there's a certain sense of urgency about it."

Novie jumped the gun. "I know what it is, too. You want some suggestions for the honeymoon, I'll bet. I have tons of places to recommend, of course. I save all my brochures, too."

"No, that's not it," Laurie replied, shaking her head. "But I'm surprised none of you has thought of this and brought the subject up on your own. I'll just cut to the chase and remind you all that once I get married to Powell, I will no longer be a widow, and this is supposed to be a widows' club. It's my studied opinion that the president of the Nitwitts should be a widow. I think I should resign my position and that we should elect my successor as soon as possible. Today over this very lunch, for that matter."

The others looked stunned and for a minute or so remained speechless at the suggestion. Finally, Wittsie said: "Oh, but Laurie, you are such a wonderful officer. You always have been. I mean, I know I wouldn't hold such a technicality as that against you. I just wouldn't. And I don't know how the rest of

you feel about it, but I just don't think I can accept your resig-
nation over a technicality such as that."

A unanimous nodding of heads ensued. "Oh, if it were just a
matter of a technicality, I think I would be far less inclined to
have reached the decision I've reached," Laurie explained further. "But the truth is, Powell and I intend to travel a great deal
even after the honeymoon is over, and I don't want to put
myself in the position of neglecting my club duties. My life is
going to change rather drastically, I think, and it just wouldn't
be fair to any of you if I pretended that I could devote the kind
of time to our beloved Nitwitts that you've all come to expect
of me."

"I suppose when you put it that way, it makes sense," Wittsie
replied, though without conviction.

"Well, I do understand about wanting to spend the extra
time with Powell," Myrtis offered. "I can't say that I blame you
in that regard. I think we'd all rather be married than widowed
when you come right down to it."

Laurie flashed her best smile and took a deep breath. "Thank
you all for understanding. I was a bit nervous about announc-
ing this, but it goes without saying that all of us have dealt with
the issue of getting on with our lives. This time for me, thankfully, change has been a matter of choice, and I want each
of you to know that I have no intention of giving up being
a Nitwitt completely. But I do think we ought to vote on my
successor."

"Right this second? Before the gumbo?" Denver Lee
replied. "I'm hungry, and I need food if I'm going to vote on a
new president. Some of the worst decisions I've ever made have
been on an empty stomach. It's like when you go to the Piggly

Wiggly, and you haven't eaten all day. You end up buying everything in sight, and then when you get it all home and start putting it away, you think you must have been possessed by a grocery demon."

Laurie squeezed more lemon into her water while carefully considering the mood of the table. Why should picking her successor be any easier than the rest of her official Nitwitt duties had been? Still, she knew she could finesse it. "All right then, we'll take nominations and a vote after we've eaten. That way there'll be no excuses for low blood sugar decisions."

Denver Lee had screwed up her mouth into a disapproving pucker. "That reminds me. Don't let me get away today without some of the best low-fat and sugar-free recipes any of you have up your sleeve. Dr. Wadkins told me last week that I might be prediabetic but that I could probably still avoid it by dropping some weight. God knows, I've tried before, but maybe I have the right incentive now."

That revelation unleashed an avalanche of comments and asides about the time-honored matronly battle of the bulge, which continued until the six steaming bowls of gumbo and side salads arrived. Once everyone had dug in with gusto, Laurie brought up the next item on her agenda.

"I did want to touch on the matter of what you ladies would like to wear for the ceremony," she began after blowing on a spoonful of her soup. "For instance, would you prefer to coordinate or each wear something different?"

"Coordinate," Denver Lee quickly replied.

"I agree," said Myrtis.

"Horse apples! I couldn't disagree more," Renza offered, furiously stirring a packet of sugar into her second glass of iced tea and then clinking her spoon noisily on the rim. "Coordinating our outfits at our age? We're not a pack of squealing sorority girls, you know."

"Oh, you just want to work in your little foxes," Denver Lee returned.

Then Novie entered the fray. "If my opinion amounts to anything, I agree with Renza. I think we would look absolutely ridiculous wearing some identical, frou-frou, frilly, puff-shouldered, pastel creation. As I'm sure I don't need to remind you, we've all been around the block a few times, and we've for damned sure earned the right to look any way we please. I've worked too hard all these years developing a little character to abandon it now."

"Never mind that," Myrtis began. "Denver Lee and I are right, Renza. What exactly did you and Novie have in mind? One of your legendary fox furs over a formal muumuu? You've probably got things in your closet that Eleanor Roosevelt would have cast off to the Salvation Army."

"Oh, really?" Renza began, zeroing in on her rival with flashing eyes. "When was the last time you updated your makeup? That preteen look of yours is wearing awfully thin. Or, shall I say, awfully thick?"

"Please stop," Laurie said, bringing her hands together prayerfully. "This is hardly going to be your average traditional wedding. For heaven's sake, we're having it in the aisles of a grocery store. I'm not going to be wearing any virginal white gown—I'll be wearing a conservative, peach-colored suit. My daughter Lizzie will be flying in to join you as the sixth matron of honor. She's going to wear something simple and conservative, too. But if all of you decide to show up in string bikinis and flip-flops—God forbid—it'll be fine with me. Myrtis, why don't you and Denver Lee go and get fitted for something together if you like? And Novie, you and Renza surprise us with whatever strikes your fancy. I just want you all there as my good friends and witnesses—that's the long and short of it."

Laurie's monologue immediately chastened the group, all except for Wittsie, who had remained unusually quiet so far and suddenly decided to speak up. "I was wondering . . . I mean, it was just a thought, not anything that's really necessary, but . . . well, my granddaughter, Meagan, is still visiting me . . . all summer, really, until her parents get back from their tour of Europe. Do you think maybe she could be in the wedding, too? How about an old-fashioned maid of honor, Laurie? I mean, it would be so exciting for her because she's just fifteen and never had the chance to be in a wedding before. What do you think?"

"Oh, I love that idea!" Laurie replied. "I think that would be charming, especially since my younger daughter, Hannah, couldn't make it. One of those family vacations she'd been planning with her husband for quite some time, you know, camping with him off the coast of Maine or something. Frankly, I can't imagine that as much of a vacation."

Denver Lee rattled her drink noisily. "Camping! Why the hell do men think that's a romantic notion? A weekend of ticks and chigger bites and insect repellent and worst of all is the, well, plumbing situation. If God had meant people to go to the bathroom outdoors, he would have made squatting look digni-fied. My late husband seemed to live for it. 'Guess what, honey,' he'd say first thing off the bat. 'Didn't catch any fish this time but really found a great place to, uh, meditate, so to speak.'

Now, I ask you, why do men think all of that is something we are just dying to hear about?"

"Oh, I agree," Novie added. "And not only that, women look like Okies in camping clothes. I mean, who thought up that ensemble — big rubber chest waders and overalls and combat boots? Men, of course, think it's absolutely great because they don't give a tinker's damn how their behinds look coming and going on the trail."

Denver Lee pressed the matter with gusto. "Hell, my behind looks absolutely huge in overalls. I look like a walking double-wide."

"Well, quickly changing the subject on that image," Myrtis cleared her throat pointedly, "if you're going to go to the trouble of having a maid of honor now, you might as well have the matrons matching the maid or vice versa."

"I've never heard such horse apples in my life!" Renza replied. "We're all of us looking at sixty in the rearview mirror. What on earth do you think we'll find on such short notice that will match the form and figure of a fifteen-year-old? Even if we should find something, do you really think the comparison will be flattering? We'll all end up looking like Bette Davis in *Whatever Happened to Baby Jane?*"

Laurie sat back in her chair, suppressing outright laughter. She was certainly making the right decision in stepping down. She was not going to miss the bickering and the sniping, even if the club and its social activities had filled many a lonely night for her. It had served its purpose during a difficult period of her life, and she had given plenty back to it as well. But she had Powell and his romantic inclinations to look forward to now.

Besides, she still intended to do things with the girls from time to time. It was not like she was never going to see any of them again.

"Let me repeat, ladies," Laurie began. "This is not a traditional wedding. Wittsie, why don't you go ahead and buy anything you like for Meagan, and the rest of you can do exactly as you please. Now, why don't we put that issue to rest and move on to our other pressing business?"

Wittsie rummaged through her purse and pulled out a notepad and pencil. "I'm ready to go whenever y'all are."

Renza posed in her customary, nose-in-the-air fashion. "Are you absolutely certain you really want to quit, Laurie? No one's ever run the club as well as you have. I think we all sort of assumed you would be running things forever."

"I appreciate the vote of confidence, but I know I won't have the time anymore. Let's be logical about this, shall we? Up until now, every one of us Nitwitts has been a widow. It's kind of an unwritten qualification, and, embracing second-wifedom as I have, I'm technically no longer qualified."

Wittsie nudged her, looking puzzled. "How do you spell it? Not second, but that wife word."

"W-I-F-E-D-O-M, I think. But why are you writing that down? That's not part of the nomination process, Wittsie. Don't write that down, for heaven's sake."

Wittsie hastily hung her head and started erasing.

"So now that you all know I'm really stepping down, we need to elect a replacement," Laurie continued. "Would anyone like to volunteer or nominate someone else?"

"I nominate Myrtis," said Denver Lee. "Need I remind everyone, she's so good with finances."

Laurie requested a second to the nomination.

"I want to nominate Renza instead," Novie said, even though she was technically out of order. "I certainly do not agree that Myrtis is good with finances. She's only good at talking about them all the time — to a fault, I might add — letting us know how much she paid for a chest of drawers she found at an estate sale or how much she saved on a case of Vienna sausages to make pigs-in-a-blanket for a reception. Hell, I think I know more about her checkbook than she does."

Myrtis drew herself up for a retort, but was preempted by Wittsie, who was quick to point out that they were not following correct procedure.

"Oh, to hell with procedure, Wittsie," Denver Lee replied. "Let's just vote and get it over and finish our gumbo before it gets cold. It's either Myrtis or Renza. Let's choose our poison."

The tense situation deteriorated even further. Since the nominees were not allowed to participate, there were two votes for Myrtis and two for Renza, and both of them looked miffed about the deadlock.

"I have a suggestion," Laurie said, determined not to let things get completely out of hand. "Why don't the two of you share the position? Myrtis, you could preside for six months, and then Renza could take over. That way, whoever's done the best job would likely get reelected for the next full year."

There was an awkward silence, but, amazingly, Renza was the first to crumble. "I suppose I'm willing if you are, Myrtis."

"I guess so. It can't really hurt to give it a try. But which of us gets to serve the first six months?"

Laurie tried not to display her exasperation. Here was yet another roadblock to her seamless escape from the fun and games and liquored-up, mental machinations of the Nitwitts. Bravely, she collected herself and said: "Shall we try alphabetical order?"

Renza narrowed her eyes and wagged a finger. "First name or last? It makes a difference, you know. If we go by first names, Myrtis beats out Renza, of course. But if we go by last names, Belford comes before Troy. Aha! Bet you thought this was going to be a snap, didn't you, Laurie?"

Laurie managed to keep that smile on her face and summoned the energy for one last try. "Flip a coin, then? Come on, ladies, you all are making brain surgery out of a simple outpatient procedure. It truly is time for me to leave the responsibilities to somebody else."

Finally, all the foolishness came to an end. Myrtis won the coin toss, and everyone, including Renza, congratulated her on becoming the new president of the Nitwitts for the next six months.

As for Laurie, she was convinced more than ever that she was doing the right thing by ending her long and impressive reign. On more than one occasion she had probably kept the group from disbanding due to the significant personality clashes within it. That responsibility would now fall to Myrtis and Renza, both of whom would be hard-pressed to duplicate her special brand of diplomacy. But Laurie felt sure that the Nitwitts could remain viable without her tireless input.

A LITTLE PAST nine-thirty that evening, Mr. Choppy was sitting beside Laurie on her living room sofa, nursing a glass of muscadine wine for courage. He felt doubly uncomfortable every time he glanced across the room to where Powell stood by the mantel with a strained expression on his face. He knew his unscheduled appearance at Laurie's door a few minutes earlier had probably interrupted some sort of affectionate exchange between the engaged couple, but they needed to know the truth. It would certainly be all over town tomorrow, and he didn't want them to hear it on the street.

"I've come to a real painful decision," he began. "I've already told my employees that I'm gonna shut down the Piggly Wiggly for good right after your wedding, and now I'm tellin' you. The dancin' and everything was a great idea—I couldn't be more grateful to you for comin' up with it, and it has brought plenty of women into the store. I guess Lucy Faye summed it up best the other day when she turned and said to me, 'Mr. Choppy, some a' these ladies look like they haven't seen the light a' day in a while, like they've been in mothballs for thirty years. You've really pulled 'em outta the woodwork, and Mr. Hampton has dusted 'em off real nice.' Funny as that was to hear, the real problem is those same ladies are just not buyin' a whole lotta groceries. I'm in practically the same financial position I was a couple a' months ago. Still hand to mouth, fallin' behind in my payments again. It's just no good. I'm afraid we're beatin' a dead horse."

Powell looked astonished as he took a seat on the sofa. "Boy, Mr. Choppy, you sure could have fooled me. I hardly have time to go to the men's room during my dancing hours every day. You mean to tell me that none of that extra activity is making a difference in grocery sales for you? And why on earth didn't you keep me posted on this a little better, Laurie?"

She looked genuinely embarrassed and said: "I didn't want

you to get down in the dumps about it, Powell. Not as hard as you've been working every day on the dance floor—or rather, the aisles. Besides, I thought everything might still work out. I didn't say anything to the Nitwitts either."

"No offense, Mr. Hampton, but I'm afraid you're just too good of a dancer is all," Mr. Choppy replied. "That's what most of 'em are comin' in for. It's not workin' out the way we'd all hoped. True enough, it's extra business in the store, but it's turned out to be what I call 'run down to the store' business more than anything else. They just run down at the last minute for one or two things they just can't do without until the next day. That's more than enough to keep a convenience store in business, but it's not near enough for a little market like mine."

Laurie reached over and gently rubbed Mr. Choppy's arm. "I hate to say it, but I had a healthy suspicion it was going to come to this after our last meeting. I kept hoping against hope that people were buying a whole lot more and that they would make the difference for you eventually."

"But they weren't—they haven't. We got that one big surge during the grand opening, and then it tailed off pretty fast, as I told you. Most folks have a short attention span these days, it seems." Mr. Choppy took a sip of his wine before continuing. "Then, when I looked at my prospects down the road, things got really grim. You two'll soon be goin' on your honeymoon, and there won't be any dancin' at all while you're gone. So even that token business from the women who just came in to dance would dry up on me. You might remember that I didn't really think it would work over the long haul anyway."

Laurie and Powell exchanged troubled glances, and she

said: "Well, maybe we could postpone our honeymoon until things start to look up again for you. We wouldn't want to go off like that if it meant we were leaving you high and dry."

"Miz Lepanto, you cain't possibly think I'd ask you to do that for me. I mean, it's your honeymoon, for God's sake. You've already done more than enough for me by loanin' me that money, and I intend to pay you and your club back like I said I would, but I think we have to face facts, here. The Dunbar family's little Piggly Wiggly is pretty much fixin' to become an extinct species these days."

Powell made a sympathetic noise under his breath. "That's a very Darwinian take, Mr. Choppy. According to your analysis, I should be dusting off your bones on a dig and calling you 'Dinosaurus Secondcreekus Dunbarus.'"

Mr. Choppy wasn't sure he got it all completely, but he smiled politely. "I don't want you folks to feel bad about this in any way. You've done everything you could, but I think the best thing for me to do is put my Piggly Wiggly to bed. I got my social security and an IRA, so I'll be okay."

"I'm kinda curious, though," Laurie began, rubbing her hands together thoughtfully. "Why did you decide to tell me about your financial predicament a few months back? As the summer went by, it seemed like you were always putting out mixed signals. Sometimes, it even seemed like you really didn't want any help at all."

"Maybe I really didn't. There was a part a' me that kept at it because it was what my daddy woudda wanted me to do. Maybe that was the part that called you into my office that day and told you all my troubles. But you're right. There was always this other part that was thinkin' it was time to move on and it was all over but the shoutin'. Plus, there are some things I just cain't go into with you, I'm afraid."

"Well, what about Ronnie Leyton's CNN coverage?" Laurie said. "It hasn't had time to really kick in yet. Maybe if you could just wait a little longer and see if that brings in the kind of business you need to stay open."

"I don't know, Miz Lepanto. I cain't see busloads a' tourists comin' by to see my Piggly Wiggly just because they mighta caught a story on CNN. Let's just say that'd be a long way to travel for a little lunchmeat. The response from the locals makes me realize I'm swimmin' upstream and fightin' the inevitable. Daddy always told me to roll with the punches but not to let myself get beat to a pulp by stayin' in the fight too long."

Laurie rose from the sofa and said: "That's a pretty graphic image, Mr. Choppy, but you may have a point. And now, if you'll excuse me, I need to go get something from the kitchen to make a point of my own."

A few seconds later she stood in the doorway with an empty plastic storage bag in hand. "Do you know what this represents?" she said, addressing them together and not waiting for their reply. "It's me moving forward. Earlier today, I led a one-woman expedition to Antarctica. That's what I call the bottom of my freezer where I've had packets of Roy's favorite foods preserved in ice for at least the last seven years, probably even longer. All this time I've been afraid to defrost them or throw them out because of my insane sentimental attachment to them. If I let them go, I would finally be letting Roy go, too. I was afraid to move on completely. But this afternoon after I got back from the store, I decided it was time to make a clean break. So I went down to Antarctica and threw out all my frozen relics. I've needed to tell someone about it, and the truth is, it suddenly feels like I've got a glacier off my back."

Powell walked over and put his arm around her. "And if I may borrow a bit from your analogy, Laurie—this defrosted woolly mammoth standing beside you in his size-thirteen dancing shoes is moving forward, too. He's proud to say he's taking on a beautiful new wife and a brand-new dance partner for the rest of his life."

Mr. Choppy was surprised by their testimonials but managed a tentative smile. "Well, it kinda sounds like you're both supportin' my decision to close down. I guess I thought you'd make more of a fuss and try to talk me out of it."

Laurie sighed. "I won't lie. There's a part of me that doesn't want you to close—mainly the part with the sentimental attachment to the produce bin. Maybe my original intention in all of this was to try and preserve that part of my personal history. But that doesn't pay your bills, and you know your financial situation better than we do. If you say it's time to let go and move on, I don't see how we can possibly not respect you on that. And you were exactly right about the dancing part turning out to be a temporary fix—I don't think Powell was up to doing it forever anyway, were you, honey?"

"Well, for starters, I was considering asking for a cutback on the hours. This is going to sound awful, and I certainly don't mean to be unkind, but between Lady Roth and some of the other less flexible women, I was beginning to feel like a therapist in the middle of a rehab session, bless all their lonely hearts."

They all smiled politely, but Mr. Choppy put his hands on the table, folding them solemnly. "I won't say this is gonna be easy for me. My whole life has been wrapped up in the Piggly Wiggly, just like your whole life has been wrapped up in dancin', Mr. Hampton. I do believe, though, there are still some things for me to work out before I leave."

That put a definite damper on the conversation, and no one spoke for a while. Finally, Laurie said: "Whatever decision you make regarding the Piggly Wiggly, Powell and I will support. You just do whatever you think best."

Mr. Choppy got up from the sofa, infused with a new resolve. "Well, there's one thing for certain you can count on. We're still gonna have your wedding and a little reception for you afterward at the store. It'll be decorated to the rafters and somethin' right pretty to look at on your special day."

"Only in Second Creek," Laurie replied, as they all made their way to the front door to say good night.

And as Mr. Choppy walked to his car in the sticky midsummer night air, he began to feel slightly better about everything. That hopeful trace of boyish enthusiasm, that ember of optimism he had never relinquished over the years was doing its best to keep him on an even keel now. Something good—no, something better than he could possibly ever imagine—was going to come out of all this, he could feel it.

Chapter Twelve

$\mathcal{S}$INCE THE DEATH of her husband, Gaylie Girl Lyons had become virtually addicted to flying first class whenever she traveled around on her pleasure junkets. But it wasn't the medium-rare filet mignon or the virtual river of champagne or even the overly solicitous service behind the carefully drawn curtain that did it for her. She had long ago decided that none of those pretentious touches were worth the pumped-up price of admission.

No, for her it was the extra space to stretch out during all that time spent in the air. She had read those horror stories in the newspapers and magazines about people getting blood clots in their legs from being squeezed into those claustrophobic coach seats for hours, and she had no intention of running that risk. Plus, there was no reason not to spend Peter's money on the upgrade. He had always traveled that way himself and would have been the first to insist that she pamper herself wherever she went.

"Can I get you just a spritz more champagne?" the perky flight attendant asked as she walked by and noticed Gaylie Girl's empty glass.

"Not just now. But you might want to check with me later. Maybe twenty minutes or so before we land."

What she really wanted to do at that moment was to sit quietly and reflect on tying up perhaps the most egregious loose end of her life. To some extent she still couldn't quite believe she was actually making the trip. If she had felt so damned guilty about what she had done, why hadn't she just hauled herself down to the Delta at any time over the past fifty-odd years to make amends? She knew the answer, of course. She had been a big fat coward about it all, afraid to face the boy, now the man, she had deceived and toyed with and otherwise manipulated — until that CNN report had lit a fire under her and gotten her off her royal duff.

She closed her eyes and let the smoothness of the flight wrap her up in a midair cocoon of sorts, the gentle humming of the engines creating a discernible rhythm that seemed to match her own heartbeat. Once the rhythm was firmly established, she turned her thoughts to music. Specifically, wartime songs. The titles conjured up images in her brain that played like snippets from grainy old Movietone newsreels—"The White Cliffs of Dover," "Rum and Coca-Cola," "They're Either Too Young or Too Old;"—"The South American Way," "When the Lights Go On Again All Over the World"—they were all part of the repertoire of her cousins, the Andrew Sisters. Oh, what a corny gimmick that was, and the trio had ultimately gone nowhere with it, even though the studio was planning a national tour for them.

Nonetheless, Gayle Morris of Chicago, first cousin to Pearl, Peggy, and Polly Andrew, had worked hard in an Evanston music store selling records from the "Hit Parade" for over a year and saved up her money with the intention of hooking up with them eventually. Then she had bought a ticket and finally taken the long, hot bus ride from Chicago along Route 66 all the way out to Hollywood in the autumn of 1944 to visit them in the cramped little bungalow they had rented near the beach in Venice.

She had such stars in her eyes that she just couldn't wait to share her adventure with someone else. In this case that turned out to be the rather large and talkative, middle-aged woman with a hint of a mustache who was sitting next to her on the bus. The woman had introduced herself as Marceline Orrigi and immediately began telling Gayle her life story.

"Most people can tell I'm originally from Brooklyn," the woman explained, tilting her salt-and-pepper head from side to side as she spoke. "But I just sold all my apartments in Greenwich Village for a song, and now I'm on my way out to Los Angeles to go live with my daughter, Anna Maria. She's been after me for years to get out of the landlord business, you know. She'd call me up every week and say, 'Mama, you gotta dump all those dumps in the Village, especially the one with the polka-dot toilet seat, and move out here with me. You gotta stop spending your life trying to collect from all those starving writers and artists and other deadbeats you rent to.' The girl had a point. So, I finally found a schmuck to take them all off my hands, and here I am on my way to the land of sunshine and movie stars. What about you, honey? What's your story? Tell me all about yourself, huh?"

Gayle chimed in eagerly, trying to sound as important as she could. "Well, I'm going to visit my cousins out there. They're a singing group in the movies."

"Oooh, would I know them, honey?" she replied, quivering with excitement.

Gayle decided to play a game with her. What the hell—she would never see this woman again anyway. "Oh, I'm sure you've heard of the Andrews Sisters. Well, they're my first cousins."

"Why, I just can't believe it. I'm crazy about their music. My daughter, Anna Maria, loves them, too. Oh, you know what? Maybe you could give me your autograph? Wait and I'll get my fountain pen out of my purse."

At first, Gayle was dumbfounded by the request. She also wondered what the woman would have said had she known that the Andrew Sisters had originally been signed as a one-shot gag group for a bit in one of the Kay Kyser movie sequences. "But why do you want my autograph? I certainly haven't done anything at all."

She winked while screwing up her pudgy face. "Not yet, anyway. Honey, as I always say to my Anna Maria, 'In life, you just never know, so you better get it in writing.' Besides, I have a good feeling about you. Who knows what great things you might end up doing?"

Gayle had done her best to autograph the back of the bus ticket stub she had been handed, and the two of them had remained practically inseparable for the rest of the ride—taking all their meals together in the bus terminals and even talking back and forth between the stalls in the ladies' rooms just like a mother and daughter might do.

But once Gayle had actually hooked up with her cousins in Venice, she decided that merely visiting them would not be enough. She needed to live up to Marceline Orrigi's vague prediction of fame and fortune.

"PLEASE LET ME go with you on the tour, Polly," Gayle had begged her cousin—the youngest, prettiest, and most irresponsible member of the trio—who was primping in front of her studio dressing room mirror while working her way through her customary pack of Camels.

"You're not serious, Gayle."

"Sure I am. Anyone would be thrilled to go on a tour like that."

"But the studio would have to okay it," Polly replied, sounding somewhat disinterested and blowing smoke at her own disdainful reflection. "We'd have to come up with something for you to do to justify it. You can't just tag along because you want to. This isn't let's-play-movie-star-in-the-backyard like we used to do as kids."

"I know. I can help with your wardrobe and makeup and stuff like that. Do you think we could swing it?"

Polly had shrugged but then reluctantly agreed to go to bat for her. Somehow, they had gotten studio approval, and the very much unknown Gayle Morris had tagged along for the southern leg of the Andrew Sisters' War Bonds Promotion Tour of various army posts, air bases, and hotel ballrooms. All along the way, she ended up spending most of her time and sharing a hotel room with Polly, since they were both nineteen and temperamentally suited, being principally concerned with themselves. There were many times, of course, when she felt exactly like Polly's dear, devoted parrot.

"Do you think this new hairstyle makes me look more like Betty Grable? How about this lipstick—do you think Alice Faye would wear it? I definitely don't like the way the peplum on this 'American Patrol' costume cuts me across the waist, do you? I think it makes me look fat with all these red, white, and blue horizontal stripes. Those horrible bitches out there in wardrobe should have thought about that. It apparently never crossed their narrow minds that vertical was the way to go. I think they enjoy making us look bad. They're just jealous. What do you think?"

And Gayle would stand nearby like a good trouper and tell her whatever she wanted to hear, fussing over her and reassuring her and otherwise playing to her overweening vanity. Anything to stay on Polly's good side so she would be invited to all the late-night parties and get to meet and flirt with the cute soldiers and other guys they went around entertaining as if there were no tomorrow. Just being around Polly, with her blond curls and Hollywood photogenic features, guaranteed extra attention from the men, and that spoiled little ingenue also seemed to know just how and when to give the studio chaperones the slip whenever something of a pressing extracurricular nature developed.

Then came the fateful decision to take a few days downtime between stops on the tour. They had just finished entertaining the troops at Camp Shelby, Mississippi, down near Hattiesburg, and Pearl and Peggy wanted to visit a distant cousin who lived near Yazoo City where the hills stopped rolling and the Delta really began to spread out to infinity. They managed to talk some of the rest of the troupe into going along with them. Polly and Gayle would rather have gone on ahead and spent the time prowling around the duck-filled fountain of the Peabody Hotel in Memphis where the trio was scheduled to become the opening act for Tommy Dorsey, but they had virtually no say-so in the matter.

They were bored out of their skulls during the Yazoo City visit. Being forced to sample grits and ham for breakfast was hardly their idea of a scintillating experience. Then they were irked to no end when their car broke down in some godforsaken crossroads called Second Creek on the way up to Memphis. After checking into the local hotel whose lobby smelled heavily of disinfectant and stale cigarette smoke, they found themselves trapped one dreary, rainy night inside a nearby Piggly Wiggly with nothing but time on their hands and plenty of mischief on their minds. They had originally gone in for a few apples and some sandwich makings—a loaf of bread, a jar of mayonnaise, and a few slices of bologna—and Polly was getting her period and desperately needed some Midol to keep her demons at bay. But the thunderstorm outside that had accompanied them into town was growing more and more severe, showing no signs of letting up.

Inside the Piggly Wiggly, things got schmaltzier and schmaltzier. The hospitable owner seemed awed by their presence and brought his RCA Victor radio out of his office. Somehow, he managed to talk the troupe into dancing and singing for the locals right there in the aisles of the store. Polly, who was cranky enough already, could barely conceal her disgust at being forced to socialize with such ghastly bumpkins, as she put it. At one point she took Gayle aside near the dairy case and unburdened herself, angrily aiming a stream of cigarette smoke at the ceiling.

"You see that skinny kid over there I just finished dancing with?"

Gayle nodded and smiled. He was cute in a rough-edged sort of way, she thought, maybe a little like Tom Sawyer with just a hint of coltish sex appeal.

"He's the owner's son. They're both named Hale, as in what the Hale are we doing here? Anyway, he must have stepped on my feet a thousand-million times while we were jitterbugging, the jerk. He's under the impression that he knows how to dance. Of course, I kept right on smiling, but if we've got to stay here another day waiting on the car, I'd like to have a little fun and get even with him and this entire hick town. I have just the thing in mind, too. Are you up for it?"

"Sure. What's the deal?"

"I want you to go over and dance with him next. He's got this really ridiculous notion about being a movie star. He even told me he thinks he could be the next Humphrey Bogart. He tried to do the overbite thing, but he doesn't have the teeth for it and he ended up spraying me. It was perfectly hideous, but I could tell he thought he was being charming. He's as goofy as they come. Says he's watched every detective movie that's ever come out, so he knows all the good dialogue and all the moves. Can you imagine? It's really pathetic. That's where you come in. Tell him something like, oh, your brother is a big studio talent scout, and you might be able to get him into the movies. String him along for the laughs and see what he does. Maybe he'll even

want to do some dialogue for you—wouldn't that be a scream?"
Polly laughed raucously. She had a way of losing control that
was highly infectious, drawing those around her into her mean-
spirited scheme of the day.

"I still think he's kinda cute."

"You can't be serious," Polly replied, this time blowing her
smoke sideways in conspiratorial fashion. "Wait until you hear
him open that rural Mississippi mouth of his. Honestly, Gayle, I
never thought you'd be one to go for a hayseed like that."

Polly's intimidation tactics did the trick, and Gayle hastily
said: "I was just kidding."

"Then you'll do it?"

"Of course."

"Good girl. Now I'll introduce you to him, and you tell him
your brother is . . . let's say, Murray Morris, the famed Hollywood talent scout. The rube won't know the difference, and the
rest is up to you. I'll expect all the hilarious details later on back
in the hotel room."

"SO YOUR BROTHER'S a talent scout out there in Hollywood,
huh?" Hale Dunbar Jr. said as they were slow-dancing a few
minutes later alongside several other couples near the meat
department. His father's radio was playing "You'll Never
Know," and the entire store seemed alive with a spontaneous
energy. People were laughing and talking and now and then
pointing fingers at each other during their more inventive dips
and twirls on the linoleum floor.

At first Gayle found it very easy to play along. "Oh, yes,
Murray's discovered quite a few major stars in his time. He's

hot on the trail of some brand-new ones out in California right this minute."

"Would I know any of the ones he's already discovered?"

"Oh, I'm sure you would. Errol Flynn. Gary Cooper. Bette Davis. Tyrone Power. Celebrities of that magnitude. He tracked down every one of them, and you wouldn't believe some of the places he had to look—many of them were as out of the way as Second Creek."

They concentrated on the music for a few bars. It was Frank Sinatra's recording, and there seemed to be some sort of choir backing him up. "I liked Miss Alice Faye's version of 'You'll Never Know' better," he told her. "She sang it in that movie *Hello, Frisco, Hello,* ya know. I saw that one five times—right here at our Grande Theater."

Gayle watched the boy's eyes light up, and something about the youthful enthusiasm he was projecting made her want to back off her ruse. Plus, he wasn't stepping on her feet the way Polly said. Maybe it was because she had been forewarned and was maintaining a polite distance as they danced, but nonetheless she found herself growing increasingly interested in him.

"How old are you, Hale?" she said.

"Eighteen."

She began to feel even guiltier about the trick she had agreed to play on him, but doggedly kept it up. "Well, I'm nineteen. We're closer together in age than I thought. I wonder if that's some sort of sign?"

"Yeah, it could be one a' those things where people get together through fate or one a' those meant-to-be things, you know."

She nodded her head and tried her best to avoid his gaze. If

he just wouldn't look at her that way, with such trusting inno-
cence and admiration. If he just wouldn't sound so eager and
enthusiastic about everything. He was like a friendly, tail-
wagging puppy in her arms, and she felt like he might even try
to lick her face at any moment.

"I'm maybe the biggest movie fan in the whole world," he
continued. "I go to the Grande Theater here all the time. I guess
you can tell it's the only one we got. Sometimes I like the musicals, but my favorite movies are the detective stories. I really
liked *The Maltese Falcon.* Didja ever get to see it?"

She told him she had.

"I memorized lots of the dialogue because I went to see it all
eight days it played here. I do that with a lot of the movies I go
to see, that is if I really like 'em. I told Miss Polly Andrew, and
I'll tell you—I'd halfway like to try and be a movie star myself
someday. I'd really like to be a detective in the movies, you
know, the kind that always gets the girl. Sometimes, when I'm
sittin' in the theater in the dark, I imagine that the man up on
the screen is me, and it's my name that comes up on the opening
credits. Do you think someone like me would ever have a
chance out there? Do you think maybe your brother could help
me out sometime?"

Gayle swallowed hard. This was just too much. After all, the
boy had stepped on Polly's toes, not hers. She had just about
made up her mind to tell him the truth when Polly caught her
eye from her lookout post beside the bread aisle and gave her
a knowing wink. How could she even think of letting Polly
down after Polly had gone to bat on her behalf with the studio
moguls?

"Well, Murray might be able to. It would all depend on his

schedule, you know. He has such demands on his time. But with the right introduction . . ."

"I guess the odds are against me, but you read all the time about the crazy ways folks got their big breaks. Take Miss Lana Turner sittin' at the counter in that drugstore, for instance. I read all about it in *Photoplay*. Imagine just sippin' a soda and then walkin' out with a contract. Hubba, hubba!"

Gayle decided to apply the brakes a tad. "I'm afraid it's not that simple, Hale. The studio publicity mills can shovel it pretty fast and furious. The business isn't nearly as glamorous as it seems. This tour, for instance, is a lot of hard work with lots of bad food and not much sleep. Then things happen like our Studebaker breaking down and the garage doesn't have the right part in stock and it'll take at least another day to get it in what with the war and all, and then you're stuck in the middle of nowhere."

His expression clouded over considerably. "Yeah, I guess Second Creek is pretty much nowhere. Maybe that's why I wanna get out."

"Well, I suppose anything could happen if you happened to be in the right place at the right time."

The gleam returned to his eyes, and they danced for a while in silence. Eventually, Gayle made the mistake of locking onto his appealing gaze, and that was when she knew she wanted him. To hell with Polly's miserable little plot—she wanted to go back to the hotel room with him and see what unfolded.

The music came to an end, and a local news broadcast started up. Hale Jr. thanked her for the dance, but she had no intention of leaving it at that.

"No, I want to thank you, and I'd like to go even further than that. Perhaps you'd be interested in coming to my hotel room tonight, and we could discuss my brother and Hollywood and your ambitions a little bit more. I'm in two-oh-three at the Second Creek Hotel. I'm sure you know where that is."

She couldn't tell from his reaction whether he was reading between the lines or not, but she didn't care. If he showed up, she would play it by ear. If not, no harm done one way or another. There was Polly to deal with, of course, but she would probably spend the night in someone else's bed as she'd done more than once already on the tour.

Apparently, Polly's Midol had kicked in enough to allow her to hook up with one of the actors who had tagged along for the detour, and she was therefore conveniently absent from their hotel room for the remainder of the evening. Nonetheless, Gayle received a mild shock when Hale Dunbar Jr. actually knocked on her door just past eleven o'clock, and she opened it to find him standing there holding a small bouquet of zinnias. He had changed from a gray flannel shirt into a nice, starched white one with a dark brown tie, and he reminded her for all the world of some nervous teenager picking up his new girlfriend for their first big date. She couldn't remember when she had encountered such a guileless example of young manhood.

"Why, thank you," she said, taking the flowers from him. "Where did you get these at this time of night?"

"Picked 'em from my mother's front-yard flower garden. Got tons of 'em shootin' up this time a' year."

She was at a momentary loss as to what to do with his offering since there was not so much as a vase in the room—just a couple of ashtrays Polly had filled up with butts earlier in the day and a lamp without a shade and a Bible on the dusty nightstand—but she eventually ducked into the moldy-smelling bathroom and filled the rust-stained sink with water, floating the zinnias on the surface.

"I suppose your parents don't know you're here, do they?" she said, returning from her task and posing invitingly on the edge of the bed, her dress hiked up slightly above the knees.

"No, they don't. I snuck out. But I'm a big boy. I call my own shots."

She could tell he was trying to sound as manly and experienced as possible, but she had sensed the truth from the moment they had started dancing. What was driving her crazy was her overwhelming suspicion that he was a virgin and that she would be the one to break him in. She had heard about the excitement of such a scenario from hanging around fast cousin Polly too much, listening to her filing her nails while dropping phrases like "letting the guy dip his stick and check your oil for the first time," and "helping him with the plunger before anyone else does." With a mighty surge of adrenaline, she decided to go for it before she lost her resolve.

"I suppose you know what an audition is, Hale?"

He sat down in the only armchair in the room—a dingy, tatty affair if there ever was one—his legs pushed together in an awkward defensive posture. "Yeah, sure I do. That's when you try out for a part."

"You say the part you want is the detective who always gets the girl. Wouldn't you like to do a little investigation right here and see how you do with me? It could pay off for you in the long run after I get back to Hollywood and mention you to my brother." She stood up and gave him her best come-hither look. "And you could get off to a good start by helping me unzip my dress."

She could see his very prominent Adam's apple bobbing up and down as he swallowed hard. For a while he just sat there frozen, looking like a frightened fawn, but eventually he got up out of the chair and approached her, taking hold of her zipper and gingerly working it down her back.

"You're, ah, unzipped," he said with an adolescent crack in his voice.

She stepped out of her dress and stood before him in her shiny, cream-colored slip, and she thought his eyes were going to fall out of his head. "I do believe you must like what you see, Hale."

He could do little more than nod.

"Now it's time for me to help you off with that nice starched shirt of yours. Here, let me just unbutton you."

He stood before her paralyzed while she took her time unfastening each button in a stylized ritual of suggestiveness, and she found the freshly shaved smell of his face and neck strangely alluring. Even the few small nicks he had hurriedly visited upon himself while cleaning himself up for her had a certain boyish charm.

"There now. All done," she said, removing his shirt and throwing it dramatically across the room onto the armchair.

Like an agonizingly slow session of strip poker, the disrobing continued until they were both completely naked. She could not decide which was more fascinating to observe, the healthy pink glow on his face or his impressive equipment standing at rigid attention. Soon, however, they were both beneath the sheets kissing and fondling each other, and she knew immediately that she had been right about his experience with the opposite sex. More than once she had to guide his hand to this spot or stop him from pressing too hard against that, but finally everything was in the place it needed to be, and they were on their way.

He did not last long, of course. But that hardly stopped him from going back for more. She found him insatiable, as all young men that age were, and she let all other earthly considerations fall by the wayside during their workout that night in Room 203 of the Second Creek Hotel. Nothing seemed to matter to her except harnessing this earnest young creature for her pleasure.

When he had finally exhausted himself—and her in the process—he gave her the sweetest, tenderest kiss on the cheek and said: "I think I'm gonna call you my Gaylie Girl. Is that okay with you?"

She was totally unprepared for such a touching display of affection, but somehow managed to maintain her composure. "Yes, I'll be your Gaylie Girl."

"Swell," he said, sounding more like a kid on the playground than a young man who had just emptied himself in the name of romance. He wanted to spend the entire night with her, but she told him no, he'd better get on home to avoid any problems.

"If they don't get your car fixed and you have to stay another day, can I come by again tomorrow night?"

"I guess so, but we'll have to be careful. I suppose we could work around Polly again. She's always got her hand in something. But you do understand that we need to keep this private, don't you?"

He said he did, but it took him forever to get dressed and leave. She was fairly certain she recognized what was going on. If it had indeed been his first time, he might just be falling in love with her, and she wasn't sure she knew how to handle it.

WHEN THE PART the garage had special-ordered for the Studebaker failed to arrive from Memphis, the troupe had to spend yet another night in Second Creek, and Hale had shown up again at her hotel room door with another hasty arrangement of plucked zinnias, a desperate, hangdog expression on his face and a line she unwisely chose not to resist.

"Tonight, I'm gonna show you what a fast learner I am, Gaylie Girl."

She gave in, and once again they tunneled beneath the covers to satisfy themselves. He did indeed seem more self-assured on this second night, paying particular attention to her nipples—an area to which she had aggressively directed him the night before.

"Is that the way you wanted me to lick them, Gaylie Girl?" he said, interrupting his patient work for her approval.

She managed a breathless reply. "Yes, but don't talk about it. Just do it."

He went back to work and quickly drove her over the top several times.

It was in the sweaty afterglow, however, that he revealed he still had a lot to learn, causing her to become unhinged with his boastful but unsettling slip of the tongue.

"You didn't have to show me near as much this time, didja? Pretty good for sixteen, huh?"

She sprang up from the sheets. "You told me you were eighteen, Hale!"

He still did not appear to fully appreciate her predicament. "Okay, so I lied. But how does that change the fact we love each other now, don't we? And your brother is still gonna help me when I come out to Hollywood, right?" He repeated the word *right* when she did not answer him immediately, and she watched him quickly wilting like last night's batch of zinnias the maid had thrown out that morning. "Are you mad at me, Gaylie Girl? Please say you're still my Gaylie Girl!"

"Oh, Hale, can't you see this is one big mess!" she said finally. "You lied to me! Don't you understand the terrible position I'm in? Dammit to hell, I never should have listened to Polly! Her and her damned period!"

"You mean Miss Polly Andrew? What's she got to do with this? All she did was introduce us. You can't blame her because I lied to you."

Despite her anger, Gayle still didn't have the heart to level with him about the whole miserable scheme. But she knew she had to make a clean break of it, or he might get her into real trouble. "This is no good, Hale. It can't go on. You're only sixteen. You can't tell anyone about what we did, and I can't see you again—ever. I could get in real trouble over this. I want you to get dressed and leave right now and don't come back!"

"But I won't be sixteen forever, Gaylie Girl. I'll be seventeen in three more months and then eighteen the year after that. I was hopin' maybe you could put in a good word for me with your brother, and I could even come out to see you. I could get me a job doin' just about anything until the big break comes. I'm a hard worker—I believe in goin' after what you really want with all your might. Don't say this is over already—it's just gettin' started. And besides, I love you, Gaylie Girl, I really do love you!"

"You have to leave, Hale! I'd run out of here myself fast as I can if I had someplace to go!"

She watched him pull on his clothes so fast he appeared to be working against a stopwatch. Then she spoke to him forcefully and deliberately. "Get this straight, Hale. It's over. O-V-E-R—over!"

The veins in his neck and forehead began to protrude as he absorbed the crushing verbal blow. Then with his teeth clenched so hard she thought his jaw might break, he reached into his pants pocket, pulled out an envelope, and tossed it at her feet. "I should be tearin' that up, but maybe it'll give you somethin' to think about!" With that, he stomped out of the room, slamming the door behind him, and that was the last she had ever seen or heard of him until that CNN report had invaded her palatial home last week.

"Did you want that champagne now?" the flight attendant asked just as Gaylie Girl returned to the twenty-first century and the tranquillity of the first-class cabin.

"Yes, I believe I do need a little something to lift my spirits. I've got some difficult work ahead of me."

While she waited for the champagne to arrive, she checked her purse one more time to see if everything was in order. Yes, they were both still there. The two key components to the success of her trip. A letter over half a century old. And a freshly cut cashier's check in the amount of eighty-seven thousand, three hundred forty-six dollars and twenty-seven cents.

It was time to take care of long-overdue business.

Chapter Thirteen

*I*T MAY HAVE been his wedding day, but Powell found himself in a totally unexpected place that hectic Saturday morning. He was standing near one of the Delta baggage carousels at Memphis International Airport holding a hand-lettered posterboard sign that read HAMPTON, SECOND CREEK—in hopes of grabbing the attention of incoming Chicago passenger Lizzie Lepanto Graham. Her flight had been delayed at the other end but was taxiing to the terminal at this very moment, the gate agent had explained.

"You're a prince for doing this for me," Laurie had said just before kissing him good-bye on the front porch of her little Victorian cottage. "Here. Slip this little wallet photo into your pocket just in case, but you'll be able to spot her anyway. Lizzie's just a more petite version of me."

And so he had driven all the way to Memphis to pick up

Laurie's daughter for the wedding because the newly elected president of the Nitwitts, Myrtis Troy, had decided to throw a girls-only brunch that morning at her country estate, Evening Shadows. It was going to make his schedule a little tight, but there would still be plenty of time to complete the round-trip and then get all spruced-up for the four o'clock ceremony at the Piggly Wiggly.

Powell held the sign high above his head and kept his eyes peeled when the Chicago carousel finally came to life with a lurching groan, rotating pieces of luggage for deplaning passengers to claim. For a while every young woman seemed to be a suspect as he compared the photo of Lizzie with the selection of females approaching the carousel. At one point an attractive, exquisitely groomed, older woman with streaked blond hair began staring intensely in his direction, giving the impression that she recognized him and might be heading his way. Then she shook her head and seemed to lose interest as she spotted her bags and focused on retrieving them, disappearing into the throng.

A few seconds later, a waving hand went up at the edge of the crowd, and Powell zeroed in on the rest of the person. Laurie had been more than accurate with her description. Lizzie was indeed a more petite tintype of her mother—same fair coloring and charming smile—with the undeniable freshness and animation of youth.

"Powell?!" she cried out, rushing over to his side and embracing him warmly as soon as he put down the sign. Then she pulled back. "You're just as Mom described you. I would have known you anywhere with that wonderful head of silver hair, and my goodness, you really are tall, aren't you?"

"That I am, and it's come in handy all these years. Being able to see over everyone's heads on the dance floor, that is. And by the way, your mother really didn't do you justice, and neither does this picture of you she gave me." There was an awkward pause as Powell flashed the photo, but he soon recovered, pointing to the carousel. "Do you see your luggage yet?"

She hastily scanned the parade of bags and suitcases and shook her head. "Just my luck, they probably lost it. That's happened to me before."

"Sometimes I think they have a quota to fill on lost luggage. Otherwise, there's just no explanation for it."

Lizzie nodded her head, then looked suddenly inspired. "You know what? As long as we're waiting, I have an outrageous idea. Mom has told me all about your affinity for dancing in public places—like grocery stores, for instance. Maybe you'd care to whirl me around right here and let me see for myself what all the fuss is about? I know that sounds like an outrageous proposition, but I'm very much my mother's daughter. There's very little I won't take on for the hell of it."

Powell cocked an ear in an attempt to decipher the generic music pouring out over the airport intercom. "Can't tell what that cacophony is. Maybe the elevator version of 'McArthur Park.' In any case it's totally unsuitable for our purposes. How about if I sing something a cappella?"

"That would be just too perfect for words. I sing in the shower, and I drive my husband crazy. I'm ready whenever you are."

He took a few moments, working the muscles of his mouth and lips into casual singing mode with a mischievous look on his face. "Cheek to Cheek" was the classic he chose.

Some of the passengers gathered around to gawk with either incredulity or delight, and Powell quickly noted that Lizzie was an even better partner than her mother. "Did you ever take lessons?" he said, briefly interrupting the lyrics. "You're very agile."

"Thank you, kind sir. But no, I didn't. I guess I'm just a natural."

By the time they had finished with "Cheek to Cheek," practically everyone in the baggage claim area, including one of the security guards, was on board applauding and cheering with gusto. But Powell couldn't help but notice that the attractive older woman who had caught his eye before did not join in and was staring him down even more conspicuously, this time with the suggestion of a frown on her brow.

He soon put her out of his mind, however, and focused on helping Lizzie claim her luggage.

EVENING SHADOWS was surely the most misnamed formal home in the Mississippi Delta, if not the entire Deep South. Raymond and Myrtis Troy had unwisely chosen to build the Greek Revival mansion in the middle of what had once been one of the Delta's largest soybean farms, a parcel of land they had inherited unexpectedly from her bachelor uncle. There was not a real tree worthy of a woodpecker within two miles of the building, only a few scrawny, transplanted saplings trying their best to make a difference but failing miserably. Not only were there no evening shadows, there were no morning, noon, or afternoon shadows. Oh, perhaps the fleeting shade from the occasional cloud passing overhead, but nothing more substantial than that. Being right out in the open the way it was, the house baked in summer and shivered in winter. As a result the utility bills were nothing short of phenomenal, giving Myrtis yet another grand expense to boast about.

Among the peculiar extravagances at Evening Shadows was a formal boxwood-and-brick maze in the so-called backyard, part of the inestimable plain of dusty acreage stretching to the horizon in typical flat Delta fashion. Worse yet, since her husband's death, Myrtis had developed a penchant for entertaining in and around this immaculately trimmed puzzle, usually in weather more suited to hothouse plants than human beings. For Laurie's wedding brunch, however, the members of the Nitwitts had been spared that indignity. Reason had evidently prevailed, and Myrtis had chosen to stage the festivities on the air-conditioned back porch—within full view of the maze, it was true, but thankfully without that unhealthy touch of the ultraviolet to further wrinkle mature skin.

Laurie would rather have gone to Memphis with Powell to pick up her dear Lizzie, but Myrtis had made a big to-do out of the brunch. "I want my first official act as president of the Nitwitts to be to honor our illustrious outgoing leader with an unforgettable party," she had said over the phone. "Not only that, all the girls want you to unwrap their wedding gifts to you right then and there, and you have to admit there's some practicality to that concept. I mean, why have all our presents dribble in piecemeal and such? Wedding showers are good for weary souls like us Nitwitts."

And true to her seamless, diplomatic nature, Laurie had given it her blessing without hesitation.

Everyone had arrived by eleven o'clock to find a generous

gourmet buffet laid out on the sprawling back porch table. Eggs Benedict, Eggs Sardou, stuffed mushrooms, miniature spinach quiches, a variety of mini-muffins, layered salad, fruit juices, coffee, Bloody Marys, Mimosas, and muscadine wine. Yet the predominant odor throughout the room was something vaguely resembling coconut oil. Laurie kept thinking that any second she would blink and find herself down on the beach at Biloxi until she realized that most of her friends had anticipated brunch in the maze and applied sunscreen as a precaution. With everything else she had to remember on this eventful day, she had let that particular detail slip her mind.

"We all took your fashion advice," Myrtis said to Laurie as they stood around the table sampling the sophisticated goodies on their plates. "I think each of us is going to wear something different this afternoon at the ceremony. I'm not going to tell you anything about my outfit. I'm just going to let it be a surprise."

"Now that's the Second Creek spirit of doing as you damn-well please," Laurie replied, thankful the controversy had been resolved.

Denver Lee sidled up and gave Laurie a mischievous wink. "I can hardly wait for you to open my present. I admit it's something a bit different, but I'm hoping you're going to like it anyway."

The slight reluctance in Denver Lee's tone instantly gave Laurie the clue as to what the gift was going to be. She began psyching herself up for the inevitable. She would grin and bear it and be a good sport—no matter what it took. The more things changed among the Nitwitts, the more they essentially remained the same.

Sure enough, when the time came to open the presents,

Denver Lee made a point of offering hers up first, and there was no doubt about its identity. That big square shape all clumsily wrapped in tissue paper gave the game away, but Laurie played along like the true champion she was.

"Oh, I wonder what this could possibly be," she said, batting her lashes coyly at the conspiratorial-looking group, who further resembled excitable girls at a slumber party on a giggly sugar high.

Finally, the payoff: it was indeed one of Denver Lee's alphabetized produce undertakings in oil, and Laurie sucked in her breath with a mile-wide grin.

"It's my 'B' painting," Denver Lee explained after belting back the last of her Bloody Mary, while a succession of raised, but hardly surprised, brows simultaneously appeared around the room.

Laurie held her grin steadfastly. "I see that. I see the beets. Those are beets, right? And all the different kinds of berries and—oh, look—you've even added broccoli for good measure. You must have made an extra trip to the Piggly Wiggly for that, you sly thing, you. I can tell you've been pinching and squeezing and thumping in the produce section with the best of them, haven't you?"

"Oh, I have, I did. And I believe Powell and I danced to 'Takin' a Chance on Love' that particular time. My best outing in his arms."

"Fox-trotting around for broccoli. Well, it was certainly worth the extra effort, Denver Lee. Thank you so much for something so original and so lively and personal."

"Do you really like it? You know, that's organic broccoli I used for my model, and besides that, I've somehow felt an obligation to include and depict broccoli because it's gotten such bad press ever since the first President Bush pooh-poohed it so. It's supposed to be so healthful for you, even though it is rather hard to digest. When it's raw, I mean. The gas seems to go on for hours. I do prefer it steamed, however. The florets are a bit tastier than the stalks, don't you all think?"

Renza snorted into her Mimosa. "I'm quite sure Laurie doesn't plan to eat the painting. And as for the organic angle, I'm sure pesticides can't possibly show up on a canvas."

"It's the principle of the thing," Denver Lee insisted.

"Ah," Renza continued. "Nothing like a politically correct painting of horse apples!"

"Never mind all that, ladies," Laurie interjected. "Why, in my opinion, it's your best work yet. It's so vibrant and full of color and, as you point out, healthy . . . looking."

"So thrilled to hear you say that, Laurie. I have, in fact, entitled it *Healthy Eating, Three*. Of course, I should take my own advice there, considering my recent prediabetic diagnosis."

"Oh, yes," Laurie replied. "How is that going?"

"I'm afraid it's not. I've gained two pounds since my last visit to the doctor. I've got to stop watching the Food Network on cable. I watch those programs where all the ingredients look so tasty and they fix everything up so colorfully that I just get so hungry, and I end up eating my way around the entire pantry, or I go out to eat and order practically everything on the menu that I shouldn't."

"Perhaps you should concentrate on eating what you paint, dear. And on that note I think I'll have another eye-opener," Renza said, hauling herself, her foxes, and her empty glass to the wet bar where the big ceramic pitchers of mixed cocktails of the orange and red varieties awaited her continued consumption.

Laurie placed the painting on a nearby armchair while clinging to her smile for dear life. "Now, who's next?"

Novie stepped up with a small, neatly wrapped package, and Laurie steeled herself even further. Please, God. It was approximately the size of a large set of slides, but maybe Novie had thought of something else. Imagine her relief when it turned out to be a fancy Wusthof carving knife!

"I know what a wonderful cook you are," Novie said. "And you mentioned last time we were over that some of your knives had gotten a little on the dull side. Now if you don't like it, don't hesitate to trade it in for something else you might want at the Second Creek Wedding Shoppe."

Laurie doled out her second hug of the day, this one delivered without a sense of guilt. "I adore it, Novie. You'll have to come over for dinner the next time I fix a pot roast."

"Good. I'll hold you to that."

Next, a thoroughly tipsy Renza presented a red and blue, porcelain potpourri bowl. "It's one of those dynasty things," she explained. "Not the TV show with all the shoulder pads and the attitudes, you understand. One of those Chinese dynasties, but I forget which. If you don't like it, you can trade it in for another dynasty."

"Oh, I wouldn't dream of trading it in. You're in rare form today, Renza," said Laurie, laughing brightly.

"People tell me I should drink more often than I do. I've been told I let down my hair only when I'm well lubricated. Tell me honestly, Laurie, do you think I have an attitude? Am I too snooty except when I've had a snootful?"

Laurie heard the spontaneous intake of breath and surveyed the expectant stares around the room, wishing she could avoid the question, but she was able to find her way home nonetheless. "I think we all mellow out a bit when we've had our daily toddies, but let's just say that I appreciate all our differences whether we're stone sober or we're crocked. How's that for an answer?"

Renza cut her eyes to the side with a smirk to beat the band. "That explains why you've been elected so many damn times. You always have an answer for everything. Are you sure you want to give up all that authority? No one really does it like you do—or ever has. No offense, Myrtis, dear."

"None taken," Myrtis replied, shrugging off the comment. "Now, shall we get back to the presents?"

Wittsie took the cue, stepped up nervously, and presented a set of beige terry-cloth washrags and towels with dark-brown piping and the initials LH inscribed, and was her usual flustered self trying to justify her choice. "I hope you don't think it was too forward of me to go ahead and give you something monogrammed. I wondered if I should have had them read LLH instead of LH. I mean, you were married all those years to Roy Lepanto . . . but now this is a new start for you. I hope you think it was appropriate for me to do that. I'm really hopeless at gift-giving most of the time. I think I hold our family record for having presents returned."

"Oh, it's very appropriate, Wittsie. Don't give it a moment's thought. I'm sure I would have done it myself soon. The monograms, I mean. It is, after all, the beginning of a new life for me."

President Myrtis brought up the rear with a selection of Laurie's favorite Estée Lauder toiletries. "I knew I couldn't go wrong with these," she said, looking very proud of herself in the process. Despite Renza's earlier remarks, further sarcasm and catty asides never materialized. Instead, there seemed to be a genuine and unexpectedly easy camaraderie flowing through-out the group.

In the afterglow of all the gift-giving, however, Laurie dis-creetly requested a moment with Myrtis apart from the others, who were busying themselves refreshing their brunch-time toddies while still buzzing over the presents, and the two of them quietly ducked into the kitchen without essentially being noticed.

"What is it?" Myrtis said, as they stood together at the butcher block countertop. "Is anything wrong? Have I over-looked something?"

"No, everything's just fine. I'm having a wonderful time. I guess I just had one of the monumental epiphanies of my life," she began. "I was noticing how you were all gabbing and laugh-ing and joking around with each other there at the end when I opened my last present. Not a hint of one-upsmanship any-where to be seen or heard, and, of course, I've come to fully expect that sort of behavior every time we get together."

Myrtis flashed a hint of surprise. Or maybe it was the tiniest bit of guilt. "Are we that bad? I've often wondered how we come off to outsiders. I guess you've seen us at our worst over the years."

"And at your best. No, it's just the way we are. It's the way we've always been around each other from the beginning. But what I suddenly realized is that I've truly been the enabling cul-prit of the club all along. Or at least since I assumed the presi-dency on practically a permanent basis."

"What do you mean?" Myrtis replied, this time with a definite frown.

"I mean that I've always been around to keep the peace. I was the one who always ended up soothing the bruised egos. I've been the luxury we Nitwitts could afford, allowing us to bark and nip and growl at each other because we all knew subconsciously that I could step in and restore order at any moment if things got out of hand."

"I understand that much. But can you run this epiphany you've had past me again? I think I may have missed it."

Laurie's laugh was relaxed and spontaneous. "Yes, I kinda wandered off the plantation there for a moment. It's just that I truly think we all like each other a lot more than we let on, but we'd rather give up happy hour than admit it too openly. What I think is going on out there right now is the realization that since I am no longer going to be around as much as official club peacemaker, the group is going to have to be a bit more straightforward and behave more graciously toward each other. That's just what I think the girls are doing out there right now, whether they realize it or not."

Myrtis gently patted Laurie's shoulder, looking slightly skeptical. "You are so analytical about things, Laurie. I guess that is quite an epiphany. But it does make me feel a bit better about you leaving us full-time and myself and Renza taking over. Maybe we'll be coming of age for all the right reasons, and maybe I can do my part to help hold things together."

"Oh, I doubt the needling will stop completely. I would still expect to attend a meeting now and then and hear opening remarks like 'Good God, who fried your hair? That perm looks like it was done with a blowtorch!'"

They both laughed and fell into a heartfelt hug, and then Myrtis said: "You know, there's one thing I guess I've always known about our membership in the Nitwitts. None of us would spend this much time together if we still had our husbands. To a certain extent, I think we're still taking the loss of our men out on each other just a tad bit, don't you think?"

"You may have something there. And, you know, as time went on, I think you all might resent me being the one who has a husband again if I stayed in the club full-time. I've had that notion in the back of my mind as another reason I should step down."

Myrtis frowned, turning down the corners of her mouth. "I think the word *resent* is a bit strong. We grew up expecting to be with men and wanting them to cater to us. Frankly, I don't see a damned thing wrong with that. I call it the car door syndrome."

"As in a gentleman holding the door open for a lady? That type of thing?"

Myrtis winked. "Precisely. And Renza is right about one thing. Or at least she's buzzing all around it. We all tend to get a little too lubricated in order to forget how things used to be for us when we had husbands to squire us. We are always talking about the way things were back then and in that year and this year and when we were that particular age or another. But we are what we are, and we miss those good times with our dear, departed heroes."

"I have to agree with you there. I told Powell when we first started seeing each other seriously that we Nitwitts had all come together—and stayed together for that matter—because of our losses." Laurie squared her shoulders. "But let's not get too philosophical and serious on my wedding day, shall we?

Hell, I'm going to get married in a damned grocery store. Can you believe it?"

"Actually, I can't, but we should get back to the others. I have some important club business to attend to."

Once they had returned to the gathering, Myrtis chimed her spoon on her water glass to get everyone's attention. "As the new president of the Nitwitts, I've been giving considerable thought to our image. I think it's time we improved the way we come off in the eyes of the community."

Still feeling her liquor, Renza interrupted. "What's wrong with our image? We're a bunch of aging widows, and that's that. Are you proposing to disguise that fact somehow? If you are proposing that we all get facelifts, you can dump that idea right in the trash can. I've worked too damned hard to acquire these frown lines and I'm proud of the way I hold my face."

"Now you know good and well I wasn't going to suggest anything of the kind," Myrtis replied, looking exasperated and amused at the same time. "I was simply going to suggest a new project now that the Piggly Wiggly thing has just about played out. Something that will continue to show our propensity for good works."

"Propensity?" Renza said, rolling her eyes. "Somebody go get me a damned *Webster's* so I can pass my vocabulary lesson!"

"Oh, do hush, Renza!" Myrtis replied. "You know very well what the word means."

Renza cut to the chase. "Is this image thing all because I trumped your ace in bridge club last week? I suppose you'll be wanting me to do seven hours of community service or something like that."

"Nonsense, Renza. I've found a worthy cause for us to

pursue, and I'd like for us to vote on it this morning. At least allow me to describe it for you."

"I like the idea of doing these civic things every now and then," Denver Lee interjected. "It kind of makes me think of us as Robin Hood and his Merry Men, except with girdles, of course."

There was a generous sprinkling of laughter, and then Myrtis proceeded, catching Laurie's nod of approval out of the corner of her eye.

"Well, we don't have nearly as much as we used to in the slush fund because of our commitment to Mr. Choppy and the Piggly Wiggly, but there is a wee bit to play around with should we decide to take this on." Myrtis closed her eyes and shivered slightly. "It's a tad bit icky, but still worthwhile. I received a phone call this morning from our ever-devoted librarian, Lovita Grubbs, a couple of hours before you all showed up. She was quite agitated—almost hysterical really."

"Why?" Laurie asked, both surprised and concerned.

"It seems the rains we had recently down in that part of the county have caused some unwelcome visitors to take up residence in the South Cypress branch. This morning Lovita was dusting the shelves and realized at some point that she was dusting off a water moccasin. It was all curled up on a row of large-print books."

"Good God!" Laurie exclaimed. "Seeing pictures of snakes in the books is bad enough. Did anyone get bitten?"

"Fortunately not. But I'm sure you realize the trauma of the entire situation," Myrtis replied. "Anyway, after Lovita had backed away and stopped screaming, a further inspection revealed two more moccasins—one wrapped around the base of the video carousel and another in the new arrivals bin. Fortunately, all of this happened before she had opened up to the general public. But the upshot is, she's going to go to the library board to suggest they shut down the South Cypress branch permanently and move their collection to headquarters in town. If those snakes could get in that easily, there's probably some structural problem that will be expensive to repair. As for the move, there will be a little expense involved, and she wondered if we might help her offset it."

"So, the Book Sheriff needs our help now, does she?" Renza said, pausing for an ironic little chuckle. "Lovita's always after me about my overdues. She says I'm nearly as bad as all the expectant mothers who keep the pregnancy books for nine months."

Myrtis smiled briefly and then grew serious again. "We don't want people to have to carry antivenin in their purses just to go to the library, do we? And after all, Lovita is looking after the taxpayers' money by being so vigilant about overdues. I say we vote to help out. We can build up the slush fund again." Then she gave a dramatic shudder. "I simply cannot abide snakes, particularly moccasins. The idea of them taking up residence amongst the *New York Times'*, bestsellers just chills me to the bone."

That statement seemed to strike a very responsive chord, and Laurie watched in amusement as a unanimous vote was taken. A new day had dawned for the Nitwitts, it seemed. The well-lubricated group was finally acquiring some substance over style.

"What a lovely morning this has been. You don't know how much this has meant to me, Myrtis," Laurie said later at the front door after all the others had left. "I think you handled things like a pro today. Particularly the business about the snakes and the books. I'd have to say that in my long tenure, I had to handle many a snake-in-the-grass, but never any in the library. That has to be a first."

Myrtis gave her a perfunctory peck on the cheek. "I've watched how you do things over the years, Laurie. I've learned a trick or two by osmosis, I believe. I guess you could say that I'm an apt pupil and that you were a great teacher."

"I don't know about that, but keep up the good work. And, of course, I'm sure I don't have to add, keep them from throttling each other. They really mean no harm, but you still can't let things get out of hand."

It was only after Laurie was driving down the gravel road to the front gates of Evening Shadows that she realized Myrtis had not quizzed anyone all morning about the cost of anything, including the elaborate and surely expensive brunch she had staged for them. Apparently, being president of the Nitwitts was more than busywork for the woman. It was going to be excellent therapy for her as well.

POWELL AND LIZZIE were speeding southward from Memphis along Highway 61. Soybean fields as far as the eye could see flanked both sides of the road. But the distant horizon near the Mississippi River was punctuated in surreal fashion by gleaming high-rise hotels plunked down in the middle of nowhere — an unexpected and startling sight.

"Casinos," Powell explained. "Scores of them. Looks kinda like a Picasso painting out there, doesn't it? Maybe that's what

Las Vegas looked like when it was first being developed way back when. Something in the middle of nothing. One thing I can tell you for sure, though. Half of Memphis and a healthy percentage of Arkansas and the Delta pours into them every weekend to gamble and drink and see all kinds of shows. Ten years ago this part of the Delta was home to nothing but local sharecroppers out of luck."

Lizzie kept her eyes glued to the scenery. "All that development has happened since I got married and moved away. Mom tries to keep me posted on all the things that are going on through her letters, but I still have all kinds of trouble explaining my home state to our new friends up in Chicago. My husband, Barry, and I were married in the Second Creek First Presbyterian Church, and he still hasn't recovered from being bombarded by all my relatives with their stories of the night the famous finger was lifted off and just flew away out of sight."

Powell gave her a knowing glance. "Everyone does seem to have their own take on that one."

"Well, I think the theory that flabbergasted Barry the most was the one from Mom's fire-breathing cousin, the late Miss Kittykate. She blasted him but good with her sherry breath and insisted that God had just gotten sick and tired of Second Creek giving him the finger that way all the time, and therefore had sent those powerful winds to spirit it away in all its pointed wickedness."

Powell laughed heartily. "Had that been me, I believe I would have pointed out to Miss Kittykate that there's a great deal of difference between a display of the middle finger and the index finger. Certainly God could tell the difference."

"Believe me, you didn't want to tell Miss Kittykate anything when she was in her cups. I'm afraid Barry got entirely the wrong impression of my extended family. He's a typical solid-citizen midwesterner, and some of our small-town southern peculiarities have left him scratching his head."

"Is that why he didn't come down with you?"

"Oh, no, nothing like that. He had a sales meeting he couldn't get out of. I know he'd get a real kick out of meeting you and hearing all about your activities at the Piggly Wiggly. He even asked me to give you his best. I think he feels just as I do."

Powell momentarily turned his head, arching his brows expectantly. "Would you mind sharing?"

"Not at all. We both feel you're the best thing that could possibly have happened to Mom at this stage of her life. She's tried to busy herself with the Nitwitts since Dad died, but, of course, that's no substitute for a lost loved one. But now, her letters are filled with her old zest for life. It's not just the dancing and the fun you two have been having together. She's says more than anything else it's that she no longer feels something is missing. You've filled the void, and she's ready to embrace the rest of her life full-speed ahead."

"Wow. That's quite a testimonial. It works both ways, you know."

"Yes, I think I understand. Mom did tell me a little bit about your wife. I just can't imagine what you went through."

He drove along in silence just long enough to gather his thoughts. "I know all about that 'something missing' business. My wife, Ann, kissed me good night just like it was any ordinary night, but she just never woke up. You never know which day or night — or minute or hour, for that matter — is going to be the finale."

"I'm sure that must have been awful for you."

Powell exhaled. "It felt like I was melting into a big, messy puddle on the floor. When someone you love deeply leaves you that way, without the slightest warning, and the chance to really say good-bye is taken from you, it takes a very long time to get over it. Closure creeps along, slow as molasses."

"Do you think you have closure now?"

He tilted his head to one side, looking particularly thoughtful. "As near as someone in my position could ever have it — yes. What really did it for me finally was your mother asking me to start waltzing with the ladies at the Piggly Wiggly. I had centered my whole adult life around dancing with my Ann, and even though Laurie's crazy idea couldn't give her back to me, it did give me back that playful vision of life I had before. It had just enough of an edge to it to get me off my rear end."

Lizzie was nodding and looking down into her lap at the same time. "I've never really thought of dancing as being playful, but I suppose that's exactly what it is. I know it makes me feel alive to get out on the dance floor."

"Yep. Same here. It got to the point where I genuinely believed I was going to dance my way to the pearly gates because they needed someone to teach the angels the latest steps. Can't be behind the times when you've got the clouds for a dance floor, can you?"

"I have to say, Powell, you're nothing at all like Dad was. I don't think I ever saw him dance a step in his life. That was not one of his gifts."

"Well, the truth is, your mother and I have a different kind of partnership than she and your dad did. It's just what we both need at this time in our lives, and I hope you understand. I can't replace your father and would never want to try."

Lizzie reached over and rubbed his shoulder. "Oh, of course I understand. It's all so romantic, I can hardly stand it!"

"You haven't seen anything yet. Just wait till your mother walks up to our indoor wedding arbor at the Piggly Wiggly and says, 'I do!' We're gonna break that old marriage ceremony mold and throw it away where no one can find it!"

Lizzie leaned back in her seat with a sigh of contentment. "I'd say so. When Mom told me you were going to get married in a grocery store, I couldn't believe it at first. But people do things like that all the time in Second Creek. I told Barry it was par for the course."

"Do you miss not living in Second Creek anymore?"

Lizzie's brow wrinkled expressively. "I do and I don't. You can live in Chicago like I do and still think like a Second Creeker and come up with Second Creek solutions to your problems. We never played by the rules, but we have our time-honored standards. Mom has no patience with people who don't appreciate that. In her letters to me she gets so mad at that Mr. Floyce and the things he does all the time. She thinks he ought to give it up and move to California where anything goes."

Powell pursed his lips thoughtfully. "Good suggestion. He definitely seems to have a different agenda than most Second Creekers."

Lizzie chuckled softly. "I told Mom she ought to run against him in the next election. Who knows? First, the Nitwitts, then

mayor of Second Creek, and finally the first woman president
of the USA."

"I like the sound of that," Powell replied. "I would be the
First Gentleman, and upon my wife's executive order, we would
have waltzing on the floor of Congress every day. It's virtually
impossible to filibuster when you're dancing, you know."

Up ahead loomed the green-and-white metallic sign demar-
cating the city limits of Second Creek and declaring it, in no
uncertain terms, A Certified Retirement City, and Lizzie said:
"I always get this great adrenaline rush whenever I come home.
I have a theory about Second Creek that I've never told anyone
before, and I've decided that you're going to be the first to
hear it."

"Shoot."

"Promise you won't think I'm a crackpot?"

"Promise."

"Okay. Here goes. I think it's a spiritual resort."

There was a brief silence, and then Powell said: "I think I
know what you're getting at. Go on."

"Well, I've heard something similar to this expressed by
other people who live there, but it's my particular belief that it
takes many lifetimes to work all your problems out and get
wherever you are supposed to get in the universe. The thing is,
we all need a break from time to time. Vacations from the hard
work of just being alive are essential. And so, I think Second
Creek is one of many spiritual resorts available to certain
people."

Powell turned his head sharply. "So in your scheme of
things, we're on vacation here, is that it?"

"I know that sounds crazy, but look at all our so-called eccentrics. Maybe they're not really eccentrics after all. Maybe they're just getting reinvigorated by taking a little down time. They're just getting their tanks refilled."

"I would agree with you there," Powell replied, smiling broadly at the road ahead. "Yes, Miss Lizzie, I like that take of yours very much, and I'm very happy you told me about it today. It's probably the reason I feel so comfortable living in Second Creek."

She reached over and patted his shoulder affectionately. "No problem. You're going to be part of the family now."

Chapter Fourteen

*L*AURIE AND POWELL had tried to ensure their quirky little wedding would remain the manageable private affair they had envisioned. No scroll-length guest lists on either side, no engraved invitations, not even the perfunctory announcement in *The Citizen*. Here and there hurt feelings had popped up, and Mr. Floyce had sent out feelers via Minnie Forbes that he might like to attend. Laurie had walked on eggshells over the phone in politely turning him down.

"The Piggly Wiggly just isn't that big, Mr. Floyce. You have to admit this is a somewhat unusual venue anyway."

"Surely you can squeeze me in, though," he had continued, pressing her further.

"Perhaps. But I could make it up to you with a cocktail party or a backyard barbecue somewhere down the line if we just can't spare the room."

"But imagine what I could bring to the table, Miz Lepanto. As an expert master of ceremonies, I could propose a toast to the happy couple. Even do one of my monologues. That'd add a special touch, don'tcha think?"

Laurie had struggled to suppress a groan and mightily redoubled her efforts to put him off. "Let me get back in touch with you on this, Mr. Floyce. At the moment, I'm trying to restrict this crazy little affair to immediate family and, of course, my Nitwitts." And finally, he had backed off.

That had not stopped the paper's social columnist, the Gossiper, however—the redoubtable, if somewhat cynical, Erlene Gossaler—from sniffing around the proceedings like the journalistic bloodhound she was. Erlene brazenly wangled an invitation from Laurie at the last minute.

"The Gossiper called just before you arrived and wanted to know if she could come with a photographer," Laurie said to Powell as they prepared to lift their wineglasses in a prenuptial toast. They were standing in her kitchen. She was tastefully attired in her pale peach suit with matching pillbox hat, while he was all spiffy and fragrant with aftershave in his black tie and tails. To hell with all that superstitious business about the groom not seeing the bride on the wedding day—they were mature adults, and this was their second time around.

"Ah, yes! The inimitable Gossiper—never met a story she couldn't sully with her catty asides. I thank whatever gods may be that she never showed up to lumber around at the Piggly Wiggly. What did you tell her?"

"I decided to split the difference. She would probably have managed to crash the party anyway, so I said yes to her but no to her photographer. I don't want a lot of flashes going off every few seconds. This could so easily turn into a sideshow if we let it. I'm sure some people already think it is. Lizzie's going to take some pictures for me, though. In fact, that's where she is now — at the drugstore getting some film."

"Well, while we have this quiet moment to ourselves, let's have our toast." He raised his glass, and she followed suit. "To Laurie, the woman who brought back the gleam in my eye and the snap to my dance step. May it ever be thus!"

They clinked rims and sipped their Delta muscadine wine. Then it was her turn. "To Powell, who took me in his masterful arms, lifted me out of the deep-freeze, and thawed me out with the rhythms of his love!"

"Now that's a whole lot to live up to, but a very nice touch there at the end, if I do say so." And they repeated the ritual, adding a warm, lingering kiss at the end.

He put his glass down on the counter, moving back slightly to take her all in. "You look so ripe and peachy and delicious, I could just take a big bite out of you right now. I think I'll nick-name you Melba—as in Peach Melba."

"Please, I'm most definitely not a Melba. I'm a Laurie. I love my given name and have no intention of ever forsaking it."

"I would never dream of asking you to. The name Laurie shall forever be music to my ears, but I still feel like taking a big ole juicy bite right out of you."

"Don't you dare. You'll muss me. There'll be plenty of time for that kind of nibbling when we get down to New Orleans and Jamaica."

Laurie had not been to the French Quarter since that insur-ance convention with her dear, hardworking Roy a year or so after they were married. Roy had spent so much time in sales meetings that she had not truly taken advantage of the Crescent City's myriad attractions. This time she intended to see as much as she and Powell could pack into each day—strolling around Jackson Square and watching the pigeons strutting and the artists at work, having beignets and cafe au lait at nearby Cafe Du Monde, riding the St. Charles Avenue streetcar past the Garden District all the way up to Audubon Park and back, browsing the antique shops on Royal Street and, of course, eating at elegant restaurants like Galatoire's and Commander's Palace for a tidy sum. Before, after, and in-between all of that, there would be plenty of time for romance and room service in their hotel room. It would be a honeymoon to treasure forever, and Laurie was fully prepared to "laissez les bon temps rouler."

"How are you coming with your packing?" he said. "I've been ready to go for days, but I know it takes women a lot longer to get their traveling act together."

"Just a few odds and ends left to put into my suitcases. Some tricks of the trade we women don't want you men to know about. Without them, of course, you might not recognize us. But don't worry, I'll be ready to hit the road bright and early Monday morning."

Laurie could hardly wait for her new life to begin. Four leisurely days in New Orleans, and then on to Jamaica for a week. No doubt Powell would teach her how to move her body to that reggae beat once they settled in at Negril And who knew? They might even find time for a little dancing besides.

ERLENE GOSSALER waddled into the Piggly Wiggly in a tent dress with her notepad and pencil and a skeptical expression for good measure. She was large enough to begin with, but her size was exaggerated even further by her towering hairdo—a pale, frothy tangle that looked remarkably like a swirl of cotton candy growing from her scalp. Although she had largely chosen to ignore the ongoing activities at the Piggly Wiggly over the past few months, she simply had not been able to resist the opportunity to witness and comment on a wedding in a grocery store.

She had arrived almost an hour early for the ceremony and was now pressing Mr. Choppy into service for a grand tour of the somewhat altered premises. "My God!" she exclaimed as he pointed out the scattered but colorful collection of patchwork and calico quilts hanging from the ceiling. "Who's getting married here today—Raggedy Ann and Raggedy Andy? I'm still having the hardest time believing this whole setup."

Mr. Choppy did not find the comment amusing but forced a smile anyway. "Those are contributions from our most experienced and devoted cashier, our dear Lucy Faye Stiers. She belongs to a quilting club, and she thought they might make interesting decorations for our little wedding ceremony here today. Just a little somethin' to give it that personal touch, and I have to say I think it looks nice."

Erlene made a quick note and said: "Reminds me of one of those interstate restaurant chains that tries to sell you countrified memorabilia that, if you turn them upside down, you see they're all made in Taiwan. Pure, manufactured country."

Mr. Choppy remained silent, and they moved along. "We had originally thought we were gonna set up our wedding trellis in the canned goods aisle, since that's the widest in the store, and that's also where Mr. Hampton did most a' his dancin' with

the ladies who came in. But then—and here's that human interest angle you newspaper people always like—Miz Lepanto,
soon to be Miz Hampton, was almost born in the produce section here. Her mother's water broke while she was handlin'
canteloupe—I know because I was a witness—and they whisked
her away to the hospital right after that. But, anyway, we decided that since Miz Lepanto was almost born right over there,
we oughta set up the wedding trellis over there, too. So, there it
is in all its special glory."

Erlene shuffled over to the makeshift arbor, masterfully
entwined with roses and ivy, and took more notes. "And our
Bob Yates, not an ordained minister, will be performing the ceremony?"

"That's right. Plain ole, crusty Bob Yates. Voted for him
myself. It's really gonna be a simple ceremony with just a few
people, including my employees here at the store—Lucy Faye,
Jake, and Kenyatta. There they are over by the refreshment
table in their suits and ties. Fine-looking young men, I do
believe. I just couldn't be prouder of 'em if they were my own
two sons."

Erlene ignored the glowing tribute to his young employees
and pressed on. "Mr. Choppy, there's something I need to get
your insights on. Specifically, I'd like to hear more about your
closing down—"

"No, I don't wanna talk about that, Miz Gossaler. We will no
longer be open for business once the ceremony is over, and
that's all I care to say on the subject. If you wanna write about
the wedding, fine, but I have nothin' to say about why I'm
closin' down the Piggly Wiggly. Period. End of subject."

Erlene looked decidedly miffed and heaved her ample chest. "Then I suppose we should move on to something else."

Mr. Choppy pointed in the direction of the bread and rolls, where a long table covered with a lacy, white tablecloth had been set up. In the middle of it sat an exquisite crystal punch bowl and ladle, a couple dozen matching cups, a three-tiered wedding cake, assorted hors d'oeuvres, and all the other para- phernalia necessary for the serving of food and drink during a reception.

"That's quite an impressive spread," said Erlene, circling the assortment with the ominous precision of a large vulture. Mr. Choppy wondered if she might just dive-bomb headfirst into the cake. "Did you have to spring for all this yourself?"

"It was a joint effort. I pitched in for half, and the ladies of the Nitwitts did the rest. I think that punch bowl set belongs to Miz Myrtis Troy. Miz Renza Belford supplied the silverware, and I mostly fixed up the hors d'ouevres—the pigs in a blanket and rumaki and such. They all brought the cake. Anyway, every one of those ladies are gonna be here as the matrons of honor. You might wanna interview 'em when they show up. I imagine it'll be quite a fashion show, if nothin' else."

Erlene hesitated, looking perplexed. "You'll just have to forgive me, Mr. Choppy. I just don't get this grocery-store staging—even with Laurie Lepanto's mother having labor pains in the produce section. This just doesn't seem like a very romantic place to get married. Pardon my French, but it smells like overripe fruit and cold cuts in here. Frankly, it's not what I'd want to remember on my wedding day."

To his credit, Mr. Choppy remained surprisingly calm. "I

guess you haven't been payin' much attention lately, Miz Gossaler. More ladies than you can shake a stick at have been comin' to my Piggly Wiggly and havin' a very romantic time these past few months. This place means a lot more to some people than just a grocery store, especially Miz Lepanto. She preferred it to any traditional church wedding, she said. Besides, you've lived here in Second Creek all your life. You know what kind of off-the-wall things people come up with here. And a lot a' those people have genuine affection for this store a' mine."

"And yet you intend to close it down."

"Old news. And I told you I don't wanna talk about it, okay?"

Erlene made a noncommittal noise under her breath and changed the subject. "Will there be music? Obviously, it would be extremely difficult to have an organ. Or is there one hidden around here somewhere I haven't thought of? Perhaps a piano hidden in the freezer compartment?"

"No organ, no piano, nothin' hidden anywhere, but we got us some music. Got it all set up on the cassette player. We had a rehearsal and everything last night. Miz Lepanto and the maid and matrons of honor will walk up to the trellis to 'Beautiful Dreamer.' She's right partial to Stephen Foster. Then there'll be a wedding waltz with Mr. Hampton to the tune of 'True Love.' That's the song Bing Crosby sang to Grace Kelly when they were out sailin' on their yacht in that wonderful MGM musical *High Society*. Saw that one seven times when it came to the Grande years ago. I'm quite a fan of Hollywood, you know. Maybe not so much the Hollywood of today, but definitely yesterday—the golden years, as they say."

Mr. Choppy paused, his expression suddenly pained. "That reminds me, Miz Gossaler, how come you nor nobody else at The *Citizen* didn't write somethin' about the Grande Theater when they tore it down? There was a lotta history tied up in that wonderful place, but all the paper did was run a picture and mention that the bricks had been sold to some subdivision builder over near Greenville. You call that decent coverage?"

Erlene looked decidedly uncomfortable. "I was on vacation when they started, and by the time I got back, it was old news. Everybody had been to see it come down anyway, so what was the point? It's not exactly like it really fit into my social column either. It was one of those fine-print things about city ordinances. That's just not the sort of thing I write about, and I can't believe anyone would really have been that interested in hearing about it anyway."

"There I beg to differ with you. I think the Grande meant a whole lot to Second Creek society."

"Well, maybe, if you stretched a point. But I still didn't think it was worth including in my column. They hadn't shown a movie there for years."

Mr. Choppy drew himself up defiantly and said: "I think that's the trouble with this town, Miz Gossaler. Nobody, except for maybe a few people like Miz Lepanto and her club, seems willin' to stand up for and talk about the things worth savin'. Second Creek is changin' before our very eyes, and we all seem to be goin' along with it and not askin' any questions. Mr. Floyce calls it progress during one of his press conferences, and maybe some of it is, but this town of ours is a special place to live and that didn't come about by our linin' up to be just like everyplace else in the country. Second Creek is different, and people come from all over the South to see for themselves what's different about it. I think it's time someone —"

He brought himself up short as he suddenly realized he had meandered into speech-making, and Erlene Gossaler was writing down his every word.

"Go on," she said. "You sound just like a politician running for office. That was a pretty good speech you had going there."

"Nah, forget it. I got carried away, that's all. Guess you could say I got a stronger sense of the past than most folks."

Erlene checked her watch and gave an impatient-sounding sigh. "Well, thirty more minutes to the festivities. Should be something for the record book."

Mr. Choppy matched her sigh with one of his own, combining elements of relief and anxiety. Relief that he had finished up with the Gossiper. Anxiety that the long history of the Dunbar family's involvement with the Piggly Wiggly was about to come to an end.

IT WAS TWENTY MINUTES to four, and the ladies of the Nitwitts were something to behold in their full, matron of honor regalia—each outfit as distinctive as the personality of its owner. Styles ranged from the sublime to the nearly ridiculous, but no one seemed to mind in the least. Mr. Choppy informally greeted each Nitwitt inside the door, whereupon the Gossiper took control of the proceedings and immediately launched into an individual fashion inquisition on each matron of honor.

"And how would you describe your outfit, Miz Troy?" the columnist began. "I can't find the words."

Myrtis briefly narrowed her eyes, took a moment to collect herself, and then rattled off a ready-made description. "Floor-length turquoise evening gown. In the past I would have made sure you knew who the designer was and how much it cost me, but I'm just not going to go there anymore."

The Gossiper looked puzzled, made some quick notes, and then moved on. "Now, what about you, Miz Chadwick?"

Wittsie managed to gather herself and pointed to her grand-daughter, Meagan, who at the moment was off flirting with Jake, the bag boy. "We're wearing matching outfits today—my granddaughter and I. She's the only maid of honor, you know."

"That's very pink and white—what you've both got on," said the Gossiper. "Almost like a birthday cake with those little rose-buds everywhere."

"Well, I was worried that it might be a tad too frilly at first, but I thought I should make this a special occasion for Meagan and go all out for something a fifteen-year-old would like to wear. I mean, it's her first wedding to be in and all."

The Gossiper's smile seemed a bit forced. "Your grand-daughter is very cute, what with all those freckles, but—"

Denver Lee, who had been lurking nearby, interrupted. "That little Meagan is a precious, darlin' girl, and don't you dare write anything else, Erlene Gossaler."

"I wasn't going to," she replied. "Meanwhile, would you call your outfit a caftan or a muu-muu?"

Denver Lee bristled. "It's a caftan. Muted gold. And don't play games with your copy. I know where you live."

Then it was the Gossiper's turn to produce attitude. "What is that supposed to mean?"

"Never you mind. This is a special day for Laurie. I just want to be sure you keep that in mind."

Obviously sensing that a further escalation in the conversation was possible, Renza stepped up and offered a quick description of her outfit. "What I'm wearing is a black, sequined pantsuit. No foxes."

"No what?"

"Just an inside joke among us Nitwitts," Renza answered, winking.

"That leaves me," Novie added, moving in with an imperious grin. "You can put down that I was wearing an off-white power suit with a dramatic silver scarf adorning my neck and that I looked impossibly breezy."

"Uh, huh," said the Gossiper, sounding entirely unimpressed while she wandered off with her notes. "I think I'm through here for the time being, ladies."

Then Denver Lee turned to Renza and said: "This is the first time in recent memory that I can remember you making an appearance anywhere in public without one of your fox furs around your shoulders. I'm mystified. What happened? Did they all run away from home or something?"

For once Renza lowered her profile. "Nothing of the sort. I just decided to turn over a new leaf. Try something new. Why not? If Laurie and Powell are adventurous enough to exchange their vows in a grocery store, then I can leave my little foxes at home once in a while. They'll still be there for me when I get back. Besides, I'll be president of the Nitwitts in just six months, so I thought I'd better get used to making tough choices and weighing my options. You can't do that very well if you're stuck in a rut. You've got to shake things up in your life every once in a while. There now. How about them horse apples? Do I sound like a future president of the Nitwitts?"

"You do, indeed," Myrtis said. "And I've recently come around to that way of thinking myself, Renza, dear."

Then Laurie and Powell arrived, and all the Nitwitts practically adhered themselves to the couple, drawn like gnats to a lightbulb.

"How handsome you look, Powell!" Denver Lee exclaimed. "And I adore your outfit, Laurie!"

"Powell thinks I look just peachy," she replied, gazing up into his eyes.

Myrtis butted in. "Oh, it's definitely your color. So much more interesting than off-white or beige. Those are such boring second wedding choices, I always say."

But when the ladies saw Erlene Gossaler heading back in their direction, they closed ranks quickly, forming the kind of defensive front line that the late Bear Bryant would have been proud to grade on film.

"Do you want to talk to her right now? She's already grilled us on our outfits," Denver Lee whispered to Laurie. "Her big behind won't get past me if you say the word. This is one line she won't break through."

"Good. But no tackling today. To answer your question: no, I don't want to deal with her yet. Tell her I'm too nervous right now. But after the ceremony I'll give her an interview. That ought to placate her for the time being."

And the Gossiper was turned away posthaste, to be dealt with later.

"I'd like to elaborate on something, Denver Lee," Laurie continued. "It just didn't occur to me at Evening Shadows this morning at the brunch, but when I thought of it later, I didn't worry about it because I knew I'd be seeing you here at the wedding. It's about the painting you gave me."

Denver Lee looked momentarily nervous but soon collected herself with an expectant smile. "Yes?"

"You were a wiser artist than you knew. Than even I knew until I thought about it for a while. What could be more appropriate for someone like myself than a painting of Piggly Wiggly produce? Here we've gone to all this trouble to commemorate my near-birth over there so many long years ago, but that will soon be relegated to a fond memory. But I will have your produce painting hanging somewhere on my walls to remind me of it all forever. How subconsciously wise you were to zero in on one of the important themes of my life."

Denver Lee gave her a peremptory smooch on the cheek. "You got all that out of my beets and broccoli? Hell, they're just vegetables, girl. Despite what all of you may think, I do realize I don't have any real talent for this. I'm not completely deluded."

"Now don't spoil the genuine sentiment of my little speech," Laurie replied, while everyone enjoyed a good laugh. "I gave it a great deal of thought, just as you obviously gave the same to the painting."

"That's so sweet of you to say, Laurie, and I do appreciate it, but I think the time may have come for me to admit that perhaps I shouldn't be overly encouraged in this area of endeavor. I've just about decided it's time I took up another hobby. Goodness, I don't know what's come over me saying something like that out in the open. Maybe it's the festive occasion. We all seem to be letting our hair down a bit more than usual, don't we?"

"Well, I haven't let mine down," Novie added. "If you all are expecting me to say I'm going to give up my traveling and take up badminton or crocheting or growing little cherry tomatoes in a little backyard plot, you are all out of your minds. I have a trip planned to the Philippines next month, and I definitely intend to go there and have a wonderful time and take plenty of slides to add to my collection."

"The Philippines?" Denver Lee said. "Aren't they having an insurrection over there or something?"

Novie frowned. "Not as far as I know. I think you're thinking of Somalia. Or is it Haiti? Well, no matter, I've been to them all, girls, and I've always come back alive and kicking. A few guerrillas in the grass never worried me in the least. As long as they don't shoot up my camera, I'm just fine."

"There are some things that should never change," Laurie replied. "Long live my wonderful Nitwitts."

"Well, now that you all have solved your personal problems as well as the many problems of the world," Powell said, "I think we'd better see about getting things started. I spy Bob Yates coming our way from the parking lot, and it's almost four. The grand occasion is almost upon us."

THE STRAINS of "Beautiful Dreamer" echoed through the Piggly Wiggly, as one by one, Meagan, the maid, and the six matrons of honor slowly approached the arbor with their bouquets of pastel summer blooms and peeled off to the right and left. Laurie thought her Lizzie looked particularly stunning in a lavender gown, adding yet another shade to the rainbow of outfits her friends had selected for the ceremony. Mr. Choppy, whom

Powell had chosen as his best man, was also a revelation in his dark, three-piece suit. In fact, Laurie could not remember when she had seen him looking so starched and pressed and presentable in all the years she had known him. It was almost like he was waiting for his own bride to show up.

And then there was her Powell, waiting for her beneath the arbor in his dashing formal attire. She had wondered, when they had decided to stage the wedding in the Piggly Wiggly, how it would actually work out, how she would feel about exchanging her vows in such a pedestrian setting. But any worries and fears she might have had were vanquished by the conviction that everything and everyone had come together in exactly the right proportions to witness and bless her new union.

The vows themselves were a virtual blur to Laurie. She could see Powell's lips moving and forming the familiar words and phrases, and she thought she had followed suit correctly when stodgy old Bob Yates had turned to her with that craggy face of his and asked her to repeat the same spiel. She eventually heard herself saying "I do" very softly, and she stood mesmerized as Powell slipped that breathtaking diamond-and-sapphire ring on her finger, but it was still mostly one, big, wonderful blur of warm, fuzzy emotion ending in a celebratory kiss.

The Beautiful Dreamer awoke, in a manner of speaking, during "True Love." She thought Powell had never danced this gracefully before, and for a while there she had no conception of where she was. She might have been in a cathedral or out on the highway, in the mountains or at the beach. She didn't care one whit—it was one of those delicious, defining moments she would treasure for the rest of her life in her album of memories.

"Are we really married?" she said, smiling up into his eyes.

"Of course we are. Don't you remember Bob Yates pronouncing us husband and wife a few minutes ago? And how could you forget that kiss I gave you?"

Reflexively, she ran her tongue over her lips. "Now that part is definitely coming back to me. But don't mind me, I guess I'm in another world."

Then the wedding waltz ended to the applause of the gathering, and it was time for the intimate little reception with punch and cake and all the rest. Laurie had only one pesky little task to dispatch—the interview with Erlene. She managed to wedge it in just after the official cake-cutting ceremony, moving well away from the crowd for a measure of privacy.

"I understand your mother nearly gave birth to you over by the produce section many years ago," Erlene began in between sips of her punch. "And Mr. Choppy has indicated that that was the inspiration for the wedding to be staged here. Has this unconventional setting actually worked out the way you expected, Mrs. Hampton?"

Laurie detected a possible journalistic ambush by the Gossiper and decided to head her off at the pass by going straight to and then over the top. "Has it worked out, you ask? Why, it was the childhood vision of a Beautiful Dreamer, and I was that dreaming slip of a girl. I awoke from my romantic slumber to find my husband whirling me around the floor with such aplomb I nearly fainted from delight. Ah, to faint from delight! The consummate wedding wish! As I danced about, the linoleum floor beneath my feet was seemingly paved with gold, the fluffy quilts dangling above me turned into precious calico clouds, the refreshments on the table across the way prepared just so for the tastes of the Olympian gods themselves. And this company surrounding me? Could it be more divine? Could the ceremony be more brilliantly conceived? I think not. Has it worked out, Mrs. Gossaler? Oh, yes, yes, and yes again. It was the first and last wedding to be staged at Mr. Choppy Dunbar's Second Creek's Piggly Wiggly. Need I therefore say more?"

Erlene dropped her jaw and then cleared her throat. "Well, I suppose that just about says it all."

"Doesn't it, though?"

And with that Laurie flitted off to track down her brand-new husband for another round of dancing.

"AND HOW DID it go with the Gossiper?" Powell asked as they were whirling around to "You Do Something to Me."

"I kept it short and sweet."

"Really?"

"No. I actually went on like a monologue from a seriously overwrought romance novel. I truly outdid myself. The words just kept coming and coming, and I wasn't even half-trying. I was on a serious roll."

"I bet that shut her up but good, huh?"

"I think she beat a path back to the wedding cake. In fact, I can see her over there right now, chowing down. When she can't get the gossip, I think she settles for the calories, and as her appearance clearly indicates, she settles for the calories more often than not."

Powell glanced over at the refreshment table and smiled. Everyone was eating and drinking and mixing with ease—from widows and relatives to bag boys and cashiers. Then out of the corner of his eye, he caught a glimpse of a woman standing out-side the front door waving to get someone's attention inside. He momentarily halted his dancing and frowned. "That lady out there looks familiar to me for some reason. I've seen her some-where recently. Now, where the hell was it?" I can see her clearly in my mind's eye, but I just can't recall the setting.

Laurie turned and focused. "I don't recognize her, but can't she read the sign? We're closed."

The woman persisted in her waving, and Powell decided to walk over and point her out to Mr. Choppy, who then marched resolutely to the entrance shaking his head and mouthing the words *We're closed!*

But the woman would not go away, knocking on the glass and mouthing her own words: "Let me in, please!"

Finally, Mr. Choppy decided to bring the matter to a head, unlocked the door and addressed her directly. "I'm real sorry, ma'am, but we're closed and in the middle of a private party."

She was looking him straight in the eye with a generous smile. "You look very nice today, Hale. I guess you don't recog-nize me. It's been a very long time."

Mr. Choppy swallowed with great difficulty.

A few feet away Powell turned to Laurie and said: "Now I remember. I saw that lady this morning at the Memphis airport."

Chapter Fifteen

MR. CHOPPY'S FAMILY HOME wasn't much to look at. It was just a modest bungalow with side screen porches set beneath the shade of a solitary pecan tree on a corner lot. Even the pecan tree had seen better days—at the moment it was home to several cottony nests of voracious tent webworms. On the ground below, the patch of zinnias and other flowers his mother had once tended with devotion had long since gone to weeds. Along with the store, Mr. Choppy had inherited all of it from his father and had never had any incentive to move out once he had resigned himself to running the Piggly Wiggly until the day he died. Of course, he had often wondered what his life would have been like had things worked out with his Gaylie Girl—or even if he had never met her at all—and suddenly here she was back in Second Creek after more than five decades. But for what?

Aware that Powell and Laurie were approaching, he had managed to cover his total shock and bewilderment when she had revealed her identity to him earlier at the Piggly Wiggly entrance. "Why, yes. You'll forgive me if I didn't recognize you after all these years," he had said, trying his best to sound as if he were merely discussing the prospect of a summer shower later in the day. "But as you can see, we're a little busy here right this minute. Could we possibly meet in, say, about an hour at my house? It's at thirty-four Pond Street, just a few blocks from here. If you get lost, anyone'll be able to give you directions. Would that be okay with you?"

She had responded in kind, obviously picking up on his concern for privacy. "Of course. I'll just browse around your charming town square until then. Maybe do some shopping or get a cup of coffee or something."

He had continued to cover his tracks with a curious Powell and Laurie as the three of them watched her walking back to her car in the parking lot. "That was just someone who said she'd dropped by to discuss the possibility of leasin' this building from me. We're gonna go for a cup of coffee a little later and get the negotiations started," he told them, leaving it at that and hoping they would buy it.

"Ah, so that explains it," Powell replied.

Mr. Choppy tried to sound nonchalant, but his guts were churning. "Explains what, Mr. Hampton?"

"Well, I saw that woman at the Memphis airport when I went to pick up Lizzie, and there was a moment or two when she seemed to be reacting to my Second Creek sign. She'd obviously flown down for your business meeting, and perhaps she thought I'd been sent to meet her or something."

"Yes, I'm sure that was it," Mr. Choppy answered, though without any real conviction in his voice.

An hour later he found himself standing nervously at his front door, ushering in his unexpected guest and apologizing profusely for the clutter of the living room. "As you can see, I have a little bachelor haven carved out for myself here. Afraid it's nothin' to brag about."

In fact, though it was clean, it could have used a woman's touch, perhaps a dash of color at the windows, maybe just a throw pillow or two as a lively accent. Everything seemed drab, tattered, and washed out—almost like a scene from an old black-and-white movie. There was a stack of assorted movie magazines on the coffee table, another stack of newspapers occupying one end of the sofa, and the lingering odor of bacon grease emanating from the nearby kitchen. The only family touch Mr. Choppy had allowed himself was a generous collection of framed and faded photos of his parents, chronicling their journey from wedding day up to advanced age.

Gaylie Girl kept a forced smile on her face as she entered. "I didn't come here to comment on your interior decorating, Hale, but thanks for seeing me like this. I'm sure it must have been a great shock to you to have me show up after all these years."

"That's an understatement." He indicated a spot for her on the sofa, then offered to get her some refreshments from the kitchen, which she refused with a polite shake of her head. Then, he said: "I'd, uh, like to compliment you on how nice you look, though. You musta took real good care a' yourself, Gaylie Girl. Truth is, you'd never know we'd once been almost the same age."

"That's one way of putting it, I suppose," she began, allowing herself a wry smile while he settled into a somewhat frayed armchair across the room. "And I appreciate your vote of confidence. I'll willingly admit to you it hasn't been just a matter of genes with me. I've had lots of extra help of the elective medical variety. The money was always there because I married up, as they say. But I'm a widow, now. I live alone with servants of both the upstairs and downstairs variety in Lake Forest, Illinois—that's a little north of Chicago on the shores of Lake Michigan."

"Yeah, I know where it is."

"Have you been there?"

"Not exactly. But that's where Robert Redford filmed *Ordinary People*, if I'm not mistaken."

Gaylie Girl seemed impressed. "You're absolutely right. Some of us inclined to get up at ungodly early hours even got to watch some of the scenes being shot with Tim Hutton and Mary Tyler Moore. From a healthy distance, of course. They wouldn't actually let us on the set for security reasons, though."

"Yeah, I'm sure it's nowhere near as glamorous as everybody thinks. I've read articles in the movie magazines about how borin' it can get on a set shootin' the same scene over and over again until they get it exactly right. Some a' those directors are downright perfectionists."

The conversation quickly dried up, and Mr. Choppy couldn't help but wonder if she was experiencing anything like his own internal turmoil. She sounded calm and composed, but maybe it was just a clever act. He was certainly dredging up all of the old emotions where she was concerned. He kept gazing into her eyes and seeing his own reflection at the raw, impressionable age of sixteen. It may have been practically another lifetime ago, but here at last was the face he had tried to suppress over the years, and though it no longer had the power of youth behind it to cast a spell over him, it was still capable of conjuring up the toil and trouble of his first time."

"I was wondering how I would be received," she finally said when the silence was just too much to bear. "I know we hardly parted on the best of terms, and I'm certainly not very proud of the way I handled things."

"I can beat that," he replied, his voice tinged with anger. Then he raised his maimed hand in front of his face and watched her wince. "This was how I handled things not long after you left. After I'd nearly driven myself crazy relivin' those two nights in bed with you, I finally just flipped out and lifted my daddy's keys to the store late one night and took his meat cleaver to every piece of meat in sight. Chopped it all up into little pieces. Only in my rage, I got a little careless. Cost my daddy a tidy sum with the spoilage and the medical bills to dress up this nub you're lookin' at. I guess I got off easy, though. Mighta bled to death if a patrol car hadn't happened by."

"I'm so sorry, Hale," she said, her eyes drooping and filled with remorse. "You can't know how sorry I am."

He tossed off her remark with a contemptuous chuckle. "Be that as it may, that's how I got the nickname, Mr. Choppy. Yep, that's what they call me now. And everybody in town knew what I'd done, but they never knew why. Not even Mama and Daddy. When they got to the hospital, I just told 'em I had fallen desperately in love with Miss Ava Gardner and thought I'd never be able to have her, and I guess my folks bought it because they knew how hooked I was on the movies and how I always spent my allowance at the Grande Theater. A movie theater rat, they called me, livin' on popcorn and big dreams."

Gaylie Girl bit her lip and briefly shut her eyes. "I guess you were trying to chop me up that night."

"I forget exactly what I was thinkin' while I was doin' all that, but I do know I had to take my anger out on somethin'. So I started with the frozen meat but ended up with a piece of myself. I think the truth is more like I was tryin' to make mincemeat outta the pathetic way I acted over you. I felt like such a betrayed fool."

"I can't say I blame you. Sometimes I worried about what you might have done to yourself. I even had nightmares from time to time. The one that really stuck with me had you running across a field and falling into a pit covered over with zinnias like the ones in that sad little bouquet you brought me. I rushed over and looked down to see if I could do anything to help, and there you were at the bottom of this deep hole with your hand outstretched, but there was no way I could reach you. Instead, I just stood there and threw you some more zinnias, which you caught and made into another bouquet to offer me. I woke up feeling so helpless and embarrassed and guilty."

Mr. Choppy hung his head and did not look up for a full minute or so. "Yeah, well, I think I mighta dug part a' that hole myself. I was just a country kid with unrealistic big-time dreams. I think we both know now that I was never gonna come close to endin' up as a leadin' man in detective movies out in Hollywood. What a crock!"

"And I'm so ashamed of myself for taking advantage of your hopes and dreams, Hale."

He shrugged and sighed at the same time. "Hey, we were both off-base, I guess. The fact that I was willin' to stay right here in Second Creek and butcher things in my daddy's little grocery store until the new millennium tells me I really didn't have the determination to go for it. Somebody that was meant to go before the cameras woudda never give up that easy and settled for makin' sausage and choppin' up stew meat at the Piggly Wiggly." He pointed to his nub once more. "In a strange way I think I've kinda used this as a justification for stayin' right where I am. The ultimate commitment to my career decision. See, I could always say, I can chop things up and off real good."

Gaylie Girl was focusing on the worn throw rug in the middle of the floor as she spoke. "I don't talk much about what I'm going to say to you now. But I, too, know what it's like to have a missing part. Despite my creature comforts, I've had a terrifying bump or two in the road." Somehow, getting that much out enabled her to look him in the eyes again. "About twenty years ago I was diagnosed with breast cancer and had to have one of them removed."

His eyes widened as he cast furtive glances right and left. "I'm sorry to hear that, but I would never've known if you hadn't said anything."

"Well, it was the left one, in case you were playing that particular game," she added, careful to keep a note of amusement in her voice. "I had it completely reconstructed, even though that wasn't my original intention. My husband really didn't care one way or the other, bless him. He wasn't just saying that to be a supportive husband either. He genuinely adored me, no matter what. But I just got damned sick and tired of keeping track of my prosthesis. It was damned hot and it itched, and I couldn't wait to get home and take it out and throw it across the room onto my easy chair. The cat would end up sleeping on it all the time. After a while I thought to myself, 'Well, I can do better than keep the cat happy.'"

The anecdote had done the trick, and they both laughed heartily and at some length. "I guess we've both learned to deal with our troubles pretty well."

"Be that as it may, I still feel bad about leading you on the way I did. I guess it wouldn't surprise you to discover that I never had a brother of any kind named Murray out in Holly-wood who was a talent scout. That was part of my cousin Polly's nasty little, premenstrual plot. I'm afraid she wasn't the all-American sweetheart she appeared to be. Although she got her comeuppance. Gained about forty pounds one summer and the studio dropped her at the speed of light. She was practically unrecognizable, and she refused to cooperate with the studio's insistence that she go on a strict diet. I guess there is some jus-tice in the world after all."

"Yeah, I remember Miss Polly Andrew. All this time I had her up on a pedestal like she was a Roman goddess or some-thin'. I even felt guilty about steppin' on her feet out on the dance floor the way I did."

"I'm afraid I made the mistake of looking up to her, too, and all that did was get me in serious trouble. She was so full of her-self all the time, she never even noticed the damage she left in her wake."

Mr. Choppy was reliving the clumsy way he had danced

with Polly, trying to rid himself of the memory with a barely perceptible shiver. "I suppose I musta seemed like a movie monster with bolts in his neck to somebody as graceful as her."

Gaylie Girl lifted a judgmental right eyebrow. "Polly, graceful? She had no idea what real grace was all about. She was the real monster, Hale, and I suppose I wasn't very far behind in that department."

Oddly, her self-deprecation failed to dissipate Mr. Choppy's anxiety. He couldn't see where she was going with all this. "So you came all this way just to admit somethin' like that to me? Why now, after all this time has passed?"

She looked decidedly uncomfortable, as if fidgeting around with that one patch of fabric on the sofa that might grant her forgiveness. "I'm surprised you haven't asked me how I tracked you down. I happened to see that CNN report about your store and all that dancing in the aisles. I'd made an uneasy sort of peace with myself about you over the years, but that little news story slapped me sideways to Sunday. Maybe it's an axiom of life: just when you think you can take a little down time and breathe easy about the way things are going for you, something else comes along to remind you to heat up the stew and stir the pot."

He debated briefly whether or not to tell her the bad news. Why the hell not? She was his captive for at least the next few minutes. What was the point of sparing her feelings at this juncture? "Well, things are plenty stirred up down here, too. My Piggly Wiggly's gonna close down after today. I'll write off the perishables and donate all the canned goods to the Salvation Army like my daddy would have done. So it looks like you showed up for the final scene of my little home movie."

"You sound so serious about it all. Are you planning to retire or completely disappear off the face of the earth?"

He gently moved his head back and forth with a hint of a smile on his face. "That's what I've heard some people say about Second Creek, ya know. That this is one of the places where people come for their final hurrah. But to answer your question seriously, I'm not sure which way it's gonna go yet. On the bright side, I know I could rent every movie in town and sit around all day and eat buttered popcorn waiting for the end to come, but I betcha that would take all the thrill out of it for me."

"Sounds familiar," she replied, making a clucking noise with her tongue. "I have a much too intimate relationship with my remote and big-screen TV. My secretary, Harriet, says I need to get out and do more, although she's a fine one to talk. She's one of those computer nerds whose relationships are of the e-mail variety."

"I don't understand computers at all. I like doing things the old-fashioned way, although I think that might be part of why my store's in trouble and goin' under. I haven't really kept up with the times, and the local MegaMart has. They've got all the bells and whistles, and all I've got is the loyalty of a generation of customers who are slowly dyin' on me."

"That is a depressing scenario," she replied. "But as for that last part, time takes its toll on all of us."

Mr. Choppy decided the conversation was beginning to drift into an imitation of a casual visit with an old friend, and this outing definitely did not fit the bill. In his mind she still had a lot to account for, and he was going to dig in and hold on tight. So he stopped being polite and went for the jugular.

"We've been talkin' some about the movies, and I want you

to know that that part of what happened between us was the easiest to get over. I mean, my silly ambitions and all. What did I really know about bein' an actor, even if you didn't have a brother out in Hollywood? Hey, anyone can sit in a dark theater, get real worked up, and then dream all the way home. People do it all the time, and I was no different. You have no way of knowin' this, but our Grande Theater was recently torn down. It went all the way back to the first talkies. I thought of it the way some people think of their church, but it's gone now — sold off as a big pile a' bricks to some contractor to make way for some tacky service station. But my actor ambitions were torn down way before that." He paused briefly before pressing on, his fingers curling up slowly into white-knuckled fists.

"What I really had a hard time with was gettin' over you. I don't mind trottin' it out in the open here before you and God. You musta had a pretty good idea it was my first time. Boy, I thought you might just jump outta the bed and your skin besides when I literally started rubbin' you the wrong way — "

"I was no model of experience, Hale. I just knew that what you were doing didn't feel good," she interrupted.

"Yeah, well, you told me, 'Not so damned hard!' I remember your exact words. 'Slow down, take your time!' you said. 'There's no fire!' A young boy, green as I was, would remember every little detail of his first time. And you had to know from that pitiful letter I wrote you that I really fell for ya. I know now it was only a dumb, adolescent kid thing, but it sure felt like love to me. I would've followed you anywhere after those two crazy nights. You were in all my dreams for a long time after that. We'd be tourin' the country together, and everyone would know we were a couple. Mr. and Mrs. Hale Dunbar Jr. of Hollywood, California."

Gaylie Girl's breasts—natural and reconstructed—heaved dramatically. "I'm sure it must have been awful for you."

He gave a wry little hiccup of a smirk. "I think the hardest part has been wakin' up in my bed at thirty-four Pond Street in Second Creek, Mississippi, and goin' to work and butcherin' the hell outta things to make up for what I didn't have—and that was my life. Never got any better. Never got any worse. And I eventually got used to it and people seemed to count on me for certain things and I listened to all their troubles and even came to like bein' called a gimpy name like Mr. Choppy. Can you imagine that? I gave up my Christian name without a fight."

"Well, if it means anything at all to you, I've never stopped remembering you all these years as anything but Hale."

"I guess it doesn't mean anything then," he replied, trying for aloofness but realizing it was an act. "Second Creek's a town that seems to create characters as fast as some little kids draw stick people with their crayons. It wasn't a real fancy place for me to end up, but I decided it was still someplace dependable to settle for. And even though it took me a real long time to do it, I somehow found a way to put you outta my mind—that is, except for days of the week endin' in 'y.'"

Gaylie Girl continued to avert her eyes at his revelations. "Funny, how I've sort of ended up doing the same thing in a different way. I married a man I was very fond of and respected quite a lot. But I never really loved him the way he loved me. I settled for pleasing him and being what he wanted me to be, a glamorous prop of sorts. My job was to be his cuddly lapdog who went to the beauty parlor every week. It cost him a fortune to keep me well-groomed, but I was his best in show."

"Maybe you're bein' too hard on yourself. He got his money's worth. You're a very handsome woman." He paused, looking slightly embarrassed. "Maybe I shouldn'a put it that way. That sounded kinda rude."

She quickly put him at ease, waving her hand at him as if it were a wand. "No, it happens to be the truth. He got what he paid for. He could afford me. But I had no great passion for anything—just a long list of creature comforts I could count on. After my husband, Peter, died, that point was really driven home to me. I'm secure with no real worries, but there's nothing challenging going on in my life either. I've often thought how thrilling it would be to have to fend for myself as I did when I knew you, or have things open-ended with all the possibilities before me, or maybe even finish some things I once started. That's what my little visit is really all about."

"You're not sayin' to me you've come back here to pick up right where we left off, are ya?"

She seemed momentarily startled, jerking her head back almost as if something or someone had jabbed her with an invisible needle. "Oh, no, Hale. I think you misread me completely. But I had hoped to tie up some loose ends and maybe make amends for the way thing worked out, or didn't work out, between us."

"And how're you gonna do that? I think it's safe to say that our lives are windin' down now, maybe even mostly over. You think there's somethin' you can say or do that'd make any real difference at this late date?"

She opened her purse and put a hand in, mixing and stirring

the way women do. Eventually she pulled out an envelope and opened it up, displaying a creased and yellowed sheet of paper. "I suppose you can guess what this is. Would it bother you if I read it out loud now? I don't want to make you feel uncomfortable, but I can assure you I am going somewhere with all this. It will be worth your humoring me."

He gave his permission with a reluctant nod. The truth was, he really did not wish to revisit those words. But she had insisted there was a point to be made, so he straightened himself up in his chair, holding on to the arms execution-style, thereby alerting his muscles and nerves to the emotional onslaught that lay ahead.

"Dear Gaylie Girl," she began. "I never have had a coupla days and nights like this. You are just my dream come true. My gosh, I guess a lotta people wanna go to Hollywood and be movie stars, but how many people get to do it for real? I know I have a lot to learn and far to go, but you have give me hope that the door might be open just a little bit for me. And you have give me more than that. I have dreamed of a girlfriend like you, I guess a lot of boys my age do. But you have shown me the way. You have even let me call you my Gaylie Girl. I hope you have a special name for me, too. If you do, please let me know soon.

"I really think this is fate for us. Why else would your car have broke down right here in Second Creek after all the miles you have traveled all over the country? They say Second Creek brings people here for a reason. They even say the weather brings them here and plunks them down, just like it brought you. So I know it is meant to be. I think from the moment Miss Polly Andrew introduced us at my dad's store, I knew it would be something special. And then you invited me back to your room, but at first I wasn't quite sure I would go. I guess I knew what you meant by inviting me, but as I'd never done anything like it before, I just wasn't real sure. You should of seen me sneaking around picking those zinnias in the dark. My mama would of pitched a fit if she knew I had done that. Maybe there was a weed or two in there and even some ladybugs and stuff crawling around, huh? I hope not." Gaylie Girl paused to catch her breath and turn the letter over.

"I'm a very lucky guy, I know that. You could've chose any guy you liked, but you chose me. I want you to know I will listen good to any advice your brother gives me about how to get in the movies. I'm a good learner, I really am. Maybe I haven't done so good in school as some of the others in this town, but I do know the movies and all the dialogue. I think maybe I have seen more of them than anyone else in Second Creek. It's a good start that I've made, but I know there will be lots more to learn if I want to be up there on the screen. I know it is hard work, but I'm not afraid of that, believe me. Nobody in my family was ever afraid of hard work.

"Most of all, Gaylie Girl, I want to be with you from here on. I hope you feel the same way. Today, I did something to prove it to you. I went to the bank and withdrew all the money in my savings account. It is what I have managed to save from my work for my daddy at the store. I want you to give it to your brother as a down payment so he can start doing things for me and telling people that I am coming out there. If this fifty dollars isn't enough for your brother to be my agent out in Hollywood, and I am smart enough to know you have to have one to get anywhere, I will work hard and get you some more. You just tell me what I need to do, and I'll do it.

"Well, that's it for now. I'm the luckiest guy in the world. Love, Hale Dunbar."

The silence was unbearable when she stopped reading. Mr. Choppy had tried to send all the proper signals to the various parts of his body, but to no avail. His execution had been completely successful, and the smoke was rising from his ears.

"You musta got a real good laugh when you read that," he said, leaning back in his chair.

"No such thing. That's why I wanted to read it for both of us again, so you'd get some idea of the true impact it really had on me. I was still so upset with you when you threw it at my feet, I didn't even open it until we got back to Memphis the next day and Polly and I had checked into our room at the Peabody Hotel. If I'd opened it right then and there in Second Creek, I would certainly have thrown that fifty dollars back in your face and made a clean break of it. Believe me, Hale, when I finally did read it, I took it very seriously. It made me feel like so much dirt, and I've been dealing with the fallout ever since."

Mr. Choppy took a while to speak, and finally said: "I guess that's why I threw it down instead of tearin' it up right there on the spot. I guess I was hopin' it would make you feel bad enough to change your mind about us, but that just shows you how mixed up I was—just a stupid kid in a blind rage." He inched his way to the edge of his seat, still unwilling to let go of the bad taste in his mouth and staring her down grimly. "Why didn't you just send me the ridiculous fifty dollars later? That was all the money I had in the world back then, and you were runnin' a scam with that business about your brother, whether it was your idea or not."

"But you also had me running scared when you told me how old you were. As bad as I felt, I also wanted to get as far away from what I'd done as possible," she replied, leaning in earnestly and pleading with her voice. "Try to understand. I wasn't sure what you might do or say. Don't forget, I wasn't all that much older or more sophisticated than you were, and I had trouble shaking all these paranoid notions about the Second Creek Police and your mother eventually tracking me down and shaking me senseless somewhere in the middle of that miserable war bonds tour. I had visions of jail, since I knew you were jailbait."

"Funny to hear a man referred to as jailbait, huh? Always seems like somethin' you hear about with older men and young girls," he observed.

"True enough. But if it's any consolation, though I doubt it will be, I never told anyone about our little affair, not even Polly, and believe me, she pressed me to within an inch of my life every chance she got on what actually happened between us. 'What was that letter you were reading in bed?' she would say. 'Who was it from—your secret lover? Are you trying to outdo me in the romance department?' Oh, she was practically a pit bull about it, but I managed to fend her off and keep the letter out of her devious little hands."

He was shaking his head in a contemplative manner. "Wicked things sometimes come in pretty packages, huh?"

"Right you are."

Just then, something resembling catharsis suddenly surged throughout Mr. Choppy's body. It took the unlikely form of awkward, intermittent laughter, causing Gaylie Girl to pull back with a look of bewilderment. A minute or so passed before he had gotten it all out of his system, but when he had, his head was clear, his heart had been purged, and he took a deep, cleansing breath for good measure.

"I just had the funniest damned thought," he continued. "It popped into my head that you'd come all this way after all this time to give me back my puny fifty bucks. Is that what you had in mind to settle the score?"

She puffed herself up on the sofa, managing to look sly and proud at the same time. "No, but I did come to return your eighty-seven thousand, three hundred forty-six dollars and twenty-seven cents." Once again she played around in her purse, this time retrieving what appeared to be a folded slip of paper, handing it over to him promptly.

He unfolded it and frowned while closely reviewing the impressive numbers on the cashier's check. "What the hell are you up to here? What is all this?"

"That check is my way of dealing with the guilt of what happened between us. I never spent your fifty dollars, Hale. Instead, I opened a special account with it once I'd calmed down and thought everything through. I decided to call it my conscience money. I told myself I would do something sensational with it one day, maybe even find the courage to come back here and give it all back to you—"

"Wait a minute!" he interjected. "What if that CNN story had never happened? Would you have ever found the courage then?"

His questions stopped her dead in her tracks, and it took her a little while to recover. "You have a point. I can't deny that."

"Well, you're at least honest about it," he said, temporarily placated.

"But let me just finish my thought about the money. Over the years I kept on investing the money in various funds, pulling it out of this one and transferring it to that one. My husband, Peter, who ran a Fortune 500 company, gave me some fantastic tips from time to time, even though he had no idea how I got the money or what I intended to do with it. I'm sure he thought of it as indulging his pet poodle. And the balance just kept on growing and growing, decade by decade. You'd be surprised how much you can accumulate under such circumstances, and you also don't know how many times I was tempted to check up on you just to see if you were still alive and kicking. A phone call is probably all it would have taken, but I never could bring myself to do it."

"There it is again. I wish you had. Called me, I mean. Not bein' able to put this thing to bed all these years has been a trial for me."

"I can imagine, Hale. But instead of doing the right thing, I just got more and more complacent and settled into my life of leisure and luxury, deluding myself that maybe you weren't around any longer and that the healthiest thing I could do was to stop obsessing about the whole shameful thing. But then that CNN report came along and reminded me that I had left Second Creek fifty-five years ago with some unfinished business to settle. And so, here I am, and there's your money."

He cast another doubtful glance at the check, still not particularly excited about the whole concept. "Well, maybe the original fifty dollars is. But you have to admit you did the rest, though. This is a whole lotta money for me to accept from you outta the blue."

"Please, Hale," she replied, desperation gripping her face. "You simply have to accept the money. It's my last chance to make things right, and it was your money from your savings account that started it all—literally thrown at my feet in your innocent good faith. I know I really can't buy my way out of a lifetime of regret, but if this money can help you in some important way at this time in your life, please take it in that spirit."

Her pleading began to take its toll, and he relaxed a bit. "I can tell you're sincere about all this."

"Yes, I am. I don't believe it was an accident that I saw that CNN story, Hale. What are the odds, anyway? This was meant to happen the way it did for a reason. Something seems to have been set in motion with that story—call it a ripple effect of some kind. Your teenage letter mentioned the weather plunking people down here for reasons unknown. Maybe that was what that strange hailstorm was all about the day I saw the CNN piece up in Lake Forest. That just never happens up where I live. I don't know, maybe we won't ever understand it completely, but something tells me we have to follow through. I've done my part. Now, you have to do yours and see where it leads you."

He could appreciate the challenge she had just issued him, and the mention of her Chicago hailstorm won him over completely. The weather as God's messenger service. It was all a part of Second Creek lore. Punishing her by refusing the money now seemed both foolish and childish, so he told her yes, he would take it and then decide what to do with it later.

She reached over and grasped his hand. It was the first time they had touched in more than fifty years, and the contact had the instantaneous effect of resolution, reconnecting all his frayed emotional wiring. He sensed that at last he was going to be able to put his lifelong frustration and sense of failure to bed.

"Now that you have this money, one possibility is that you could keep your Piggly Wiggly open after all," she said, as they both rose together from their seats. "Think of the check as the cavalry riding in to save you from being scalped."

"I don't know. I'll have to think about it. My mind seems all set in concrete about the store. All the dancin' hoopla was good fun and games, but I think I've prob'ly known for some time now that it's past time for me to move on to somethin' different in my life. In a way you comin' down to see me is gonna make that even easier for me to do because I agree with you that somethin's been set in motion. I can feel it, too. Don't know where and why it started, don't know where or how it'll end, but I can definitely feel it."

She started to reply, forming the first word, but then shook her head and slowly closed her mouth.

"Were you gonna say somethin' else?"

"Well, Hale, I wasn't sure how you would react to his, but I'll go ahead and venture it anyway. I wanted to extend an open invitation to you to come and visit me up in Lake Forest any-time you'd like. No strings attached. Just a friendly visit if you'd like to see the sights in Chicago sometime. I have a lot of time on my hands, and maybe you wouldn't be interested, but there it is, for what it's worth. I'd like to think we could leave this world as friends."

His immediate reaction was muddled. This was far too much information to process all at once. But then, out of nowhere, he made a gracious gesture borne of years of dealing successfully with the public as a businessman. "I appreciate the offer. And now let me make one. Maybe you'd like to go to dinner with me at the Victorian Tea Room? It's just a few blocks from here. We could even walk if you'd like. They have right good food if you have a little time to spare and don't have to leave right away."

She seemed both surprised and pleased and said: "Will you let me treat?"

"No way. Hey, I've got eighty-seven thousand dollars I didn't have before the sun came up this morning. That means I can certainly afford to treat you."

"All right. Your treat," she said with a brief, pleasant smile. Then she grew somber. "There's something else I'd like you to know. Over the years I've had trouble even admitting it to myself, but here it is. I had some genuine feelings for you, Hale Dunbar Jr. I was attracted to you the first time Polly pointed you out to me at the Piggly Wiggly, but then she suggested in that snotty way of hers that I should somehow be ashamed of that because of where you came from. So when you admitted you were sixteen, that gave me the easy way out and permission to explode. You were too young, you were a hick from nowhere, and what the hell was I thinking? But I still want you to know that I thought you were adorable and insatiable those two nights with your sad little bouquet of zinnias, and under different circumstances, I think we might very well have become an item. There, I've finally said it."

Mr. Choppy pointed in the direction of the front door and

made a little whistling noise. "I don't know how much more a' this I can take on an empty stomach. Let's go get somethin' to eat, huh?"

"Sounds good. We can take my car."

And with that they headed out to a date that had been on hold for the last fifty-five years.

GAYLIE GIRL was sipping a Kahlua-laced coffee after they had finished off a superb dinner of quail, wild rice, and asparagus at their Victorian Tea Room corner table. "So, Hale. Do you have any inkling of what you're going to do yet?"

"Not a clue," he had answered without hesitation. "Suddenly, everything seems up in the air."

"Will you at least write and let me know what you decide? I'd really like to hear what you're up to. I realize I'm probably asking a lot, but this time you have complete control of the situation. Maybe you always have, but this is the first time you've actually realized it."

"Yeah, I'll keep in touch. I think it'll be good for my head to keep everything open between us now."

She put down her cup, smiled warmly and said: "I won't lie to you. I was so full of knots and butterflies coming down here after all these years, and then wondering what you would think about me throwing all that money at you. I wouldn't have blamed you if you'd refused to even talk to me. I'm sure I had that coming."

"Hey, what happened between us happened. What I've got to figure out is what to do next. But just this second I think I got a little flash of sorts. Back at my house, I remember sayin' to you that I thought our lives were almost over. Maybe I was still lettin' my anger speak too much at that point. Maybe that was a bit too pessimistic."

"I don't quite follow," she replied, between measured sips of her after-dinner drink.

"What I mean is: who's to say it's almost over? People go by counting the years too much. When there's work to do, it's never over. It's not a matter of age, it's a matter of purpose, and somethin' keeps gnawin' at me now that I've got some important work to do. I've just gotta find out what it is."

"You have no idea how intriguing that sounds to me. If you really feel that way, you absolutely must keep at it until you discover what it is you're supposed to be doing. I can't tell you how often I've wished I had a purpose in life. I guess as long as my Peter was alive, I didn't much question my reason for being. Having money is not a purpose, I can assure you, but my wish for you is that the money I've given back to you will help you find your answer."

He looked directly into her eyes and gave her a playful wink. "Fair enough. I'm gonna bear down and work that out, and when I do, you'll be one of the first to know about it. I'd say I've taken long enough to figure out my life."

Then it was time for him to pay the check. They walked out of the restaurant together and stood awkwardly in front of her rental car. "Do we, uh, offer a handshake here, or what?" he said.

Disdaining a handshake, she offered a hug instead, and the two of them let it linger somewhat longer than was necessary. When he finally pulled away, he said: "That was nice."

She ventured a peck to his right cheek and said: "Good. I

think we should leave it like this for now. We were both stupid kids who made some stupid mistakes, and I'm not sure the slate can ever be wiped clean. But if you ever care to come up to Lake Forest, I assure you I won't run away from you again."

"Understood. And thank you for that."

Then they walked around to the driver's side of her rental, where he opened the door for her and watched her slide in, and he stood there in the street, waving good-bye to her and watching her drive away—this time without the overwhelming sense of loss he had always associated with his Gaylie Girl.

Chapter Sixteen

MR. CHOPPY had never liked sundays. Without store hours to occupy his time, he often found himself moping around the house and dwelling far too much on the insufficiencies of his life. Mondays, when he could ask the bag boys and cashiers about how they'd spent their day off, could never come soon enough. There were never enough videos to rent to get him through the long hours of numbing and worrisome inactivity on his so-called day of rest.

This particular Sunday had started out even more problematical than usual. Suddenly, every aspect of his life was up for grabs for the first time since he had been a teenager intent on conquering the world via Hollywood. His Gaylie Girl had materialized out of nowhere with an amount of money that had blown him away, not to mention essentially apologizing for messing with his life and even leaving open the prospect of a future friendship between the two of them. Wasn't that an unexpected blip on his radar screen!

This Sunday, though, was beginning to feel more like a dream sequence in one of those crafty, convoluted Hitchcock movies he had rented so many times over the years. Suddenly, he was Cary Grant or James Stewart confronted with a twist in the plot, and nothing was what it appeared to be or very easy to figure out anymore.

The question that kept tumbling around inside his head like an enormous boulder was: should he completely ditch his plans to close the store now? After all the effort that Laurie, Powell, and the rest of the Nitwitts had put into helping him keep his head above water, didn't he owe it to them to follow through now that he could? The money would allow him to keep it open indefinitely, but it no longer seemed as simple as that.

So when Sunday dawned, he realized he had some pressing issues to resolve. With his mind finally cleared of the emotional baggage he had carried around for more than fifty years, he began to perceive things differently. For some reason, it came into his head that the town of Second Creek, itself, might give him both the right question to ask and the answer he needed to hear. All he needed to do was listen and observe. The signs might be anywhere. In the sky. In the trees. In the grass. On a dusty road in the distance. If he remained open to the living, pulsing grid of possibilities that was Second Creek, he would read the signals correctly as so many had before him.

So he began making the rounds. He walked all over the pedestrian mall lost in thought for the longest time until a voice called out to him from a sidewalk table shaded by a big yellow umbrella in front of the Town Square Cafe.

"Mr. Choppy! Come on over and join us! We're having coffee and Black Forest cake on this glorious Sunday afternoon!"

He looked up to see Hunter and Mary Fred Goodlett waving and smiling, and he quickly headed in their direction with a wave of his own. Now midway through their sixties, the handsome couple had grayed and plumped up together gracefully. Up until the Lepanto-Hampton wedding, they had remained Second Creek's most famous example of setting out on the road to matrimony with an assist from the Piggly Wiggly.

"You looked like you were gonna wear a path in the pavement out there," said Mary Fred, after Mr. Choppy had pulled up a chair and ordered a cup of coffee. "I turned to Hunter just a few moments ago and said, 'I'll betcha anything he's thinkin' about the Piggly Wiggly closin' down? Was I right?"

"Pretty much," he answered, finding it difficult to focus on conversation when he had so much on his mind.

"We were so sorry to hear about you goin' outta business," Hunter added, swallowing a mouthful of his cake. "As you well know, your daddy's bulletin board was the thing that got us together."

Mr. Choppy leaned in and gently shook his head. "Nonsense, Hunter. You folks got yourselves together. You were meant to be. That's how it works, ya know. The bulletin board just got you both off dead center, that's all."

Mary Fred reached over and grasped her husband's hand warmly. "We've always thought it was destiny, but we still have a soft spot in our hearts for your store because of your daddy's contest and the way things worked out for us. You know who won it, don't you? It was Lillibelle Parker of all people. And she never stopped phoning people all over town to tell them she'd won free groceries. You'd have thought she had won a lottery or something." Then Mary Fred cleared her throat and changed her tone. "I don't suppose there's a chance you can keep the Piggly Wiggly open? I don't look forward to dodgin' all those brats in the aisles of the MegaMart. They just run wild and break things. What money you might save is more than canceled out by the stress and the size and the noise."

Mr. Choppy's coffee arrived, and he took the time to fix it up the way he liked it. "Believe it or not, folks," he said at last, "I've reached a point where everything's up for grabs. You caught me wanderin' around The Square thinkin' about my options. It's been a long, long time since I've been so undecided about things."

Mary Fred seemed almost girlish in her excitement. "Oooh, you mean the Piggly Wiggly might not close down after all?"

"It's possible. But it's also possible the little wedding we had yesterday was the curtain call."

"Oh, I read all about it in Erlene Gossaler's column in the paper today," Mary Fred replied. "You could read between the lines and tell she took a rather dim view of the proceedings. Not that that's a big surprise, of course."

Mr. Choppy was stirring his coffee absentmindedly. "Miz Lepanto and Mr. Hampton were happy with everything, and that's all that counts with me. I did it for them, and I don't really give a damn what anybody else thought about it."

Hunter finished his cake and put down his fork. "Well, you let us know if you change your mind about the store, Mr. Choppy. We want to do everything we can to support the businesses in and around the square. That's the true, living, breathing heart of Second Creek, and we wanna help look after it as long as we're alive. This place has been good to us, kept us happy and secure."

Hunter's words seemed to resonate strongly with Mr. Choppy long after they had all downed the last of their coffee and gone their separate ways. Indeed, Second Creek seemed to treat people especially well. And there was frequently a show in the skies to keep the citizens alert and active—meteorological flights of fancy to beat the band.

Mr. Choppy continued to hang around The Square and took the time to notice the deserted storefronts the MegaMart had recently left in its wake, each one sticking out like a missing tooth in an otherwise disarming smile.

Then he moved on to the park, briskly circling the shady cypress pond several times. Was it his imagination, or were there fewer and fewer people frequenting it these days? After all, it was part of the downtown area, not the Bypass where so many of the newer franchise businesses had set up shop. Was it simply no longer fashionable to be seen holding hands and smooching there? And he was reasonably certain that kids still liked to fly kites, but he was also positive he hadn't seen any of them doing so in the park that spring. And yes, the Annual Delta Floozie Contest showed that The Square was still a viable attraction for tourists, but that was only one day out of the year. There were plenty of days when the same square was exclusively the domain of the trickle of locals visiting the courthouse to pay a traffic ticket or buy a personalized license plate.

Next, Mr. Choppy marched purposefully over to all that was left of the Grande Theater—an ugly, fractured concrete foundation waiting to be crushed into manageable pieces, then excavated and eventually transformed into one of those self-serve gas station monstrosities. Hadn't anyone at all in the current lamentable municipal administration ever heard of zoning? He remembered the art-deco perfection that had once been there, how many times he had sat up in the balcony with his popcorn and soda and memorized the plots of hundreds of movies from the golden days of the studios and beyond. What a thrill it had been for him as a young man to round that corner and catch a glimpse of that big white marquee trimmed in neon, imagining his name—HALE DUNBAR JR. (yes, he would insist upon the junior)—up there in huge red plastic letters beside a knockout like AVA GARDNER or LAUREN BACALL or VERONICA LAKE as his seductive costar. He had even made up titles for his forthcoming films: *Red Hot Ice, The Mystery of the Blue Monkey, The Beale Street Bandit,* and his personal favorite—*Murder at the Peabody Hotel.* That was the one where, as famed detective R. Keene Lee, he would solve the mystery by observing an important clue left behind among the pennies cast into the bottom of the duck fountain, and the final scene would involve everyone in the lobby applauding vigorously as he dipped his leading lady in very dramatic fashion while planting a big juicy kiss on her moist, inviting lips.

For his final act of reconnaissance, Mr. Choppy got into his car and headed away from the town, taking one of the many farm roads that bisected the soybean fields, not particularly caring where it would lead him. It might dead-end in the middle of nowhere, or he might end up in somebody's front yard. He just needed to drive, be in motion, anything to help him sift through the blizzard of input he was experiencing.

The first few miles of his journey were uneventful, but after about five minutes of staring blankly out at the flat, dusty fields, something dramatic happened. The sky suddenly darkened, the way it does during an eclipse, and he glanced up to see that an enormous bank of angry-looking clouds had blotted out the sun. A playful wind began to swirl outside the car, almost as if it had appeared to escort him to an unknown destination. At first he put it out of his mind. Just Second Creek's peculiar weather, that was all it was.

But the wind began to pick up even more, and the sky grew even darker. The weatherman hadn't predicted rain that he could recall.

Another five miles passed, and he found himself parked on the side of the road in front of what appeared to be a pecan orchard—there could be no other explanation for the distinctive arrangement of the trees. The unbearable heat of the day had returned when the clouds had suddenly vanished and released the sun to do its customary damage. He got out of the car and walked around. That he might be trespassing on somebody's property never entered his head. Instead, he seemed to be following an urge or an instinct he couldn't explain. He kept thinking about Gaylie Girl's observation that something had been set in motion.

He continued walking down an alley of pecan trees, thankful for the respite they provided from the intensity of the sun. Up ahead, just beyond the shade of the orchard, was a small pond that looked as if it might have once functioned as a watering hole for cattle. Now it was nearly encircled by tall grass and weeds, except for a few stretches of dried mud here and there. There was something enticing about this shallow pool of water, as if it had been waiting for him all this time to come and discover its secrets, whatever they were.

He carefully made his way to one of the mud flats, keeping an eye out for snakes that might be lurking in the nearby brambles to escape the heat, and gazed out across the dark, mirrored surface. It was well on its way to drying up, he could easily see that, and things that had once been completely submerged and resting on the bottom were now uncovering themselves — mostly tree trunks and limbs that had been tossed or fallen in. One such object looked particularly arresting as it protruded out of the water in the exact center of the pond.

Mr. Choppy squinted hard to try and make it out. What the hell was that thing? It had no business being there. It seemed too smooth to be a tree trunk, and it was an odd color besides. He picked up a rock and took aim, missing the first time. But the second throw was accurate, bouncing off the object with a distinctive pinging sound. He threw a third time. Another ping.

All the more intrigued, he walked around to the other side of the pond to observe it from another angle. From that vantage point he could make out more of the submerged portion of this curious creation, discerning the outline of an enormous hand, cracked straight through the palm. The realization hit him like a bolt of lightning. Here was where the famous finger off First Presbyterian had come to rest during the straight-line winds of 1963 — at the bottom of somebody's shriveling pond in the middle of a pecan orchard. It had not gone over the rainbow to Oz after all. Though damaged goods, it still remained in the Mississippi Delta, tentatively poking a finger out of the water and still striving for sunlight.

He laughed and then pinged another rock off the gold-plated symbol. He decided then and there that he wasn't going to tell anyone about it. This was a definite sign. The fate of the famous finger had been revealed to him, and apparently no one else, as the climax of a remarkable weekend that had seen a couple get married in his store and the woman who had turned his life topsy-turvy return to make amends. Now, what was he to do with all this incredible bounty?

His reconnaissance finally completed, Mr. Choppy returned to his homey little nest on 34 Pond Street and sank down into his favorite armchair to collect his thoughts. The Sunday edition of *The Citizen* was spread out all over the floor where he had left it after his breakfast of al dente grits and fried eggs with runny yolks. Staring up at him was a society column mug shot of the far-from-photogenic Erlene Gossaler just above her gossipy recounting of the Lepanto-Hampton wedding at his Piggly Wiggly the afternoon before.

Then he noticed one of the pictures on the nearby front page. There was Mr. Floyce in all his cheesy glory—out at the MegaMart, mugging his way through another photo op, this one apparently in honor of the deal he had just cut with the chain to market his corny "She's a Doozie, She's a Floozie" CD throughout all their outlets in Mississippi with an option to go nationwide if all went well. Mr. Choppy picked up the paper and zeroed in on a quote from Mr. Floyce.

". . . and I am so pleased to have formed this alliance between myself and one of the great merchandising chains of the new millennium. Now that my initial offering will be out there for the public to sample and enjoy, I'll be hard at work on other CDs that will combine my unique music with my down-home humor. There is no telling how far Mr. Floyce Productions,

Incorporated, and the MegaMart will go together. This will be one of the great collaborations and success stories of the early 21st century. . . ."

Who would have guessed that these two seemingly unrelated items, courtesy Erlene Gossaler and Mr. Floyce, would become the final pieces of the puzzle he needed to bring everything into sharp focus? Both the question and the answer he had been searching for suddenly materialized, floating down into his lap like an angel feather.

He had it back completely now. That sense of wonder at what the world could offer him, could offer anybody who was open to it. That glorious belief in the benign nature of the universe that had once permeated his childhood.

So, being an actor was never in the cards for him. So what? Nothing in life, no trial, no heartbreak, no triumph, no aspiration was ever pointless or wasted energy. It was never too late to discover what you were actually born to do in a particular lifetime. For the first time ever, Hale Dunbar Jr. knew what his mission was. Hallelujah! So this was what Sundays were supposed to feel like. This was the purposeful feeling at his very core that he had been missing all these years, and he could hardly wait to share the good news with someone.

Chapter Seventeen

*L*AURIE AWOKE on monday morning with the promise of Christmas, Easter, Thanksgiving, and New Year's stuffed into every nook and cranny of her brain. In a couple of hours they would be leaving on the honeymoon trip to New Orleans and Jamaica. She glanced over at Powell, still sound asleep, and couldn't help but smile at the way her life had turned around in recent months. Once again it had taken on the charmed qualities she had enjoyed all those years with Roy. The point had been driven home to her rather unexpectedly as she and her daughter had enjoyed Starbucks' cappucinos at the Memphis airport while waiting for the first boarding call of Lizzie's flight home.

"I always have such mixed emotions when I leave Second Creek," Lizzie was saying. "I feel so safe here. Like even if something bad does happen, there'll be something to help cushion the blow."

"I know what you mean. I still miss your father terribly, but then Powell came waltzing into my life. I realize I had something to do with that in a roundabout way, but Second Creek is the type of place that encourages you to view things from unusual angles. Once you do, you are generally rewarded."

Lizzie wiped foam from her upper lip with her little scalloped napkin and smiled. "Oh, I think you and Powell are going to make a great team, and I've already told him so. We had a wonderful conversation on the way down from the airport. He really opened up to me, which I thought was so dear."

Laurie took a sip of her coffee and glanced at her daughter affectionately. "I appreciate the vote of confidence, but I really don't see the two of us talking like we are now all the time over the breakfast table. You always were the more philosophical of my two best girls, but a heaping helping of the metaphysical with my corn flakes is a little heavier fare than I prefer. I guess I'm more the 'oatmeal keeps you regular' type of girl."

"Well, you and Powell don't have to OD on the whys and wherefores of life. Just live it out together."

"Such a cerebral sweetheart you are." Then Laurie grew somber for a moment. "I'm glad you told me this. To be honest with you, I thought when you married Barry and moved away to Chicago, it meant you didn't really like Second Creek all that much and that you were turning your back on your upbringing. Not that you ever said anything to that effect, but a mother has a way of reading between the lines all the time that usually ends up getting her into trouble and driving her crazy. It sort of comes with the territory, as you'll eventually discover."

"My marrying Barry had nothing to do with Second Creek. But sometimes it's nice to get a different view of things for a while, so to speak. If it's any reassurance to you, I've already told Barry that I'd like to return to Second Creek for our retirement years. After we get here, we can compare notes with the other crazies."

Laurie reached over and patted her daughter's hand. "Well, it'll be waiting for you, and there'll probably be an incredible thunderstorm or something of a meteorological nature to announce your arrival. Maybe one of these days someone will actually figure out what's been going on around these parts and why people act the way they do."

With that prediction and observation Lizzie's flight to Chicago began boarding, and mother and daughter hugged for the longest time, neither one wanting to be the first to let go.

Once again, Laurie's thoughts returned to her Monday-morning bed and her tall, sleeping husband with his feet hanging off the end of the mattress. She marveled at his physical dimensions. He was not only tall, he was also long where Roy had been thick and stubby. She had never imagined she would have a point of comparison, or that that could possibly be important to her, but now she did, and it was. And despite her extensive history with and undisputed love for Roy, she found herself much preferring length to width these days. It had surprised her—the renewed interest in sex—and she truly was a woman who had been thawed out in every sense of the word.

When Powell finally roused himself into wakefulness with a couple of amusing little snorts, she decided to give him the benefit of her insights after a perfunctory "good morning." "I'd just like to say that the main reason I moved away from the

Nitwitts was because of you. Specifically, the fact that I'm getting some."

He sat up in bed, quickly propping up his pillow, and smiling wickedly. "Well, that's quite a good-morning opener. Matter of fact, we're both getting some. Even lots more than most, I'd say."

"I just think it's tacky to lord it over your friends, and I don't even want to be tempted to give away anything about us to those women."

"Would you? I mean, if they pressed you hard enough?"

She considered briefly and then turned to him with an impish grin. "To be truthful, it's not as if that subject hasn't come up before in our many social conversations. We women do a bit of comparison gossip behind your backs now and again. As for myself, though, I believe I'd rather keep the delicious details of our relationship all to myself."

"Such as?" Powell replied, an expectant look plastered across his face.

"Such as nipping at earlobes and nipples with precision timing." She pointed to her forehead. "It's all up here in the emotional diary I keep in my head."

"And I intend to keep supplying you with more of those entries, starting with our honeymoon."

Laurie sank back onto her pillows and began conjuring up mental pictures. Soon they would be exploring each other even further as only people on their honeymoons can do, and she could hardly wait to get underway. She was going to prepare an especially hearty breakfast to stoke their fires and tide them over until their arrival later that afternoon—a sweet and savory omelet stuffed with chopped Vidalia onions and sliced

Portabello mushrooms and a side of French toast dusted with cinnamon and sprinkled with pecan pieces.

"You're going to spoil me for those grand New Orleans restaurants," Powell said later, after finishing up the last bite of his toast and then pushing away from her kitchen table thoroughly sated and feeling like royalty.

"Not even remotely possible, sir. I'll gladly relinquish the culinary spotlight to someone else for the next two weeks — that is, assuming gourmet food remains your number one priority for the duration of our honeymoon. I predict you'll have other things on your mind."

He rose, walked around the table, and stood behind her, gently massaging her shoulders. "I don't intend to miss anything. Not a crumb of delight, whatever the source." Then he leaned down and gave her a peck on the cheek.

The doorbell rang, and Laurie said: "And that would be Mr. Choppy with his news that just couldn't wait."

"What do you suppose this great news of his is going to be that he just couldn't tell us about over the phone?" Powell added, making his way over to the front door while Laurie shrugged her shoulders.

"And a grand Second Creek good mornin' to you, Mr. Hampton!" Mr. Choppy exclaimed with an energy that seemed to be oozing from his every pore. Laurie joined them with a smile, and he greeted her with the same infectious enthusiasm.

"I know you're both prob'ly wonderin' why I called and asked to see you just before you set out on your honeymoon," he continued as they all headed to the kitchen. "I guess it coudda waited until you got back, but out of everyone here in Second Creek, I feel closest to you two, so I didn't think you'd mind puttin' up with me for just a few minutes while I explain what's up. I promise you won't be disappointed."

"Of course we don't mind, and I can't imagine that we'd ever be disappointed in anything you had to say. You sounded so excited over the phone," Laurie replied. "We can hardly wait to hear what your great news is. But first, can we offer you some breakfast—maybe some juice or coffee?"

"Already had a great big healthy one myself. Two big bowls of cereal with sliced bananas. Boy, did I have the appetite of Atlas this mornin'. In fact, I feel like I could carry the whole world on my back now that I got the weight of the world off my shoulders. I know that sounds like a big fat juicy contradiction, but, believe me, I've got everything straight in my head for the first time in my life, and it feels terrific."

Laurie and Powell exchanged amused glances, and she said: "Well, let's sit down then and hear all about it." She quickly cleared the breakfast dishes, and the three of them settled in around the kitchen table for the skinny.

"It's actually a real long story," Mr. Choppy began. "But I'm gonna try and cut to the chase because I know you've gotta get rollin' soon. First, I'd like to share somethin' with you two and only you two. I'd appreciate if you didn't tell anybody else the part I'm gonna tell you now. Would that be okay?"

Laurie made eye contact with a nodding Powell and smiled. "I speak for both of us when I say that whatever you tell us will be held in strictest confidence. You know you can trust us with anything."

"Good. Well, the first thing is that I lied to both of you the afternoon of your wedding. That lady that came to the Piggly Wiggly wasn't interested in leasin' my store. She was the girl I thought I was in love with way back when I was just an empty-headed teenager, and she came back to Second Creek the other day to settle an old score." Without self-consciousness, he held up his hand, pointing to the nub with the other. "She was, in fact, the reason this happened to me so long ago."

Powell remained relatively calm, arching his brows, but Laurie was instantly captivated. "So she's your mysterious lady, is she? And surfacing after all these years. Does she have a name?"

"I just call her my Gaylie Girl. Did from the very beginning. She lives up near Chicago now, but I believe that's all I'd really care to go into about her. At least for now. Maybe another time when things aren't so rushed."

"Of course. We understand completely," Laurie replied, genuinely respecting his plea for privacy but secretly wishing he had spilled more. It was the gossipy side of her personality that the Nitwitts had nurtured all these years.

Mr. Choppy resumed his story. "Anyway, she sorta set things right between us after all these years, and it got me to thinkin'. As you know, I plan to close down the Piggly Wiggly. But I was at loose ends as to what to do next. That is, until Gaylie Girl showed up, and I did some thinkin' and got a brand new perspective on things—"

Laurie couldn't help herself, interrupting impulsively. "You've decided not to close down the Piggly Wiggly after all? Is that your news?"

Mr. Choppy didn't answer right away, giving her the impression that she had guessed his secret. Then he quickly dashed her hopes. "I'm afraid not. I'm definitely gonna close down the Piggly Wiggly. The time has come to bring that long chapter of my life to an end. I don't wanna upset you, but it's the right decision at the right time."

"Okay. Me and my big mouth," Laurie replied. "So now, no more interruptions on my part. What's the real deal?"

Mr. Choppy seemed to be milking the moment for his own enjoyment, continuing to beat around the bush. "Do you know what's gonna happen here in Second Creek in another six months?"

Laurie drew a blank, and she could see that Powell was struggling as well. "Tell us, Mr. Choppy. Please tell us before we both explode."

"All right. Here it is. The mayoral election. Mr. Floyce, our zoning-challenged, ham and cheesy master of ceremonies and bargain basement recording artist, is up for reelection, and I intend to run against him. Not only that, I intend to win. And not just squeak by either. I expect to win by a large and impressive margin. As God is my witness, I will be the next mayor of Second Creek, Mississippi, and give it the respect it deserves. There now, the rabbit's outta the hat. Whaddaya think?"

Laurie was stunned, completely unable to speak. Powell sat there with his jaw hanging.

Mr. Choppy laughed good-naturedly at their expressions. "Talk about your somethin' outta left field, huh? But I know what this town is all about. I was born and raised here, and I really understand what's goin' on with every brick and window and doorstep inside the city limits and even some of the pecan orchards and cattle ponds way out in the country. Yessir, I got the inside track on all of it. Most important, I care about Second Creekers and their so-called solutions to everything. I don't think Mr. Floyce is the right man to appreciate that anymore —

if he ever was. He's got some strange notions in his head, I do believe, and I've always felt he was sent here to stir things up and keep us on our toes. Now, it's time to return Second Creek to the reign of the angels."

"That's it!" Laurie proclaimed, nodding her head emphatically. "Those are the exact words I've been searching for all these years about Mr. Floyce. Sometimes I've even felt he was more an idea than a real person we were fighting against. No one ever could find out where he was from, no matter how hard they tried. For all practical purposes he is the Devil with a pencil mustache and a karaoke voice. Nothing worthwhile ever proceeded from that combination."

Mr. Choppy smiled and returned to his agenda with even greater gusto. "All that's very true, and furthermore, we need someone runnin' things who can strike a balance between the old and the new, between what's worth preservin' and what we should say good-bye to for our own good. No matter what, though, the things we treasure most shouldn't be for sale to the highest bidder." Mr. Choppy paused for a much-needed breath and then continued with his spontaneous stump speech.

"Miz Lepanto—I mean, Miz Hampton, please excuse me, I gotta get used to your new name—you put it best that day you and me were watchin' that crew tear down the Grande Theater. We gotta stand up for the people and the buildings that make us unique, and that's what I intend to do. That's what I'm gonna talk about durin' my campaign, and I'm gonna wipe the streets of the town square with Mr. Floyce and his corny CDs. I've run a business in this town for many years, so I know what it takes to make a go of it here, and I aim to do everything I can to give every business a fair shake."

"Unlike someone else whose name we shall not mention," Laurie said, squeezing a word in edgewise.

"Right," Mr. Choppy replied. "And I'll be fair to everyone who darkens my door, newcomers and crazy veterans alike. Hell, even if Lady Roth barges into my office one day all done up as the Queen of Sheba with her eyes lined to Kingdom Come, and I have to fix myself up and dance with her as the Prince of Babylon, I promise I'll listen and do what I can to help. I've got the patience and understanding to deal with every problem there is — big or little — 'cause the truth is everybody in this town has brought all theirs to me at one time or another. The Piggly Wiggly has been Second Creek's shoulder to cry on, but now I'm gonna offer my own shoulder in an officially elected capacity. And because of all that, I'm gonna make a damned good mayor, the best Second Creek's ever had!"

This time Laurie and Powell responded with applause. "Bravo!" they both shouted, nearly in unison.

"I wish the election were being held today because I'd go right down to my precinct and vote for you!" Laurie exclaimed.

"And I'd be right behind her!" Powell added. "Or maybe we'd just waltz our way down there together."

"That's just what I wanted to hear from you because there's more, folks. I'm gonna ask both of you to be my campaign managers. Hell, if you could bring every woman in the county outta hidin' to dance in my store, I believe you could help me bring every voter into the booth to vote for me when the time comes. Would you be willin' to do it? I'd ask you to start as soon as you got back from your honeymoon. We'd have to hit the ground runnin', as they say. And you can ask your wonderful Nitwitt

ladies to back you up. I know they'd help you run a fine campaign for me."

There was a brief silence filled with sly grins and furtive
glances, but in the end Laurie and Powell gave him an unmis-
takable thumbs-up.

"We'd be honored," she answered.

"Our great pleasure," Powell added.

"And I'm certain the Nitwitts would rise to the occasion as
they did with our Piggly Wiggly project. Give a wealthy widow
a purpose, and you've got a warrior on your hands," Laurie
continued.

"I was hopin' you'd say that, and maybe now you can see
why I wanted to run it all past you before you left. I could be
workin' on my campaign plans while you're gone, and then the
three of us could get together as soon as you get back. Hey,
somethin' like this is gonna require our top effort. Mr. Floyce
has been in there awhile, you know. I'd say he's bought himself
more than a few allies in this town, and none of 'em'll go easy into
that good night, I reckon. The lot of 'em might even resort to a
dirty trick or two before it's over. Which reminds me: got any
skeletons in your closets? I finally buried all of my old bones just
the other day. Nothin' to haunt me anymore, I'm proud to say."

"No skeletons for me," Laurie answered, her profile lifted
proudly. "Just lots of boxes of unopened junk in all of my closets from that last time Roy and I moved."

"Same here," Powell added. "I got a coupla hundred pair of
old dancing shoes I can't seem to throw away. Sentimental reasons, I suppose—kinda like all those relics Laurie had in her
freezer."

Mr. Choppy gave them his most confident smile. "Great. We'll be ready for Mr. Floyce no matter what he tries. We'll beat him by standin' up tall for Second Creek and showin' him up for who he really is."

Laurie was rolling her eyes around and chuckling at the same time. "And who is he, really? Again, that question."

"My impression has always been that he is someone who would have been booed off the stage in vaudeville and walked away with tomato on his face," Powell replied. "I know I felt like throwing a few at him the morning of the Floozie Contest."

The image momentarily amused them all, but Laurie was soon frowning. "Your idealism in all this is admirable, Mr. Choppy. But what about money? Running for just about any office these days is a pretty expensive proposition. I can't believe how much these national politicians spend. It just boggles my mind. At the national level it's become a runaway train. Could you swing it?"

"All taken care of. Let's just say my Gaylie Girl settled an old account with me. I got all the backin' I need to make a go of it politically here in Second Creek, and you know what finally made me realize that runnin' for mayor of Second Creek was what I needed to do with the rest a' my life? It was seein' Mr. Floyce's toothy grin on the front page of yesterday's paper and rememberin' a conversation I had with Miz Erlene Gossaler, of all people. That's what did it. How 'bout them wormy apples?"

"Or as Renza Belford would put it, 'How 'bout them horse apples!'" Then puzzlement crept into Laurie's features. "I get the reference to Mr. Floyce and his CD deal with the Mega-Mart, but the bit about the Gossiper completely escapes me. You're gonna have to explain that one."

"Well, it was your wedding day, and she had come in early to check out everything, and I took her to task but good for not payin' better tribute to the Grande Theater in *The Citizen*. She tried to justify herself by sayin' she was on vacation and such as that, but I didn't let her off the hook so easy. I told her Second Creek needed someone to stand up and protect what made it different from all the other towns, and I just went on and on. I even mentioned how you and your club had stood up and done the right thing by me, even if it didn't work out. She told me I sounded just like a politician, and you know what? Somethin' worthwhile finally came outta her mouth. Anyway, I finally got the message, and now you've got it, too. The three of us are gonna begin a very special journey, but, hey, it's not like we don't know how to work together. We made waltzin' at the Piggly Wiggly happen. We can make this happen, too. All we gotta do is put our minds to it."

"Fascinating," Laurie replied, turning her hands palm side up. "Utterly fascinating how these things work out if you just watch and listen for the signs and then give yourself permission."

Mr. Choppy squinted slightly. "Permission?"

"To do things like an expedition to Antarctica or to run for mayor of Second Creek. As for the election, I believe just as firmly as you do that we'll win, Mr. Choppy. Don't forget, I kept a carload of finicky widows in line for three terms. When I put my mind to something, it gets done up right. There's no way Mr. Floyce is not gonna be dead meat. Maybe we can even come up with a slogan to that effect—you know, something that plays on your nickname."

"Nah, I don't think so, Miz Hampton. I'm gonna shut down both the Piggly Wiggly and Mr. Choppy at the same time. I think it's best I run for office as Hale Dunbar Jr. It's a good, strong, grown-up name without any baggage to lug around, and it's time I took it outta cold storage and wore it proudly. I've abandoned it for too long as it is. Now I'm gonna be the man I was meant to be."

Laurie gave him an impulsive, heartfelt hug. "Hale Dunbar Jr. it is, then. Very proud to make your acquaintance."

Powell offered a firm handshake as well, and soon they were all standing at the front door saying their good-byes. Then Mr. Choppy bounded down the steps to the sidewalk with his arms raised high above his head, looking exactly like a long-distance runner who had just burst across the finish line for a well-contested victory.

"See you both in a coupla weeks," he called out as he reached his car. "And show those Jamaicans a step or two while you're at it, Mr. Hampton!"

POWELL'S CAR was packed and gassed up and ready to go, but he was standing on Laurie's front porch looking as if he had forgotten something important.

"What's the matter?" she said, studying his face closely.

"I was just thinking. We're getting off bright and early. I think we still have plenty of time to do it."

"To do what?"

They walked down the steps, heading toward his car parked out on the street, and he said: "I think we ought to ride around for a few minutes and take one last look at Second Creek before we leave."

Laurie not only didn't get it, she was beginning to worry about his tone of voice just a bit. "You make it sound like we're not going to be coming back. Do you know something I don't know? Are we going to be beamed up into a UFO and probed by aliens or something, never to be seen or heard from again?"

He laughed while opening the door for her, and she slid in. Then he walked around and got behind the wheel, starting the engine and turning the air-conditioner on high to cool off the miniature greenhouse the car's interior had become even this early in the day. Until the cooling kicked in, it was difficult for them to draw a breath.

"Sorry, Mrs. Hampton. I didn't mean to sound so ominous and cryptic. I meant that we ought to make some memories of Second Creek in our heads. You know: this is how the town looked under Mr. Floyce's old regime, before our Mr. Choppy took dead aim and hit the political bull's-eye."

"You're really excited about this campaign already, aren't you?" she said, just as he pulled away from the curb.

"That I am. You know how I've always felt about Mr. Floyce and his incessant glad-handing. Now I have the opportunity to do more than just complain and vote against him."

Powell was as good as his word, and they took a brief tour of the town square, the rest of the downtown area, and some of the residential neighborhoods. Not much was happening, and people were going about their business, watering their lawns and letting their kids play under the hose in their bathing suits to offset the rapidly escalating heat. Some were puttering around in their cars running errands and one brave soul was even walking his dog before it got too unbearably hot. No matter. It was all just the calm before the political storm that Mr. Choppy intended to whip up on their behalf.

"I just thought of something amusing," Laurie said, as they finally headed toward the Bypass and Highway 61 South that would lead them down to New Orleans. "Maybe Mr. Choppy will allow dancing in the courthouse as part of his administration's new outlook. You know, come in and do the cha-cha while you're waiting to pay your fine or do the tango to blow off steam after you've had a really rough session with the tax assessor."

Powell shook his head emphatically. "I think we've overdone the dancing-in-unheard-of-places schtick, don't you? I, for one, have had more than enough of the likes of Lady Roth starring alongside me as Carrie Nation, Madame Curie, or Elizabeth Barrett Browning. There comes a time when a little more decorum wins the day as well, even in Second Creek. Look at it this way, Mr. Choppy is taking himself very seriously and running for office as Hale Dunbar Jr. He has finally decided to put away the meat cleaver of his impetuous youth and wield instead the sword of his just maturity."

"Now that is very eloquent stuff, sir. I can see right now who's gonna be writing all the campaign speeches." Then she gave him a quizzical glance. "You do intend to waltz with me at our Mr. Dunbar Jr.'s inauguration, though, don't you? I would be utterly crushed without that to look forward to."

"Naturally. And any other time you want to dance, I'll be there. But let's try to strike a balance between decorum and spontaneity. I think maybe that's a good rule of thumb to follow about everything we do in our marriage from here on out. Losing Ann the way I did taught me the hard way that you can't take anything or anyone for granted. You can blink, and they could be gone."

He switched on the radio and tuned in the Big Band station. They were gradually driving away from the signal, so he knew they wouldn't be able to listen too much longer. "Talk of the Town" was playing at the moment, and it seemed the perfect sendoff. To anyone who had read Erlene Gossaler's snippy account of their Piggly Wiggly wedding in the Sunday paper — "the bride wore a pale peach suit and hat that seemed a calculated throwback to Jackie Kennedy and Camelot, while the maid and matrons of honor literally wore any and everything under the sun" — they were indeed the talk of the town.

A small number thought they were either out of their minds, heathens, or heretics. One or two even resented the fact that they had the social position and clout to pull off something so eccentric without being ostracized. But most Second Creekers wished them well and thought it was just business as usual. Just another mildly amusing Second Creek solution to life as they understood it.

Laurie and Powell drove along in silence for the next few miles, letting the music settle them down into a soothing travel mode. By the time the station had succumbed to a fatal attack of static, they were content to observe the dusty Delta acreage flashing by. Here and there, enormous sprinklers set between the furrows shot arcs of water high into the oppressive heat to keep the lucrative soybean crop from burning to a crisp, and the sky bearing down upon the fields seemed so white-hot it had somehow managed to crowd out even the perception of blue.

They were leaving all that behind for a while to bond for

what they expected to be the rest of their lives. Second Creek would take a back seat briefly while they dabbled in jazzy, laissez-faire New Orleans and indulged a taste of funky, spicy Jamaica. But they would soon be back to invigorate their cozy little universe of souls with a newfound sense of purpose and boundless energy.

"I've been thinking," Laurie said, gazing intently at her new husband all the while. "When we get back, we need to talk to Mr. Choppy—I mean, the Honorable Mr. Hale Dunbar Jr.— about an adaptive use for the Piggly Wiggly. So it's not exactly historical, and so it's not the most attractive building in the world. It's just an ordinary grocery store. But it means too much to Second Creek for us to allow it to fall apart like the Grande. If he's going to be campaigning on that issue, he needs to pay attention to his own building and lead by example. As his campaign managers, it's our duty to point that out to him and see that he acts on it. We can't afford that kind of simple mistake."

"So what's the bottom line here?" he replied.

"My conclusion would be that we use the Piggly Wiggly for the next six months as his official campaign headquarters. No reason to have to fork over good money for another building when we'll have that one readily available."

"God, you're good. I was thinking exactly the same thing," Powell replied. "Are we on the same wavelength or what?" Suddenly, he was grinning impishly, returning her ardent and adoring gaze. "Now, the way I see it, the Piggly Wiggly is a bit on the smallish side for a grocery store. But after the election is over and we've won, of course, it will be more than large enough for a dance studio, don't you think? I don't really like being retired, you know. It's time I put on my dancing shoes permanently again."

For some reason she wasn't the least bit surprised by his brainstorm, reaching over and patting his arm affectionately. "Aha! The return of Studio Hampton—and waltzing at the Piggly Wiggly is brilliantly reincarnated. You know, you really shine when you're dancing. You're the person you were born to be at those moments."

"I appreciate the compliments, but let's not forget that I'll definitely need a new partner for this venture."

"You're looking at her."

"So I am."

"Cheek to cheek, and you can take that any way you want to."

"I most certainly will," he replied, winking at her and then scouring the sky from left to right and back again. There was nothing there. Only the sun. Only the white. Only the hot. "I think we're going to have clear sailing from here on out," he said finally. "And I don't mean just to New Orleans."

"I feel the same way, Powell."

He turned the radio on again, searching for a new station and finally landing on a strong signal out of Jackson, Mississippi. The format was similar to the Big Band station up in Memphis, and the song that poured itself sublimely into the car, immersing them in a river of all-encompassing memories, was Doris Day's wartime recording of "Sentimental Journey" with Les Brown's orchestra backing her up beautifully. In the short time they had been dating, they had discovered it was a mutual favorite.

"Perfect choice," Powell said, relaxing at the wheel and setting his heart at ease with the machine he was driving.

Laurie sank back, listening in wild anticipation and inhaling the music like it was a whiff of her beloved Estée Lauder. "Right on time," she added. Then she closed her eyes for a well-deserved and satisfying nap.

Recipes

If there's one thing the Nitwitts of Second Creek know how to do, it's fixing their favorite recipes and serving them to their friends and family. They would also like to share them with you, the reader, in this special addendum containing a brunch dish, a dinner or lunch dish, a dessert, and two cocktails—one each of the spirituous and teetotaling variety. Of course, these have all been passed around so frequently among the Nitwitts that it's becoming very difficult to remember who originated what. No matter. Follow these quick and easy recipes faithfully and you, too, can become the host or hostess with the most or mostest at the drop of a hello, y'all!

LAURIE LEPANTO HAMPTON'S
SOUPER EASY EGGS BENEDICT

Here's a variation on the traditional eggs Benedict recipe that Laurie first enjoyed serving to her late husband, Roy Lepanto, and their now-grown daughters, Lizzie and Hannah, and still serves to second husband, Powell Hampton. She is particularly fond of whipping this up on holiday mornings. *Serves four to six.*

1 can Campbell's condensed Golden Cream of Mushroom soup	6 medium eggs
1 tablespoon Dijon mustard	6 English muffins
Black pepper	6 slices Canadian bacon
Cooking spray	6 slices American or cheddar cheese

Prepare Souper Sauce by combining into a saucepan and stirring over low heat the can of Golden Cream of Mushroom soup (do not add water or milk), the tablespoon of Dijon mustard, and pepper to taste. Let simmer while the rest of the dish is being prepared. (Laurie often discusses rumors with the other Nitwitts over the phone while this sauce is simmering.)

Spray six individual muffin tins with cooking spray. Break the six eggs and drop each into an individual tin. Heat at 350 degrees on middle shelf for ten to fifteen minutes, or until whites are firm—desired doneness of yolks (soft or hard) may be left up to individual. (Laurie says Powell prefers the yolks to lean to the runny side rather than the alternative.)

Meanwhile, brush each of the six English muffins with a bit of butter, if desired, or spritz with cooking spray, and top each with a slice of Canadian bacon. Place on cookie sheet on top shelf of the 350-degree oven and lightly toast for five to ten minutes. (Keep an eye on them and do not let them burn as Laurie has been known to do while talking too long over the phone.) At last minute, top each muffin with the cheese slices and run into oven again until melted.

Now you're ready to assemble and receive your kudos. Carefully dislodge cooked eggs from tins by running spoon around edges and placing one each on a muffin. Pour sauce generously over each egg/muffin.

Serve immediately with glasses of chilled Chardonnay or white Zinfandel. (And take the phone off the hook so you're not disturbed while enjoying, being sure to tell everyone that you spent hours at the stove on this secret family recipe!)

MYRTIS TROY'S SHRIMP AND WILD RICE CASSEROLE

This versatile dish which Myrtis enjoys serving at Evening Shadows to dazzle her guests on the back porch overlooking the maze doubles as a lunch or dinner entrée. *Serves four.*

Two to three dozen fresh or
frozen uncooked shrimp
(any variety)
Extra virgin olive oil
1 teaspoon of garlic salt
Black pepper
Paprika
Dried basil leaves

2 packets Uncle Ben's microwaveable
wild rice (or 1 cup uncooked
wild rice)
Cooking spray
1 can Campbell's Golden Cream
of Mushroom soup
2 slices American or cheddar cheese
(packaged singles)

Peel shrimp and lightly sauté for three or four minutes in skillet over medium heat in olive oil, with garlic salt, black pepper, paprika and dried basil to taste. Turn shrimp once. Remove from heat. Do not overcook, as shrimp will become too tough during baking later on. (Myrtis has sometimes run afoul of this step while arguing with Renza over the phone about running the club.)

If using microwaveable packets of wild rice, follow instructions (should take nine minutes per packet.) If using one cup of raw wild rice, bring water to boil according to instructions, lower heat and cook for fifty to fifty-five minutes. When rice is done by either method, spray medium-sized casserole dish with cooking spray and place rice, shrimp, can of Golden Cream of Mushroom soup (no water or milk added), and two slices of cheese cut into squares into dish. Mix together thoroughly. Cook in 350 degree oven for forty-five to fifty minutes. Goes especially well with garlic bread.

DENVER LEE McQUEEN'S
LEMON ICEBOX PIE

Oh, dear! Denver Lee's had to give this one up due to her recent prediabetic diagnosis, but before that happened she passed the recipe around to the rest of the Nitwitts, who have all embraced it enthusiastically. *Warning: Do not expect this pie to last more than a day. It disappears completely when any of the Nitwitts serve it at one of their tea parties. You might want to make two if you have a larger family.*

> *4 medium lemons*
> *1 can Borden's nonfat condensed milk*
> *3 medium eggs*
> *1 Keebler graham cracker or shortbread piecrust (no baking of crust required)*

Cut the lemons in half and juice them. Pour juice through strainer to remove seeds and pulp. Set juice aside in measuring cup.

Pour the can of condensed milk into a mixing bowl. Crack the three eggs and separate the yolks. Fold the yolks into the condensed milk until thoroughly mixed. (Some people have been known to save the whites and make a meringue, but that's optional.) Then carefully fold the juice into the mixture several tablespoonfuls at a time until smoothly blended.

Pour mixture into piecrust and bake in 350-degree oven for twenty to twenty-five minutes. (Try both the graham cracker and shortbread crusts and see which you like best. Renza,

Wittsie, and Novie prefer the graham cracker, while Laurie, Denver Lee, and Myrtis prefer the shortbread.) If preferred, add whipped cream or Cool Whip once the pie has cooled. Or let guests add topping later to individual slices.

RENZA BELFORD'S BLOODIEST MARY

Never let it be said that Renza Belford does not know how to mix a potent drink. Over the years, she has perfected the art of "slugging," as it is sometimes called in the Deep South. That means, of course, that you are always welcome to add another splash beyond the jigger to any given spirituous concoction for good measure, as Renza does. Be sure you have no driving to do after any imbibing of consequence, however. (And, for God's sake, don't go shopping for food or clothes!) *One cocktail.*

Zest of half a lemon
1 jigger (or a jigger and a splash)
of plain vodka, lemon-vodka,
gin, or tequila (pick only one,
of course)

2 ice cubes
1 cup of Beefamato or Clamato
juice
Cayenne pepper
Celery stalk

Zest lemon and save. Pour the jigger and the splash over the ice cubes. Add Beefamato or Clamato juice. Sprinkle in zest and cayenne pepper. Stir. Garnish with celery, if desired. (Renza suggests you try liquors other than vodka for that extra kick!)

WITTSIE'S BLOODY SHAME

The only real teetotaler amongst the Nitwitts, Wittsie nonetheless wants something to sip in the company of her good friends. Thus was born the Bloody Shame, a virgin adaptation of the Bloody Mary. To make up for the lack of a buzz, Wittsie compensates with a little extra spice. *One cocktail.*

1 cup tomato or V–8 juice	*Tony Chachere's Cajun seasoning*
2 ice cubes	*2 pimento–stuffed olives*
Half a lemon	*2 cocktail onions*
Cayenne pepper	

Pour cup of tomato or V-8 juice over ice cubes. Squeeze the half lemon over the drink and stir. Sprinkle in cayenne pepper and Tony Chachere's Cajun seasoning—less if you can't tolerate highly spiced, more if you can. Sink the two olives and onions and stir everything again. Don't breathe on anyone for a while after drinking. (And cheers from all the Nitwitts to you!)

Acknowledgments

THE FOLLOWING must take many deep bows in helping me pull this project together at the professional level: Meg Ruley and Christina Hogrebe at the Jane Rotrosen Agency, the first to believe in, take on, and champion my Second creek universe; and who led me to Rachel Beard Kahan at Putnam, my superb, insightful editor and great teacher as well. Also: Scott Matthews of Random House, who introduced me to Meg and Christina in a generous gesture of networking and professional camaraderie.

On a more personal level, I must thank Frances Alvarez, Sis Slaughter, and the rest of the original Nit Whits of Mobile, Alabama, for their amusing anecdotes and permission to use a variation of their club name; Kristi Blaes for the professional broadcasting input; Sunflower County library director Alice Shands, for her humorous and candid contributions; and my usual family touchstones — Marion and Daddy Joe.